This morning she'd been a widow on
the verge of ~~...~~
she was a wi ~~...~~
bed with her ~~...~~

But between this ~~...~~
had been switched and she'd been propelled back
into the past.

Michaela took a deep breath and walked into the
bedroom.

Heath blinked, and his lips parted. "Dear God," he
whispered softly.

As she watched, his expression hardened and the
desire in his eyes turned to ice.

His gaze held hers in a furious deadlock. "It doesn't
take much imagination to recognize that as a
trousseau gown. You were planning to wear it for
Darren tonight, weren't you?" His voice was as icy
as his eyes.

"I . . . Heath, it's all I had with me. I didn't think—"

"Damn you." He bit the words off, sharp and
cutting. "Sleep in the other room, or go to Darren
and get on with the honeymoon, but get out of
my sight."

Dear Reader,

Welcome to the Silhouette **Special Edition** experience! With your search for consistently satisfying reading in mind, every month the authors and editors of Silhouette **Special Edition** aim to offer you a stimulating blend of deep emotions and high romance.

The name Silhouette **Special Edition** and the distinctive arch on the cover represent a commitment—a commitment to bring you six sensitive, substantial novels each month. In the pages of a Silhouette **Special Edition**, compelling true-to-life characters face riveting emotional issues—and come out winners. All the authors in the series strive for depth, vividness and warmth in writing these stories of living and loving in today's world.

The result, we hope, is romance you can believe in. Deeply emotional, richly romantic, infinitely rewarding—that's the Silhouette **Special Edition** experience. Come share it with us—six times a month!

From all the authors and editors of Silhouette **Special Edition**,

Best wishes,

Leslie Kazanjian,
Senior Editor

PHYLLIS HALLDORSON
All We Know of Heaven

Silhouette Special Edition

Published by Silhouette Books New York

America's Publisher of Contemporary Romance

SILHOUETTE BOOKS
300 East 42nd St., New York, N.Y. 10017

ISBN: 0-373-09621-6

First Silhouette Books printing September 1990

Printed in the U.S.A.

PHYLLIS HALLDORSON

At age sixteen Phyllis Halldorson met her real-life Prince Charming. She married him a year later, and they settled down to raise a family. A compulsive reader, Phyllis dreamed of someday finding the time to write stories of her own. That time came when her two youngest children reached adolescence. When she was introduced to romance novels, she knew she had found her long-delayed vocation. After all, how could she write anything else after living all those years with her very own Silhouette hero?

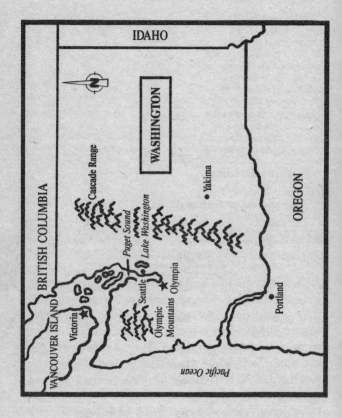

Chapter One

Happy the bride the sun shines on.

The adage had been echoing in Michaela Tanner's thoughts all morning as she dressed for her wedding. Each time it came around, her uneasiness increased.

A gust of wind blew the driving rain against the windows of the bride's dressing room in the stately old brick church, and Michaela shivered. Rain was certainly no novelty in Seattle, but cold, dark, windy storms in the middle of June were.

Why did the heavy, black clouds have to open up and pour today of all days? There would be no sun shining on her when she took her vows. Was it a portent of another failure?

She tossed her head in an effort to dislodge the unwelcome thoughts. That was silly. The sun had been dazzling bright and hot when she'd married Heath seven years ago, almost as bright and hot as the love she'd felt for her bridegroom. But the marriage had disintegrated before their first anniversary.

Her hand shook as she carefully applied lipstick in the color she'd chosen to complement both the red highlights of her hair and the champagne color of her cocktail-length formal dress. She'd been a virgin on her first wedding day and entitled to the long white satin gown and maidenly veil she'd worn. Now she had a five-year-old son.

The thought of Skippy brought another onslaught of foreboding. Her son was a boyish version of his father. The same thick black hair and brown eyes that danced with mischief. He even had Heath's single dimple at the right side of his mouth.

The resemblance made it doubly difficult to put her fun-loving, irrepressible late husband behind her and form a new relationship. She'd loved Heath so much until he'd dulled that love with his careless disregard for her feelings and well-being.

Thank goodness that type of schoolgirl infatuation was a thing of the past. She was older now, more mature, and her feelings for Darren reflected that. They were quieter, less chaotic. No more hot flushes and palpitations. Life with him would be peaceful and serene, and, even more important, he'd be the perfect father for Skipper.

Poor Skip. Yesterday he'd wakened with a temperature, and this morning the first pustules of chicken pox had appeared. He was heartbroken over not being able to attend the wedding.

Rain continued to beat against the windows as the strains of sacred music from the organ in the small chapel wafted on the air. What a way to start a marriage, with a sick child, a canceled honeymoon, and the worst storm of the year making the world dark and dreary.

A cheery voice from behind snapped her out of her gloomy thoughts. "Hey, what did you do to enrage Mother Nature? She's sure throwing a tantrum for your wedding day."

It was Michaela's sister, Catherine, three years older, five inches taller, with blond hair, in contrast to Michaela's strawberry tresses. Catherine had been married eight years and had two children with another baby due in six months.

"I'm warning you, you'll have to go through with the ceremony in spite of the chicken pox and the gully washer. If you postpone it even one day I won't be able to fit into this dress." She patted her rapidly thickening waistline.

Michaela turned to look at her glowingly beautiful sibling, who was dressed in a soft green duplicate of the bridal gown. "Since you're my only attendant, I guess I'll just have to marry the man today and get it over with," she said with a laugh.

"Well, I should hope so," her sister teased. "He's waited a long time to make you his wife."

Michaela's smile faded as her moodiness returned. "Yes," she said with a sigh. "He has. I hope..." She didn't finish the sentence but turned around to face the mirror again.

A second later Catherine's image appeared in the glass, but she was no longer grinning. "Hey, what's the matter? Surely you're not having second thoughts about this."

Michaela shook her head. "No, of course not. I wouldn't do that to Darren."

Catherine frowned and put her hand on Michaela's shoulder. "Mickey, you *are* in love with Darren aren't you? You're not marrying him just because he's been good to you and Skippy and you feel obligated?"

"If you mean do I lust after him, the answer is no, I don't," Michaela answered heatedly. "If I did, I wouldn't marry him. I learned all about the folly of passion as a basis for marriage from his brother, Heath. This time I'm thinking with my head instead of my hormones. Darren is patient, kind, and he respects me. He'd never treat me the way Heath did. He won't spend all his money on extravagances, or go partying and forget to come home for three days. He won't make me pregnant and then go off and get himself killed!''

Her words stopped as she realized what she'd said. Good heavens, where had that come from?

She felt her face flame. "Oh! . . . I mean . . .''

Catherine's hand tightened on her shoulder. "Honey, you won't be doing Darren a favor if you marry him out of a sense of duty. Are you sure this is what you want? I know it's natural to think of Heath on this day, but it shouldn't upset you so.''

Michaela reached up and put her hand over her sister's. "It's no big deal," she said contritely. "Just bridal nerves. Of course I want to marry Darren. He's a dear, and I don't want to live out my life as a single mother. I want a husband, more children, and a home in the suburbs. Darren will give me all that, plus he'll love Skipper as his own. It's important for a boy to have a father.''

Before Catherine could answer, a third feminine voice sounded, anxious and fretful. "Michaela, you haven't fastened your wreath on yet, and it's time to start. Catherine, you're supposed to be helping her and watching the clock.''

It was their mother, Lila Burdett, looking pretty in her mother-of-the-bride gown of emerald green lace as she continued to scold. "The guests are here and your father's waiting for you in the narthex. The ushers are ready to walk Alice and me down the aisle, so for goodness' sake, hurry.''

"Alice" was Alice Tanner, Darren and Heath's mother. Michaela's past and future mother-in-law. Michaela reeled as it occurred to her what a mess she was making of the Tanner family tree by marrying both of their sons.

"I'm sorry, Mother," she said as she picked up the wreath of fresh orange blossoms. "I'm all ready. Tell Dad that Catherine and I will be there to make our entrance by the time you and Alice are seated."

Lila left to go to the narthex, and Michaela adjusted the sweet-smelling wreath on her head while Catherine anchored it with bobby pins.

They'd just finished when there was a knock on the door, and Rodney Rule, the minister, called, "Michaela, there's someone here to see you. May we come in?"

He sounded anxious, but no more so than she felt. A hasty glance at her watch informed her that it was time for her to start her walk down the aisle to become Darren's wife.

She quickly crossed to the door and opened it to find three men waiting. One in a white clerical robe, one in a business suit, and the third in a navy uniform. "Rod, there's no time," she said to the white-robed, middle-aged man.

"Excuse me, ma'am," said the man in the suit, "but this is extremely important."

He took a small leather folder from his pocket and opened it to reveal an identification badge. "My name is Eli Fisher. I'm from the State Department in Washington D.C." He motioned to the other, younger, man. "This is Lieutenant J.G. Otto Quimby. May we come in?"

Taken by surprise, Michaela stepped back to admit the three men. The State Department and the navy? What on earth could they want of her?

"I'm already five minutes late for my own wedding," she said. "Couldn't this at least wait until after the ceremony?"

"Afraid not," said Lieutenant Quimby. He looked at Catherine. "Ma'am would you mind stepping out of the room for a few minutes?"

Catherine glanced at Michaela uncertainly, and Michaela felt a shiver of apprehension pass through her. What was going on here? She reached for Catherine's hand. "This is my sister, and I prefer that she stay."

"You're Catherine Wellington?" Eli Fisher asked.

Both sisters blinked with surprise. He knew Catherine's name. Michaela's anxiety heightened.

Catherine nodded, and he turned to Michaela. "For purpose of identification, are you Michaela Burdett Tanner?"

Impatience warred with Michaela's apprehension. "Yes, you already know that."

"The wife of Ensign Heath Tanner?"

For a moment she faltered. Did this have something to do with Heath? "I'm Ensign Heath Tanner's widow. My husband was killed six years ago in the line of duty."

Fisher nodded and continued. "Have you ever had that marriage terminated?"

She gasped and stared at the man who must be some kind of idiot. "Terminated?" It came out in a strangled sound. "There was no need to terminate my marriage. My husband's dead. He was killed in a naval skirmish in the Persian Gulf—"

The voice of the minister cut her off. "Mr. Fisher, I think this has gone far enough. There's a wedding going on here. Now, I suggest you either get to the point of your visit, or read Mrs. Tanner her rights and let her contact her attorney."

Fisher looked startled. "There's no need for that," he said. "I'm sorry if I seem insensitive, Mrs. Tanner, but I have to be sure I have the facts straight. Please bear with me a few minutes longer. Is it true that the man you are planning to marry today is Darren Tanner, elder brother of Heath?"

Michaela nodded, unsure of her ability to speak as alarm clawed at her. Dear God, what did these men want?

"I assume he's here in the church now?"

Again she nodded, and he turned to the minister. "Mr. Rule, would you please get him and bring him here? And then you'd better make an announcement to the guests that there will be a delay in starting the wedding."

"Now, just a minute..." The Reverend Mr. Rule was a retired army chaplain and unimpressed with authority figures. Michaela was grateful for his intervention. "I'm not going to let you charge in and ruin this young woman's wedding day. Either give me a good reason why you're here, or I'll have to insist that you leave."

Fisher looked at the Navy officer. "Go with the Reverend and fill him in, then bring Tanner here."

The two men left the room, and a few minutes later Quimby returned with Darren. Michaela's gaze lingered on her fiancé. He looked so distinguished in his tuxedo. His dark brown hair was cut short and neatly styled, and the slight paunch at his waist was hidden by the expertly tailored coat and cummerbund.

Darren was shorter and heavier than Heath, and his features were somewhat irregular, but he was a nice-looking man. Not breathtakingly handsome and irresistibly sexy as Heath had been, but he was mature, reliable and loyal. Admirable traits that had been missing in his younger brother.

His perplexed gaze sought Michaela's and apparently saw her fear. He crossed the room and took her in his arms. "What's going on here?" he demanded of Fisher. "You'd better have a damn good reason for delaying our wedding."

While the two men established identities, Michaela relaxed against Darren. It was supposed to be bad luck for the bride and groom to see each other before taking their vows, but she was glad he'd come to her.

He would straighten this out. He was the rock to which she clung, the strength that supported her in those awful days when Heath had first been declared missing, and then dead. He'd been with her during the agonizing months after Skipper was born, prematurely and with a damaged heart, and he'd become a substitute father for her son, his nephew.

The minister returned, and the expression of shock on his face warned Michaela that something was awfully wrong. Her knees trembled as Darren led her the few feet to a small couch and sat down with her.

When they were seated, with Rod standing silently in the background, Eli Fisher spoke. "I'm really sorry about this, Mrs. Tanner. I know the timing's lousy, but you've moved and somehow our computer lost track of you."

A cold breath of foreboding teased the back of her neck. "I've been living and working here in Seattle for three years," she said.

"I know, but it took us a few days to find that out." He ran his hand through his thinning blond hair. "I don't know how to tell you this."

"Just spit it out," Darren exclaimed. "We have over fifty family members and friends waiting in the chapel to watch us get married."

"That's the problem," Fisher blurted. "There's not going to be a wedding."

Michaela felt the blood drain from her face, and the room began to spin as she struggled for composure. Catherine gasped and Darren swore and practically leaped off the sofa, but the other man held up his hand for silence as he continued. "I hate to spring it on you this way, but less than a week ago our negotiators in the Middle East learned that Ensign Heath Tanner wasn't killed six years ago as we thought. He was rescued and has been held prisoner, incommunicado, in a hostile country all this time. We only learned of it now because we have a prisoner they want and they negotiated a trade."

He looked from Darren to Michaela. "Mrs. Tanner, your husband, Heath, has been taken to a hospital in Wiesbaden, West Germany, for physical and psychological evaluation. He's undernourished and understandably somewhat confused emotionally, but there doesn't seem to be anything seriously wrong with him. He's desperate to come back home, though, and within the hour will board a flight to Washington, D.C. They'll land at 11:00 p.m., eastern standard time, and he's expecting you to meet him. We have a navy plane ready to take you there."

Fisher paused and surveyed his stunned audience. When he spoke again, his tone was gentle and filled with compassion. "Ensign Tanner hadn't known that he'd been declared dead. He's expecting his wife to be waiting to greet him with open arms.

"He hasn't been told that you were planning to marry again. We didn't know it either until the manager of your apartment complex told us less than an hour ago."

Chapter Two

Heath Tanner shifted impatiently in the seat of the military transport plane. His brand-new beige uniform felt stiff and uncomfortable after six years of threadbare prison garb, and naval regulations had required him to shave off his beard and cut his hair short. He'd gotten so used to being shaggy that now he felt almost nude.

Leaning back, he closed his eyes and tried to relax, but it was no use. His nerves were strung so tight that it was all he could do to sit still, and his stomach was tied in knots that made eating or drinking almost impossible. He'd been that way ever since his captors had led him out of his cell and turned him over to his American rescuers.

They hadn't even let him know they were negotiating for his exchange!

The physicians and psychologists at the hospital in Wiesbaden had told him he was still in shock brought on by his sudden, unexpected release, and he could believe that, but mostly it was the thought of being reunited with Michaela that was driving him crazy. For six interminable years he'd clung to the memory of her in that hellhole where he'd been held.

He'd dreamed of her soft, creamy skin unblemished by the freckles that usually accompanied strawberry-blond hair; of her brown eyes that twinkled with fun and darkened with passion; and of her smooth little hands that were equally good at lulling him to sleep or exciting him to madness depending on what she was doing with them.

She'd been there with him every minute of his long confinement, stroking him when he was in pain, encouraging him when he was morose, and beckoning him on when he would have given up. She was as real to him as if she'd been there in person in that dismal, lonely cage. Without her, he would have lost his mind.

Now there'd be no more barriers. In a few more hours she'd be there waiting when he stepped off the plane. Not the memory, or the feverish apparition, but the flesh-and-blood woman he could hold in his arms, kiss in all her warm, moist places, and bury himself in to explode their long dammed-up passions and tumble them over the edge of euphoria.

My God, couldn't they fly this damn plane any faster? It seemed like they were standing still in midair over the vast expanse of ocean.

Someone sat down in the seat next to Heath, and he jerked to attention and opened his eyes, an automatic reflex.

It was Navy Lieutenant George Newman, one of his naval and State Department escorts, or "hosts" as they were officially called. "Sorry, Heath," he said, "I didn't mean to wake you."

Heath sighed. "You didn't, sir. I wasn't asleep."

Lieutenant Newman frowned. "Your doctor tells me that's something of a chronic condition with you. He says you haven't been able to sleep without sedation since you were freed."

Heath shrugged. "It's only temporary. My nerves are all shot to hell, but I'll be able to relax once I get home."

"I'm sure you will, but meanwhile, why don't you give those raw nerves a rest. How about a tranquilizer, or a shot of whiskey?"

"No, thank you, sir," Heath said. "I haven't seen my wife in six years, and I don't want anything to dull my senses when I get off this plane."

It seemed to Heath that the Lieutenant's frown deepened, but he sounded jovial enough when he spoke. "Right. How long were you and your wife married before you were...ah...lost?"

"I wasn't lost, sir," Heath snapped. "I was captured."

The words were out before he could stop them, and he realized that was no way to talk to a senior officer. "Sorry, Lieutenant." He ran his fingers through his thick ebony hair. "It's just that I can't believe everyone thought I was dead all this time. It's so...so bizarre."

"Yes, it is," Newman agreed, "and we still haven't gotten a satisfactory answer as to why we weren't notified that you'd been rescued and were being held. We'll probably never know. But about your marriage...?"

Heath was more than happy to change the subject back to happier times. He'd been answering questions about his imprisonment for days, and reliving all those tormented years was tearing him apart.

"Michaela and I were married almost a year before that skirmish in the Persian Gulf, but I'd been at sea for three months, so we actually had less than nine months together."

Heath let his memory roam as he continued to talk. "We met at the University of Arizona, where she was enrolled as a freshman and I was a senior." A smile hovered at the corners of his mouth as his mind pictured her. "She was just eighteen and a little thing. Claimed she was five-two, but that must have been with her shoes on. Weighed about a hundred pounds, but you'd never mistake her for a child, if you know what I mean."

No, Heath thought, tiny though she was, she was all woman—slim and trim but round in all the right places. Even after they were married it had been all he could do to keep his hands off her in public. In private he didn't even try.

The lieutenant chuckled. "Yeah, I know what you mean. Six years is a long time, though. She'd be about twenty-five now. Are you prepared for the possibility that she's changed since you last saw her?"

Heath blinked. "Changed? Oh yeah, I've thought of it, especially since I found out I'd been declared dead instead of missing. It's not something I can face right now, though. Things have been coming at me too fast the last few days. Michaela has been the one constant in this whole horrendous experience. She's been my lifeline, the hope I clung to, and if I start doubting her now I'll go crazy before we land."

"I can understand your reasoning," Newman said. "Just don't expect her to be a teenager anymore. She probably has a different set of values than she did as a college student. Most people do by the time they're in their mid-twenties."

Heath felt his muscles tightening again. Did they know something they were keeping from him? "Look, lieutenant, are you trying to tell me something?"

Newman shook his head. "No, Heath, I'm not. I know almost nothing about your wife except what you've told me, but I want you to be prepared for the probability that she's not the same girl you remember. She's a woman now and has no doubt matured and set new goals."

Heath wasn't altogether convinced that the lieutenant was telling him the truth about not concealing information, but he wasn't going to argue. "It's me who's changed, sir. A hell of a lot more than Michaela ever could. I look drawn and gaunt and ten years older than my age, which is twenty-nine. My new clothes are two sizes smaller than the ones I wore when I was captured, and I've learned firsthand all about man's inhumanity to man."

He could see that the officer was going to protest and held up his hand to stop him. "We both know it's true. I may not have had mirrors in jail, but there were plenty of them in the hospital I just left. I'll be lucky if my wife even recognizes me."

He leaned back and rubbed his hands over his face. "I've lost six years out of my life. How will I ever catch up on all that's happened?"

Newman stood and put his hand on Heath's shoulder. "I'm betting that you're going to be just fine. Right now you're malnourished, anemic and in need of some dental work, but in a couple of months you'll have rested up, gained weight and gotten reacquainted with your wife. The government will provide you with counseling for as long as you need it, but any man who can endure six years in a stinking foreign prison and come out more-or-less intact should be able to survive almost anything. Now try to get some sleep. It's still several hours before we land."

Heath leaned back and closed his eyes, but not to sleep. Sleep was an illusion—only a man who'd never been incarcerated could indulge in it at will. He'd learned the skill of keeping his mind active and alert even when his body was at rest. Now his mind ferreted out the possibility the lieutenant had alluded to and which Heath had as quickly banished.

Had Michaela changed? For the sake of his sanity as those long months had turned into years, he'd never allowed himself to doubt her love, her steadfast loyalty. In his thoughts she was always nineteen and unquestioningly his. It was a matter of survival, because without the certainty that she would be eagerly waiting for him when he was finally released he couldn't have gone on.

He realized that his heart was pounding and his body was damp with sweat, familiar symptoms of the panic that he'd battled for so long. He breathed deeply and forced his fists to unclench.

Michaela, my darling, my wife. I'm frantic with need for you. Please need me, too. Otherwise, I have no reason for having endured the unendurable.

Michaela checked her buckled seatbelt and braced herself as the plane taxied onto the runway, then picked up speed for the ascent. Ordinarily she enjoyed flying, but this time she was too confused and upset to react with anything but sufferance.

The plane left the ground, and she gripped the arms of her seat, then relaxed her hold somewhat when Darren put his hand over hers. Darren, who like a big brother, was always there when she needed someone.

She looked over at him sitting in the seat next to her and smiled. He squeezed her hand but couldn't quite manage an answering smile. He looked as shocked and bewildered as she knew she did, and well they might. If everything had gone as originally scheduled they would have been leaving about now to drive to Vancouver, British Columbia, where they'd planned to spend their wedding night, then board a luxury liner for a honeymoon cruise to Alaska.

They'd canceled the cruise earlier when Skipper started running a high temperature, but the idea that they might be leaving Seattle on a special flight to Washington, D.C., was too much to even imagine.

The small plane reached the desired altitude, and the Fasten Your Seat Belts sign went off. Michaela relaxed, and Darren captured her hand in his. "Are you all right?" he asked anxiously. "You look so...so..."

"I know," she answered as he groped for a word to describe the emotions that must be playing across her face. "So do you. No, I'm not all right. I'm scared, disoriented and just plain bewildered. My husband has been dead for years, and now they tell me he's coming back and expecting me to take up where we left off."

A tremor ran through her. "My God, Darren, I don't even remember for sure what Heath looked like! I mean really looked like. All I see when I think of him is the photo image in our wedding pictures. I don't remember his expressions when we woke up in the morning, or when he was elated, or angry, or hung over."

She knew her voice had risen, and she was on the verge of losing control, but she couldn't stop. "It's unnatural, ghoulish. We buried him, if not physically at least psychologically. We had a memorial service. I grieved..."

She swallowed a sob, and Darren's hand tightened on hers as she continued. "Although our marriage was in trouble at the time of his death, I truly grieved. I still loved him even though we were almost totally incompatible, but I managed to put that all behind me. I bore Heath's son, finished my education and got on with my life."

The tears she'd been striving to hold back spilled over and ran down her cheeks. She turned to clutch Darren.

"Oh, Darren, I feel like such a selfish, rotten traitor. Instead of rejoicing that my husband is alive and returning to me, I'm absolutely terrified!"

Darren held her as deep, tearing sobs shook her, and tears dampened his gray suit coat. "Go ahead and cry," he said softly as he caressed her back with the palm of his hand. "Get it all out so you can deal with it. There's nothing wrong with the way you're reacting. You've had a stunning shock. We both have."

He rubbed his cheek in her hair. "If it'll make you feel any better, I'll admit that I'm not rejoicing, either. Heath is my little brother and I love him, but I resent his assumption that he can turn up after all this time and claim you as his wife again. Only a heel would be resentful at a time like this. No, worse than a heel, a creep, so don't think you're the only one with a load of guilt."

Michaela wept in his arms until there were no tears left, but even then the shuddering sobs continued. When she finally gained enough control to take a trip to the restroom, she discovered that the makeup she'd so skillfully applied just hours before for her wedding was ruined, as was the coiffure that had been arranged to complement the wreath of orange blossoms.

With paper towels and soap from the dispenser she scrubbed her face, then layered it with hand cream from another dispenser to ease the burning of skin made raw from tears. If anything, she looked even worse. Her eyes were red and swollen, as were her cheeks, and underneath she was pale as death.

There was plenty of makeup in her purse, but she chose to use only a light coat of the lipstick that she'd selected to wear with the teal-blue dress she'd changed into from her wedding finery. It would be at least five hours before they landed in D.C.; she'd wait until later to try to repair the damage.

With the three-hour time difference, it was nine-thirty and dark when the plane approached the nation's capital. Michaela had long dreamed of someday vacationing in this historic city with its key government buildings and famous monuments. Now, as she looked out at the myriad of lights below, she'd sell her soul if the plane would just turn around without landing and take her back to Seattle.

Her nerves were strung so tightly that she jumped when Darren, who had been across the aisle talking to Eli Fisher and Otto Quimby, touched her shoulder. "Sorry," he said. "I didn't mean to startle you, but Eli wants to talk to us for a minute."

He slid into the seat next to her, and the man from the State Department sat on the other side of both. "I just want to explain what's going to happen after we land at Andrews Air Force Base," he said. "Heath Tanner's plane is due in a little more than an hour, and we're keeping the news media off base until his plane approaches. There are limousines standing by to drive us to the Mayflower Hotel, where—"

"Wait a minute, back up," Michaela said. "What do you mean 'the news media'?"

"Just what I said," Fisher answered. "When we left the airport at Seattle, the State Department released the announcement of Ensign Tanner's capture, imprisonment and exchange. We'd been keeping it under wraps before then, until you and his family could be found and notified, but we couldn't sit on it any longer. The news is on every radio and television broadcast in the country, and Andrews is going to be a madhouse of reporters and photographers."

Michaela felt as if she'd been punched in the stomach. "Oh, my God! No!"

Darren clenched his fists and glared at the man. "Couldn't you have waited until Michaela and Heath had their initial meeting in private?"

Fisher held up his hand. "I'm sorry, but that wasn't possible. A hostage exchange isn't something you can keep secret for long, and Tanner has been free for three days. We didn't want his wife to read about it in the newspapers, but there had already been leaks. As soon as we found her we had to release it to the media to prevent an unauthorized version from being circulated and blowing the whole thing up in our faces."

Michaela leaned back and fought the faintness that threatened to overwhelm her. Was there no end to this nightmare?

With a guilty cry she hid her face in her hands. *Why did she keeping thinking of Heath's return as a nightmare?*

He was alive. It should be a happy occasion, and all she could feel was fear and foreboding. What kind of wife was she, anyway?

But there was the heart of the problem. She wasn't a wife, she was a widow. Had been a widow for six years, and before that she'd been an estranged wife.

Except that her estrangement from Heath had been breached just long enough to conceive a son who had always been told that his father had been killed in the service of his country months before he was born.

How did you explain a return from the dead to a five-year-old?

The landing of the navy plane at Andrews Air Force Base was uneventful. Michaela had a few minutes alone to freshen up and reapply her makeup in the officers' club lounge before Heath's plane was due, but it did nothing to soothe her. It gave her only more time to imagine all the ways she could make a fool of herself and disappoint Heath with the whole world looking on.

When she'd finished, she stepped back to view herself in the full-length mirror. Her silk blend dress was fresh and wrinkle-free. Teal blue was one of her best colors, and the makeup had helped, but she still looked like a sad, lost waif. The inner sparkle that usually radiated from her was gone, as if someone had pulled the plug. There was no way she could reconnect it.

Michaela hated that she couldn't be a glowingly happy, loving wife. She owed Heath that much at least before she shot him down with the news that she'd been within minutes of marrying his brother.

At eleven o'clock it was still sultry and warm on the tarmac, where Michaela stood with Darren and their escorts waiting for the military plane carrying Heath and naval and State Department personnel to land.

As Mr. Fisher had predicted, the airfield was a madhouse. The artificial lighting was almost as bright as day, and reporters, photographers and curious bystanders swarmed against the ropes that had been set up to contain them. The roar of their shouted questions never let up, although it was impossible to understand what they were saying. The click of cameras was incessant.

Michaela was surrounded protectively by Darren and their hosts, and they in turn were guarded by armed naval shore patrol officers. It could have been a threatened invasion instead of a happy homecoming.

She fought the waves of alarm that buffeted her. In just minutes, Heath, alive and well, would step out of the grave and back into her well-ordered life.

* * *

Heath sat on the edge of his seat as he adjusted his hat and looked at his watch. The watch that a former cell mate had given him just minutes before being taken from the jail and shot.

Heath shuddered. Would the time ever come when the horror he'd been through could be dealt with and then forgotten? If not, how could he live out the rest of his life with the ever-present memories and nightmares?

They were approaching Andrews Air Force Base, but it seemed to take forever. If this suspense didn't end, and quickly, he was going to explode. The human mind and body could only stand so much tension, and he was long past the normal breaking point.

Would Michaela really be waiting for him down there? As soon as he'd arrived at the hospital in West Germany he'd requested permission to make an overseas call to her, but they'd told him she'd moved and they were having a little trouble tracking her down. Each day he'd inquired and been assured that it was only a temporary delay.

Still, shortly before flight time today, they'd brought him the good news that they'd found her in Seattle, and she was being flown to Washington, D.C., to meet his plane.

The voice of the navy steward broke into his troubled musing. "Fasten your seatbelt, sir, we're landing."

Michaela trembled with tension as she watched the plane taxi toward them and stop. Portable stairs were rolled to the door, and two men in shore patrol uniforms took up positions on the ground at either side. The crowd below held its collective breath for a few heart-stopping seconds until the door opened. Then a roar of welcome shattered the silence as a tall, slender man in a beige uniform appeared.

It was Heath! Michaela was too stunned to move. How could she have thought she wouldn't recognize him? Although she was too far away to see his features clearly, there was an aura about him that was unmistakable: his stance, the way he moved, the tilt of his head as he surveyed the crowd below.

A hand on her arm captured her attention, and Lieutenant Quimby said, "Go ahead, Mrs. Tanner, he'll want to greet you alone. We'll wait back here."

Alone? How could Heath greet her alone with dozens of television cameras recording their every move and expression for the country to watch at its leisure over the next several days?

Heath was moving quickly down the stairs now. Michaela took a tentative step, unsure if her trembling legs would hold her, then another, and several more until she was alone in the space between the crowd and the plane. Heath saw her when he reached the ground. For a moment their eyes met, and then he started to run.

She stood rooted to the spot, and by instinct rather than design her arms came up and out in an invitation issued by her heart against the better judgment of her mind.

When he was a few yards away he slowed to a walk, and when he reached her extended hands he took them in his and held them to his chest. His heated gaze never left her face, nor was she aware of anything but the warring emotions in his green-flecked brown eyes. Uncertainty, relief, joy and passion; each seemed to flicker briefly before being replaced by another.

"Michaela," he murmured thickly, for her ears only. "Oh, my God, how I've missed you!"

Then she was in his arms, and the moment of tenderness was gone as he clasped her to him.

He was so thin, but there was a sinewy toughness in his body that told her he'd fought his captivity with every ounce of his strength rather than capitulate and grow soft. How like Heath. That stubborn determination was what she'd loved about him, and also what had made him nearly impossible to live with.

She inched her hands up his chest and clasped them around his neck as she lifted her face to meet his mouth. It descended over hers, and a small shock jolted her and made her tingle. She'd forgotten how powerful the magnetism between them had been. How quickly he could scramble her resolve to stand up to him and insist that he start taking their marriage seriously.

He held her even closer, and the tingle became a throb in the very core of her being. The tension drained out of her, and she melted against him, as long dormant passion began to ignite. It had been six years since she'd been kissed like this, but the storm of feeling it evoked in her finally brought her to her senses.

With an effort, she brought herself to move her head and break the kiss. "Heath, we have an audience. The people and the cameras..."

The tension that had melted in him as it had in her returned, and he lifted his head and looked around. He seemed dazed, and she watched the emotions that played across his face as he slowly came down to earth.

He loosened his hold but didn't release her, and there was regret in his dark eyes. "I'm sorry, sweetheart." His voice was rough with emotion. "I didn't mean to embarrass you. I'm afraid my control is pretty shaky."

Her heart went out to him. He hadn't been the only one who'd lost control. In all the upheaval this day had wrought it had never once occurred to her that she might still respond passionately to Heath. She'd thought her passion had died with him. Apparently it had been resurrected with him, too, and that was going to complicate things.

She'd learned the first time that passion alone was too fragile a base for a lifetime commitment. She didn't intend to make the same mistake again.

Still encased in the circle of his arms, she stood on tiptoe and kissed him softly on the lips. "There's nothing to apologize for, Heath," she said huskily. "I'm just so glad you're alive and well."

He put his arms around her waist again and nuzzled his face against the side of her throat. For a long moment they shut the world out and just held each other as a silent prayer formed in her thoughts.

Help me. Dear God in heaven, help me. I'm lost and don't know which way to turn.

Chapter Three

All the world loves a lover.

Michaela could believe it. The crowd was screaming, clapping, shouting questions and going wild with good cheer as they watched the romantic reunion of the handsome young ensign and his wife. If only it could have been as simple as they seemed to think it was.

Heath shivered in her arms as he clutched her to him, and she knew he was even more tightly strung than she. Her emotions were impossibly tangled. She'd been surprised by the depth of her response to him, but this man wasn't the Heath she'd known. They'd only been together a matter of minutes, but she recognized him for what he was, a wounded stranger who mistook her for the innocent teenage bride he'd married so long ago.

That girl had died along with the boy who was her husband. The woman Heath held so desperately was a different person. Would he recognize that? And if so, would he have the strength to accept it?

Darren had been standing beside them, and now he touched Heath's shoulder. "Heath, there's a car waiting to get you out of here. They're ready anytime you are."

Heath raised his head and looked at his brother, recognizing him for the first time. He released Michaela and threw his arms around Darren, who grabbed him in an emotional embrace.

"Darren," Heath murmured.

"Yeah," Darren muttered, equally unable to speak. "Me, too."

Moisture glistened in the two brothers' eyes as they broke apart, and Heath again put an arm around Michaela and held her close beside him as they walked toward the welcoming committee of navy and State Department personnel.

The official greeting was short, for which Michaela was grateful. She was exhausted, and knew that both Heath and Darren were, too. The reporters hadn't been allowed to speak to Heath, which annoyed them mightily, and in a short time the three of them were whisked away from the airfield in a black limousine followed by a second one containing their escorts.

Michaela sat between the two men, encased in Heath's arms. The only time he had let go of her was when he'd hugged Darren. Since then, he'd kept her attached to him at all times, although there'd been no chance to speak more than a few words to each other.

She leaned against him and tried to relax, but it was a struggle. One that he was waging, too. He was as taut as she, and his body didn't feel at all familiar. He was many pounds thinner than the man she'd married, and under the artificial lights on the airfield he'd looked so much older.

A wave of pity and guilt assailed her. She should be snuggling with him, kissing him, caressing him, and telling him how much she'd missed him. How miraculous it was to have him back. Instead, she'd failed him unforgivably. Not that she'd pulled away from him physically, but he had to have noticed her reticence. She couldn't even think of anything to say to him.

Darren stepped in and helped her by breaking the tense silence and talking to Heath about their parents, their joy at his return, their disappointment that because of the shortage of time they'd been unable to be on hand to greet him, too, and the fact that their father, a career army colonel, had retired, and he and their mother were now living in Florida. After that, the brothers talked while Michaela remained silent and miserable.

It was almost midnight as they raced toward the Mayflower Hotel in downtown Washington where Heath and Michaela had been told that a suite of rooms awaited them. She tried not to shudder at the thought of what the next few hours held.

Obviously she couldn't spend the night alone with Heath, and just as obviously that's exactly what he expected her to do. Her original plan had been to spend this night, and every night hereafter, sleeping with Darren. Even though she'd felt no surges of passion in her relationship with him, she'd convinced herself that it would happen once they were married.

What she couldn't do, no matter how much she might wish she could, was switch her plans from one man to another in the short space of a few hours. Not even when the one she was switching to was her long-absent husband.

No, even though it was late and they were worn out, there were still two things she had to do tonight. The first was to tell Heath that he was the father of a five-year-old son. She was almost sure that would be a happy surprise and she looked forward to it.

The second was to tell him about her near marriage to his brother, and she was afraid that might destroy him.

They arrived at the luxurious old hotel to find that the media had discovered their destination and were waiting for them. Fortunately there was also added security, and, surrounded by their escorts, shore patrol and uniformed police officers, they were rushed up to a suite on the sixth floor.

The living room of the suite seemed crowded even after the S.P. and police officers left. Heath's host, Lieutenant Newman, looked around, then turned to Heath. "Is there anything more we can do for you? Anything you need?"

Heath shook his head. "No, sir, it looks like everything's been taken care of."

The lieutenant smiled. "All right, then, we'll clear out of here and give you some privacy. There'll be a shore patrol guard posted outside your door at all times to make sure you're not bothered. If you want to get in touch with me, tell him. Otherwise, I'll be back in a couple of days."

The panic Michaela had been fighting all day once more clutched at her as everyone but Darren said good-night and left. They'd postponed the inevitable as long as they could. Now what was going to happen? Heath wouldn't let her leave until he'd been given a good reason, that much was sure.

Heath looked at Darren. "I really appreciate your accompanying Michaela today and taking care of her," he said and clapped his brother on the shoulder. "It's great seeing you again, but I'm sure you'll understand that right now I want to be alone with her."

An expression of possessive anger flitted across Darren's face before he could bring it under control, and

Michaela understood how difficult this situation was for him. He loved his brother, but he also cared for her, and she'd have been *his* wife now if it had taken the government just a few minutes longer to find her. Their marriage, had it taken place, might even have been legal. She didn't know how the law worked in a case like this, but Heath had been declared dead by the navy.

"I understand that," Darren said carefully, struggling not to sound angry, "but there are some things you have to know first."

"The things I have to know are things that my wife can tell me," he said impatiently. "Anything else can wait."

Darren stood his ground. "I wish that were possible, but it isn't. I'm sorry, Heath, but this is important. Please, sit down."

"Now just a minute..."

Michaela could see that Heath's tenuous control was slipping, and she turned in his arm so that she was standing in front of him. "Please, Heath," she said softly. "Darren's right, this can't wait. Let's all sit down."

He looked at her with such longing that a low moan rose in her throat. She couldn't stand to see him so tormented! Her control disintegrated as once more she was inundated with a seemingly inexhaustible supply of tears. Violent sobs shook her, and she heard Darren swear and hurry toward her.

"Dammit, Heath," he roared. "Give her a little space. For six years she's thought you were dead, and it's only been a few *hours* since she learned you aren't."

Heath jerked as if he'd been hit and immediately released her. Darren helped her to the sofa and sat her down, then turned to face his stunned brother. "I know how hard this is for you," he said more quietly. "Believe me, I know better than you can understand right now. You've been gone a long time, and Michaela has had to make a new life without you. You can't expect to come back and take up where you left off."

For a long time Heath stood looking at Michaela, then slowly he moved forward and sat on the couch beside her. He looked dazed. "Do I repulse you, Mickey?" he asked quietly.

She gasped, and her sobs ceased. "Oh, Heath, no," she lifted her head to cup his cheek. "I'm so thankful that you're not dead, but it's going to take a little getting used to. This whole thing has been such a shock...."

He didn't move but sat still and let her caress his face. "Are you afraid of me?" There was disbelief mixed with anguish in his tone.

She wanted to say no, to reassure him that wasn't the case, but his gaze held hers and wouldn't let it go. She couldn't lie to him. "I... Maybe, a little. I don't know what to expect. I don't know what you want of me."

He winced. "Yes you do. I just want to know if you still love me. We need time alone together to get to know each other again. I'm not going to force you to do anything you don't want to do."

Her eyes widened and she clasped her hands in her lap. "I didn't think you would!"

"I believe you do." His tone was unnaturally calm. "I'm afraid I've been so busy trying to handle my own feelings that I haven't given much thought to yours. You've been so real to me in my thoughts and dreams all these years...."

"Don't, Heath," she pleaded. "None of this is your fault. We're all victims of a twist of fate that we had no control over."

Again she reached out to him. This time she put her hand over his. "My life has changed drastically since you've been gone, but I have a surprise that I'm sure will make you very happy.''

He shook his head. "I've had all the surprises I can stand. Please don't tease me. Just tell me—quick and all at once."

She hadn't meant to bedevil him. Taking a deep breath she plunged ahead. "Heath, you and I have a five-year-old son."

Heath looked at her as if she'd suddenly begun talking jibberish. "A son?" He paused and seemed to be trying to make sense of what she'd said. "I have a son? Are you telling me that you have a child?"

"*We* have a child. You and me, together." Michaela wanted to make certain he'd have no doubts about who Skipper's father was. "His name is Heath Skipper Tanner, Jr., and he was five years old on February 17." She saw no reason to burden Heath with the knowledge of his son's congenital health problem now. She'd tell him about that later. "He's a beautiful little boy," she continued. "I brought his picture. Just a minute and I'll get it."

She started to rise, but he grabbed her hand and pulled her back down. "Why wasn't I told about this earlier?" he demanded.

"Earlier?" Michaela was puzzled. "But you were dead. I mean—"

"I've been out of that prison for three days and nobody said a thing to me about being a father."

Now she understood and moved closer to him. "There was a computer foul-up and my records were lost. That's why the navy couldn't find me right away. None of the people with you in West Germany knew about Skipper until today, and I insisted on being the one to tell you."

She felt the tension drain out of him, and then he reached for her. She went to him willingly and as he held her close, he murmured thickly, "A son. All the time I was in that jail you were bearing me a son and raising him."

His voice was low, vibrant. "Oh, Michaela, I love you so. At first I was certain I'd never live to see you again. Then, as time went on, all I could think of was you—"

His voice broke, and she felt the sob that tore through him as he tightened his grip on her.

Michaela held him, stroked him, and murmured comforting words. It was then she realized that Darren was gone. She hadn't heard him leave the room, but she was grateful for his sensitivity.

Heath quickly pulled himself together and raised his head, as though breaking down after all he'd been through was a sign of weakness.

"Now would you like to see the pictures?" she asked.

He nodded. "Yes. Please."

Michaela got up and removed the packet of photographs from her purse. "This is the latest one." She handed him a professional portrait.

Heath's hand shook as he took it from her, and she sat down beside him again. "It was taken on his fifth birthday, four months ago."

Heath stared at the handsome little boy with black curly hair and an impish smile. Michaela had seen pictures of Heath at that age and knew that the resemblance between father and son was startling. She'd dressed Skip in dark blue slacks and a light blue slipover sweater, and he'd have looked like an angel if it hadn't been for the devilish twinkle that flashed in his wide brown eyes.

Heath swallowed hard as he gazed hungrily at the photo that shook in his hand. For a few moments he couldn't speak, and when he finally did his voice was raw with emotion. "My boy." He looked at Michaela and a grin split his face. "He's the spittin' image of me. What do you call him?"

"He's known as Skipper, or Skip."

"Where is he? Why didn't you bring him with you?"

"I would have," she said, "but he has the chicken pox. He's being well looked after by both of our mothers."

Heath frowned. "I understood you were living in Seattle now. What's our son doing in Florida? Are your parents there, too?"

Michaela bit her lip. "He's not in Florida. Both of our parents are in Seattle."

His eyes widened with a mixture of surprise and dismay. "You mean your mom and dad have moved to Seattle, too? But what are mine doing there?"

She hadn't meant to open this Pandora's box yet, and cast around for a way to distract him from the subject for a while. "Not exactly, but we'll get to that later. Don't you want to see the rest of my pictures of Skip?"

That did it, and for the next half hour she showed him photos that represented every stage of his son's development from birth to his latest birthday.

Both Michaela and Heath had relaxed as she shared the joys of parenthood with him for the first time. He overflowed with questions about the child he hadn't known he had, and she answered them in detail.

They were even laughing together when a knock on the door interrupted them. The laughter stopped abruptly as the tension returned. "Damn it, why can't they leave us alone!" Heath growled as he stood and stomped across the room. "Who is it?" he asked.

A muffled voice called from the other side of the door. "It's Darren. Let me in. I have to talk to you."

"Can't it wait until tomorrow?"

For a while, as they'd talked about their son, Michaela had forgotten that she had another secret for her recently reincarnated husband. This one was guaranteed to consign him back to the hell he'd been suffering in for so long, but there was no way it could be postponed.

She hurried over to stand beside him. "Please let him back in," she said carefully. "He's right, there's one more thing you have to know before you hear it on television or read it in the papers. Take my word for it, it can't be put off, and he needs to be here."

Heath's facial features tightened, but after a moment he reached up and unlocked the door.

Darren came in and glanced quickly at Michaela as the door closed behind him, his apprehension plain. She managed a thin smile in an effort to reassure him. "Thank you for giving us a few minutes alone," she said, "and for coming back."

He turned to his brother and his expression softened. "You have every right to be proud of your son. He's a great kid."

Heath nodded. "He'd have to be with Mickey for a mother." He looked at his watch. "I'll give you ten minutes to tell me what in hell it is that's so important it can't wait until tomorrow."

Michaela uttered a cry of protest, and Darren's fists clenched as his jaw set in the same stubborn mold as his brother's. "All right, dammit," he grated. "I was hoping to make this as easy on you as I could, but if that's the way you want it, that's the way you're going to get it."

Michaela gasped, but before she could stop him Darren continued. "At one o'clock this afternoon, when the government men found us and intervened, Michaela and I were in the process of getting married to each other. Ten minutes later and she'd have been *my* wife."

Heath didn't move. He didn't even breath, but the blood slowly drained from his face.

The two brothers stood facing each other, their features stark with fury. When Heath finally spoke it was barely above a whisper, but his voice carried around the room. "You bloody son of a bitch!"

With lightning speed he swung and hit Darren with his right fist followed immediately by his left. Michaela screamed as Darren crashed noisily into a table when he went down. A loud pounding on the door went unnoticed as Heath followed Darren, grabbed him by his shirt front, hauled him to his feet and hit him again.

This time Darren landed on a desk that stood against the wall, and he managed to remain standing as Michaela, her heart pounding with horror, shouted at Heath to stop. Heath, totally out of control now, was poised to throw another punch when the door was flung open and the shore patrol guard charged into the room.

"What in hell's going on here?" he boomed as he lunged for Heath and wrestled his arms to his back.

The guard was a big man with muscles that bulged under his uniform shirt, and he wasn't being gentle with his captive. Heath groaned as his arms were pushed high. "Sorry, sir, but you better pull yourself together and settle down. I can't allow a brawl in the hotel."

For a moment Michaela was too stunned to move. Her breathing was raspy, and she was appalled that the two brothers had exchanged blows over her.

Well, that wasn't exactly accurate. Heath had thrown all the punches. Darren hadn't made a move to defend himself. Why? He wasn't as tall as his brother, but he worked out regularly and was in good shape. She was dead sure that no other man would have gotten away with beating him up the way Heath had.

The sight of Darren swaying unsteadily against the desk as blood flowed from his nose and mouth propelled her into action. She hurried into the bathroom for a warm, wet washcloth and handed it to him while the guard, apparently satisfied that Heath was defused, led him to a chair several feet away.

"Okay now," he said placatingly, "what happened here? I understood you two were brothers."

Heath was breathing heavily as he glared at Darren and Michaela. "Not anymore we're not," he snarled. "That bastard's been sleeping with my wife!"

The words knifed through Michaela, and both she and Darren gasped. "That's not true!" she said, frantic to make him believe her.

"Like hell I have!" Darren retorted. "I said we were getting married, but that wasn't meant to imply that we've been making love."

Heath sat forward and gripped the arms of the chair. "Oh, shove it," he snapped. "We were raised together, remember? You haven't been celibate since you were fifteen."

Darren sighed as he dabbed at his face with the washcloth. "That's right," he said wearily, "but I've never slept with a woman who wasn't willing, and Michaela wasn't."

A wave of embarrassment swept over her, and she looked away. It was mortifying to have these two men discussing her sex life in front of a third man as if she weren't even there.

As if reading her mind the guard turned and let himself out.

Darren ran his fingers through his dark hair. "Michaela's very dear to me, but she was busy mourning for you, having your son and finishing her education. It wasn't until a year ago that I told her how I felt, and it was six months after that before she agreed to marry me."

He raised his head to look squarely at his brother. "You're right, I'm a male with all the normal urges. I won't pretend that I was content to wait, but she was reluctant to sleep with me until after we were married and I wouldn't pressure her."

For a moment the two men glared at each other, then Heath dropped his head in his hands and muttered a succinct oath.

Darren hesitated, then took Michaela's arm. "Come on, Mickey," he said quietly. "It's time for us to leave."

Michaela hesitated. She couldn't just walk away and leave her husband alone after a blow like that. He'd reacted violently, but it was understandable.

Darren applied pressure to her arm. "He needs to be alone for a while to sort things out. We'll come back tomorrow when all three of us are a little calmer."

Still she didn't move, and after a moment Heath raised his head and looked at her. His face was white and expressionless, but his eyes betrayed the depth of his agony. "Are you going to divorce me, Michaela?" His tone was flat.

The idea of divorce had never occurred to her, and she was shocked. "Of course not. At least, not unless that's what you want. I've been in too much of a daze to make any plans for the future."

"Then stay here with me."

"No way!" Darren said harshly. "I'm not going to leave her for you to abuse."

Heath glared at him. "Butt out," he snapped. "You have nothing to say about it." Again he captured Michaela's gaze. "Have I ever abused you, Mickey?"

She shook her head. "No, never, but—"

"But you don't want to have sex with me." It was a statement, not a question. "Well, that's no problem because your announcement has taken all the starch out of me, to phrase it delicately. I couldn't even if you wanted to, but tonight I need you with me. I don't want to be alone anymore."

She saw the look of commiseration on Darren's face, and knew that he felt as sick as she did. "Oh God, Heath," he said, "I'm sorry. I lost my temper, but that's no excuse for my behavior. I should never have blurted it out like that."

Heath didn't respond to his brother as he continued to hold Michaela's gaze. "Don't look so stricken," he said to her. "I'm sure it's only temporary, but you'd have been safe with me, anyway. Darren isn't the only one who's never forced himself on a woman. I won't even touch you if you don't want me to, and don't forget the guard. He'll be right outside the door. All you have to do is scream if I do anything you don't like."

He looked so anxious, as if nothing in the world was as important as her answer. She felt Darren's fingers tighten on her arm in warning but pulled away from him to stand straight and alone.

Heath was her husband. He had a right to expect her to be with him when he needed her. "All right," she said softly. "I'll stay with you if that's what you want."

Darren sucked in his breath. "No. Michaela, you don't have to—"

"I want to," she said, still watching Heath. "He's my husband. He has a right to ask that of me, and I trust him to keep his word and respect my wishes."

Heath's expression mirrored intense relief, but a glance at Darren revealed his dismay. She put her hand on his arm. "It'll be okay," she said reassuringly. "Are you staying here at the hotel?"

He nodded. "Yes, on the third floor, but—"

"Then we'll see you tomorrow when we're all thinking more clearly." She prodded him to move toward the door and lowered her voice. "He needs me, Darren. I can't just walk away from him. Please don't make a fuss."

She knew she was hurting both men, but it was a no-win situation. There would be a lot of pain for all of them before this entanglement was finally resolved.

Darren looked at his brother, then back at Michaela.

"Try to get a good night's sleep and don't worry," she told him.

Slowly he shook his head from side to side. "That has got to be the most useless bit of advice you've ever given anybody," he said. "Call me if you need me."

He opened the door and left, shutting it behind him.

She collapsed against it and closed her eyes. What was she getting herself into? Emotionally Heath was on the ragged edge, there was a lot of suppressed violence in him. He was no more the man she'd married than she was the wife he'd expected would be waiting for him.

Still, there was a strong emotional bond between them. Her compassion for him was almost overwhelming, and she was afraid she'd do anything to relieve the deep anguish that she and Darren had caused him. Could she honestly say no if he wanted to make love to her? More importantly, did she really want to refuse?

She'd always responded to him sexually even when her trust and respect for him had worn thin. It was obvious that she still did, but was it inspired now by love or by pity? She needed time to learn to know this stranger who was her husband before she committed herself both body and soul to him again.

Chapter Four

Heath slumped wearily in the chair, only partially aware of Darren and Michaela who had moved away from him and were talking quietly on the other side of the room. He couldn't remember ever having felt so physically and emotionally battered, not even after the beatings and brainwashing sessions his captors had delighted in giving him. He'd known those were coming at intervals and was prepared for them, but this...

Since the initial shock of his unexpected release, he'd been in a constant state of fluctuation, part of the time riding the clouds of euphoria, the rest of the time plunged to the depth of despair. The first crushing blow had been when they'd told him they couldn't find Michaela. For two days he'd worried, and fretted, and nearly gone crazy.

Then, earlier today—or was it yesterday by now?— they'd come to him with the jubilant news that she'd been located and would be at the airport in the States to meet him. Once again he'd been high on pure relief and happiness.

The long trip had been an agony of impatience and uncertainty that had set his nerves screaming, but then the plane landed, he was on the ground and Michaela was in his arms. He'd never known such exultation, and when she told him he had a son he'd gone into orbit.

It had been a long way down this time, and the crash had shattered him. He felt disembodied and knew he'd finally crossed the threshold beyond which he couldn't function. All he wanted to do was sleep.

A hand on his shoulder triggered the instant reflex of all prisoners, alarm. His eyes flew open and he jerked upright, prepared to defend himself. It was Michaela, and she jumped back, frightened.

"I'm sorry, I didn't mean to startle you," she said.

Her marvelous big brown eyes were wide with surprise, and for the first time he noticed that she looked pale and tired. Older, too, but the years had enhanced rather than diminished her beauty. They'd brought a ripeness, a look of completion, that made her even more desirable. Except that there was no desire left in him, which was a blessing tonight.

He curbed his intense need to touch her. He'd promised he wouldn't, and nothing would make him break that promise unless she indicated that she wanted him to.

Instead, he rubbed his hand over his face. "It's not your fault. I learned quickly to be always on guard. I'm afraid it'll take me awhile to get over it." He looked around. "Did Darren leave?"

"Yes, he did." She stood looking down at him, a worried frown creasing her smooth, creamy brow. "Heath, you look like you're about to collapse. Don't you think you'd better go to bed?"

Ah yes, to bed. That's what he'd been looking forward to for six years, going to bed with Michaela on his first night home.

He fought an insane desire to laugh. *The best-laid plans of mice and men*... as the Scottish poet Robert Burns so aptly put it. The thought of going to bed alone again was almost intolerable, but he knew she was right. It wouldn't do to pass out and frighten her.

He nodded and attempted to stand. "With the time difference and everything it must have been a couple of days since I slept last...."

A wave of dizziness knocked him off balance. He stumbled and grabbed for the back of the chair, and then Michaela's arms were around his waist, steadying him. He clutched at her, and the vertigo subsided as they embraced each other.

She was so soft, and she seemed to melt against him as he rubbed his face in her thick Titian hair. He hadn't meant for this to happen when he'd pleaded with her to stay with him tonight, but now that it had, how could he possibly release her?

For all those years it was his own resources that kept him alive and sane. He'd had a reserve of toughness and cunning that enabled him to bluff, and scheme and claw through that blazing hell to survive, but as time crept by, the cruelty, malnutrition and loneliness had chipped away at his will. The memory of her sweetness and her strength were all that had kept him from disintegrating.

Tonight he needed the comfort and security of her warm, familiar body in his arms.

Michaela balanced herself to absorb some of Heath's weight, but after a moment he managed to steady himself. She could feel his heart beating under her cheek. It was a fast, irregular beat much the same as her own. They were both in a state of upheaval from the continuous trauma they'd endured during this long day.

She was getting used to his thinness, and his body became more familiar each time he held her. This time she welcomed his arms around her and snuggled against him in an effort to take away some of the pain she and Darren had caused him. Surprisingly the contact comforted her, too, and she was reluctant to break it.

"Are you going to be able to make it to the bedroom?" she asked against his shirt front.

"Sure," he said softly. "How about you? I suspect that you're as exhausted as I am. It's been a rough day for both of us."

His gentleness was almost her undoing. She hadn't expected him to be so understanding. She drew a ragged breath, and her mouth trembled, making speech difficult. "Oh, Heath, I'm so sorry to have made your homecoming such a disaster...."

He moved his hand up to caress the back of her head and press her face against his chest. "No, Mickey, we're not going to talk about that," he said firmly. "There'll be plenty of time later after we've had some sleep. Now, come and show me which bedroom you want me in."

She managed a grin. "I don't even know where they are," she admitted as they began to walk, each with an arm around the other, "but I imagine we'll find them."

They did, and she led him into the first one they came to and made him sit down on the edge of the bed. He lowered himself stiffly, then just sat there, shoulders slumped and looking unutterably weary.

She couldn't leave him like that, knowing that if she did he'd lie back and fall asleep with all his clothes on. She dropped to her knees in front of him and untied one of his shoes.

"Michaela?" He sounded startled.

"It's all right," she said without raising her head. "I just want to make sure you're comfortable." She hesitated a moment, then looked up at him. "Do you mind?"

He looked disapproving but appreciative as he cupped her face with his hands. "You don't have to wait on me. I'm not an invalid."

She put her hands on his thighs for balance, and he parted them to bring her closer. "I know you're not, but I'd like to do this for you. Of course if you don't want me to, or if it makes you uncomfortable..."

He leaned down and stopped her words with a gentle kiss on the lips. "I want you to do anything for me that you want to do." He brushed a misplaced lock of her hair back from her forehead. "And if by 'uncomfortable' you mean aroused, you needn't worry. Tomorrow I'm sure I'll have to deal with that problem again, but tonight I'm just too tired."

Too tired and too shocked, she thought, feeling sick because of what she'd done to him. She was amazed that he was taking it so well. The Heath she'd lived with six years ago certainly wouldn't have.

She removed his shoes, then reached up to unfasten his uniform shirt. Her fingers shook as she tussled with the small buttons, and it didn't help any when he put his arms loosely around her waist. "You didn't used to have this much trouble undressing me," he said with a teasing smile. "Don't be so nervous, honey, I won't bite."

She felt as if she were going to splinter into little pieces, but she couldn't, wouldn't do that to Heath. She knew he was almost at the end of his tether, too, and she wasn't going to make it any more difficult for him. If he wanted to keep things between them on a fairly even keel until he was better able to deal with the mess he'd come back to, then she was going to do everything she could to help him.

She lowered her eyes shyly. "It's been a long time," she murmured. "I'm out of practice."

With a moan he tightened his arms around her, drawing her against his chest and belly. "Much too long," he said tightly. "Michaela, sleep here with me tonight."

Instinctively she tensed, and he hurried on. "I mean sleep, literally. I won't bother you for sex, I just need you in my bed, in my arms. I've been so lonely without you."

Her resistance melted. How could she refuse his request, knowing what it must have cost him in pride now that he knew about her engagement to his brother? She could always get out of bed and go to the other room if he made a pass, but she was sure he wouldn't. Heath may have been thoughtless in the early months of their marriage, but when he'd made her a promise, he'd kept it.

Besides, she'd been lonely, too. Her arms had never stopped aching for her husband, and even as she'd prepared to walk down the aisle to marry again she'd been unable to wholeheartedly accept another man in his place.

"I've been lonely, too," she said honestly. "I was telling the truth when I said I'd never been intimate with—"

Heath put his fingers to her mouth, cutting off Darren's name. "I told you we're not going to talk about that yet," he said. "I don't want to hear about you and any other man, not tonight. Will you stay with me?"

"Yes," she said, and pushed the shirt off his shoulders and down his arms, leaving a good share of his torso bare. She was appalled at how white he was. Heath had gone to college in Arizona, and he'd been a dedicated athlete. He'd spent most of his time out-of-doors, and he'd had a golden tan.

Now his skin had a pale gray pallor, and there was no flesh between it and his ribs. Each bone was distinguishable, and she pressed her trembling lips together to keep from crying out.

Instead, she reached for his belt buckle, and again her fingers were all thumbs. They kept slipping and touching his exposed stomach, sending little shivers down her spine. A hot surge of color flushed her face. Good heavens, why was this so difficult? It wasn't as if they were in the throes of an urgent passion.

She finally got the belt off and had reached for the top button on his fly when his hand covered hers, holding it in place. "Would you rather I left my pants on?" There was amusement in his tone.

She looked at him and blinked. "Do you still sleep... uh...unclothed?"

He chuckled and put his arm around her again. "I think the word you're looking for is 'nude'."

Her blush deepened and his arms tightened around her. "I'm sorry," he said, but his tone still held laughter. "I shouldn't embarrass you, but I can't begin to tell you what a relief it is that you haven't lost your innocence."

Her eyes widened. "My innocence! How can you say that? I'm married and have a son...."

"I'm not talking about virginity," he said solemnly, "although you gave me that, too. By innocent, I mean that you can still blush. It's just one of the many reasons I fell in love with you."

Michaela swallowed, and for a moment she couldn't speak. Who was this man? The State Department, the navy and her own eyes and instinct told her he was Heath Tanner, her husband, but he neither acted nor talked like Heath. He didn't even think like Heath. It was scary.

Before she could find her voice, he spoke again. "Why don't you go into the other bedroom and change into whatever it is you wear to bed, while I turn down the covers and brush my teeth?"

She felt a rush of gratitude. He was being sensitive to her feelings. She'd have found it terribly difficult to undress in front of him, or worse, let him take her clothes off. Not that she hadn't done both many times in the past.

Although she'd been a shy and virginal bride, it hadn't taken him long to overcome that and teach her the ecstasy of uninhibited lovemaking.

Dismayed at the turn her thoughts had taken, Michaela got to her feet. "Thank you, I will," she said formally as she walked across the room to pick up one of the two suitcases that someone had put there. "Can I bring you something from your suitcase?"

"Just the shaving kit there on the table. It has everything in it that I'll need."

She picked up the kit and gave it to him. "I won't be long," she assured him and left.

In the other bedroom, Michaela put her suitcase on the luggage rack and opened it. She and Darren had both had their suitcases packed and ready to leave on the honeymoon they'd later had to cancel, and she'd selected the one with all the necessities in it to bring to Washington with her.

As she sorted through it, looking for a nightgown and robe, she remembered with consternation that all her nighties were bridal gowns, silky and low-cut. She couldn't climb into Heath's bed in one of the those and expect just to sleep!

Unfortunately, she had no choice, and finally she selected the most demure one, the one she'd intended to wear for Darren on their wedding night. It was chiffon in a shade of pink that complemented rather than clashed with her hair, and it had small embroidered rosebuds sprinkled through it. The neckline featured tiny buttons to the throat, but the gown was sleeveless and the material was transparent enough to offer tantalizing glimpses of the nude body underneath.

Its saving grace was a matching peignoir that also buttoned to the throat and had long full sleeves. Like the gown, it was semitransparent, but the two garments worn together were opaque.

With a sigh she undressed, brushed her teeth and took a quick shower, then slipped into the gown and peignoir and ran a comb through her hair. As she looked at herself in the mirror, she was struck by a sense of being swept into a time warp by some force that gave her no will or choice.

This morning she'd been a widow on the verge of marrying again. Tonight she was a wife getting ready to go to bed with her husband, but between this morning and tonight the husbands had been switched and she'd been propelled back into the past. She was reliving a night that had happened seven years ago!

The comb fell from her hand, and she closed her eyes and turned away. She didn't dare dwell on the happenings of this bizarre day or she'd be convinced that she was hallucinating.

With a twinge of apprehension, Michaela walked across the hall and into the other bedroom. The bedside lamp was still on and Heath was stretched out with the sheet pulled up to his waist and his eyes closed. For a moment she thought he was asleep, but then he opened his eyes and saw her standing just inside the door.

He blinked, and his lips parted as he looked at her. His eyes widened, and his features softened with love. "Dear

God," he whispered softly, and raised himself up on his elbow.

The warmth of his reaction radiated across the room and enveloped her, as, for a few seconds, she basked in his admiration. Then, without warning, she felt a chill and was wrenched out of her enchantment. It took her a moment to realize that the chill also emanated from him.

As she watched, his expression hardened, and the desire in his eyes turned to ice. Instinctively she cringed and wrapped her arms around herself in an effort to cover the sexy garment.

His gaze held hers in a furious deadlock. "It doesn't take much imagination to recognize that as a trousseau gown. You were planning to wear it for Darren tonight, weren't you!" His voice was as icy as his eyes.

Michaela groaned. She'd been so afraid he'd think she was teasing him with the seductive outfit that she'd missed the obvious fact that any man would know it was created for a wedding night.

Her mind seemed to have shut down completely, and she couldn't think of anything coherent to say. "I—Heath, it's all I had with me. I didn't think . . ."

"Damn you, get out." He bit the words off, sharp and cutting. "Sleep in the other room or go to Darren and get on with the honeymoon, but get out of my sight." He rolled over and buried his face in his arms on the pillow.

Too distraught to do anything but follow orders, she turned and fled back to the other bedroom, where she threw herself on the bed and curled up in a ball. Her heart hammered, her breath came in gasps, and if she'd had something in her hand she'd have thrown it.

Dammit, she couldn't seem to do anything right, but who could foresee Heath's lightning changes of mood?

He'd seemed to be taking her engagement to Darren so calmly once the initial violent reaction was over.

Why was she bearing all the guilt, anyway? Heath had been dead. The navy told her so, and everybody agreed that the navy was all-knowing. Ask them. They were always happy to admit that they never make mistakes.

Everyone had encouraged her to stop grieving and think of her child. They'd pointed out that Skip needed a happy, well-adjusted mother, and all her friends had told her to find a nice man and marry again to give her son a father.

As a widow she'd been entitled to rebuild her life, so why was she so mired in remorse? If she didn't pull herself together and stop feeling as if she'd committed some unforgivable sin, she wouldn't be any good for Heath, Skipper, Darren or herself.

She lay quietly for several minutes trying to clear her mind and not think. She just went around in circles when she did. How could she possibly make important decisions when she was so tired, confused and unnerved?

She hadn't turned the lamp back on, and with the drapes pulled across the picture window, it was dark. She listened for a sound from the other bedroom, but there was none. Had Heath fallen asleep? She didn't think so; he'd been too upset. He'd said he didn't want to be alone, but then he'd sent her away without letting her try to explain.

Obviously he wasn't taking the news of her plans to remarry as calmly as he'd led her to believe. Resentment was boiling just under his surface calm, waiting to erupt at any provocation. Still, he had been making a superhuman effort to keep it under control.

Slowly she unwound herself and sat up. He'd ordered her out, but she couldn't leave him alone without trying to set things right.

She turned on the light and rummaged through her suitcase until she found a pair of underpants and a thigh-length T-shirt. If this situation was agonizing for her it must be many times more so for Heath after his long confinement. His whole world had fallen apart while he'd been gone. She had to try to understand and help him.

After removing the offending peignoir, she dressed in the T-shirt and panties, then turned out the light and once again approached the room across the hall. The light was still on and the door open as she'd left it.

Her stomach knotted with apprehension as she stepped inside. Heath was still lying on his stomach with his face in his arms. At first she thought he was asleep, but as she neared him she could tell by his ragged breathing that he wasn't.

Not wanting to startle him again as she had earlier, she spoke softly. "Heath, I'm going to turn off the light."

He gave no indication that he'd heard her, so she moved to his side of the bed and turned the switch on the lamp. The window was undraped, and the room was not totally dark but dimly illuminated by the lights from the surrounding buildings. Michaela made no sound as she walked barefoot on the carpet around the bed and climbed in.

Heath didn't move or acknowledge her presence, and for a moment she lay tense and silent on the edge of the queen-size mattress. It had been so long since she'd shared a bed with a man, and she didn't know what to expect from this one. Maybe Darren had been right, and she shouldn't have stayed with Heath.

The minutes ticked by as she reminded herself that this man was her husband, and he needed her help to adjust to the so-called civilized world again. After what he'd been through, it was unrealistic to expect him to be reasonable and predictable.

She'd almost gotten up the nerve to reach over and touch him when she felt his hand on her shoulder. She lay still as he moved it up the side of her throat and caressed her cheek. His palm was rough and callused, but his touch was hauntingly gentle.

"I'm sorry, sweetheart." His voice was as gentle as his touch, and heartbreakingly remorseful. "I should have listened to the psychiatrist in Germany and let them take me directly to the Bethesda naval hospital when I got here. I'm a real basket case."

He outlined her quivering lips with his thumb. "You don't have to put up with that kind of treatment. It would be best if you'd get a room of your own somewhere else in the hotel. I'll arrange for it. No one will blame you, least of all me. Tomorrow I'll let them check me into the hospital."

He was offering her an out. She should be relieved, but all she could feel was the tenderness of his touch and the anguish in his tone.

She reached up and covered his hand with her own. "Is that what you want, Heath? Would you rather be alone?"

She heard the groan that seemed ripped from his throat, but he didn't speak.

She took his hand in hers and held it as she rolled on her side to face him. It was too dark to see his expression, but his uneven breathing told her of his turmoil.

"If you want me to leave I will," she said as she caressed his hand, "but I'd rather stay with you. We have a lot of catching up to do, and the going will get pretty rough. I don't intend to run away every time that happens. Now, tell me honestly, would you prefer that I leave?"

He reached for her then, and she went willingly as he cradled her against him and buried his face in her shoulder. "No!" It was a strangled sound uttered against her throat. "God forgive me, but I can't send you away. I'm not even sure I could have let you go."

"Then let's not consider that an option," she said as she stroked her fingers through his thick black hair. "You'll feel better after you've had a lot of badly needed sleep, so just relax and let it take over."

She lowered her fingers to his neck and shoulders and massaged the tight muscles.

"Mmmm," he murmured. "That feels so good."

His hands moved over her back and the rise of her buttocks, then lower to her bare thighs. He caught his breath. "What have you got on?"

The muscles in his neck had started to unknot under her caressing palm. "A pair of panties and a T-shirt," she answered, and moved her fingers to rub his shoulders.

"I love you," he said drowsily, and settled his hand under the shirt on her silk-covered derrière. Within seconds he was asleep in her arms.

It was nearly noon before Michaela woke after ten hours of deep, reviving sleep, but she knew exactly where she was and that the man wrapped around her so intimately was Heath, not Darren.

Somehow, even though she'd slept well, she'd been aware of Heath's movements and responded to them, turning when he did, snuggling when he held her, and holding him when he seemed restless. Once, when he'd cried out in some nameless terror, she even sang the first verse of a lullaby to him. She smiled. It was the same one she used to sing to Skipper, and Heath had quieted down as easily as Skip had under the simple, soothing melody.

Carefully she wiggled out of his embrace and slid off the bed. He mumbled and rolled over onto his stomach but didn't waken. Michaela pulled the blanket over him to keep him warm and hoped he'd continue to sleep for several more hours.

The first thing she did when she finished dressing in cream slacks and a matching, summer-weight, short-sleeved sweater was to phone Darren's room. He was anxiously waiting for her call and wanted to come up, but she told him no. Although she didn't mention it to him, she knew that Heath's temper was uncertain at best, and she didn't want him to wake up and find her alone with his brother.

After ordering lunch from room service, an unheard-of luxury, she telephoned her apartment in Seattle and talked to her mother and Skip. In the rush to leave, so that Michaela could be in Washington, D.C., to meet Heath's plane, there'd been no time to explain the difficult situation to the sick child, and that task had been delegated to Michaela's parents. They'd done their best, but Skipper was upset and confused.

"Grandma says you didn't marry Uncle Darren," he said accusingly.

"That's right, honey. Did Grandma tell you that your daddy's not dead but has been a prisoner all this time?"

"Uncle Darren's my daddy. You promised." His tone was petulant.

Michaela winced. How on earth did you explain something like this to a five-year-old? "I know, darling, but I can't marry Uncle Darren now because I'm still married to your real daddy. He didn't even know he had a little boy, but I showed him your picture and he's so proud of you. We'll be coming home in a few days."

There was silence on the other end of the line before Skip finally spoke. "Doesn't Uncle Darren want to be my daddy anymore?" There were tears in his voice.

"Oh Skipper, of course he does, but so does your real daddy. Darren will always be your uncle. That won't change."

But it would change, and she knew it. Not the blood relationship, but the close emotional bond between uncle and nephew that had existed since Skipper's birth. It would be impossible to maintain that bond with Heath back and eager to assume his rightful role as father to his son.

"I don't want a real daddy, I want Uncle Darren," the child sobbed, and Lila came back on the line.

"I'm sorry, dear. The poor little guy just doesn't understand...."

Michaela ran her fingers through her hair. "Of course he doesn't, Mom. I wish I could be there to handle this, but I can't leave Heath. Maybe if Darren talked to Skip..."

"Now don't you worry," Lila insisted. "Darren's parents have been working with him, too. Surely between the four of us we can reassure him that it's great to have both an uncle and a daddy."

A knock on the door and a voice calling "room service" put an end to the conversation, but not to Michaela's foreboding.

It was two o'clock before she heard Heath moving around in the bedroom. She'd used the time to read the newspaper that had been sent along with her lunch, and to watch the news on television. Both featured Heath and his miraculous resurrection, and both gave more attention to his wife's aborted marriage to his brother than they did to his imprisonment. They even used pictures of Skipper and her that they could have only obtained from family members.

Michaela was outraged but knew there was nothing she could do about it except warn their families not to talk to reporters. Maybe the interest would die down in a few days.

When she heard water running in the shower she phoned room service and ordered split pea soup, a fresh garden salad, a cheeseburger with french fries and a large pot of coffee with two cups. Heath was probably starved, and she was looking forward to putting some weight on him.

He was taking a long time in the shower, and Michaela found herself pacing around the small living room while she waited. Her nerves were tight again, and the anxiety she thought she'd conquered had crept back.

How should she greet him when he finally came out? Since they'd spent the night together, would he expect her to be the loving wife now? Would he want to hold her, kiss her, even make love?

How did she feel about that? She'd slept in his arms, and after the initial uncertainty and shyness, it had been wonderful. Although they'd only spent a few months together before he'd been lost at sea, it had taken her years to get used to sleeping without him. She'd missed having a man in her bed, but, oddly, in all the time he'd been gone, she'd never been tempted to replace him there, not even with Darren after he'd become her fiancé.

Michaela was standing at the window looking out over the city when the bedroom door opened and Heath came down the short hall to the living room. She turned and smiled at him, but the smile she received in return was strained and didn't reach his eyes.

"Sorry I slept so long," he said formally. "You should have woken me up."

Her smile faltered, but she managed to keep it in place. "You needed the rest. Are you feeling better now?"

He looked better. His eyes were clearer, and the lines of exhaustion were gone from his face. He stood straighter and his walk was lighter, but she'd expected him to be more relaxed, now that he was free at last.

Instead, he was still tense and ill at ease, with an air of not so much depression, as disillusion, about him. Michaela knew that it was her fault, and the knowledge ate at her.

"Much better, thank you," he said in answer to her question. "And you?" Impersonally his gaze roamed over her. "You look rested and very beautiful."

He could have been talking to a stranger, and before she could think of a reply, there was a knock on the door and his lunch arrived.

Heath signed the bill while Michaela set the food out on the table. "I knew you'd be hungry, so I called room service as soon as I heard you stirring," she explained, then added uncertainly, "I guess I should have asked you what you wanted."

"This is fine. Aren't you eating?"

"I had my lunch sent up earlier, but I'll have coffee with you."

"I'd like that," he said as he seated her. "Do you mind if I turn on the television? There's so much I need to catch up on."

She'd hoped to spare him the newscasts for a while, but he had to see them sometime. "All right," she said hesitantly, "but I'd better warn you that you *are* the news."

She could almost feel him cringe as he turned away. "In that case, I'll eat first," he said and sat down across the table from her.

They spoke little while Heath ate. He seemed preoccupied, and she tried not to squirm as her apprehension mounted.

What was the matter with him? He'd held her so closely last night, never letting her out of reach. Why was he so distant now?

Had she done something to displease him? He didn't seem angry, but maybe he was disturbed because she'd gotten out of bed while he still slept. Or had he expected her to throw herself into his arms and kiss him when he did get up? That should have been the normal reaction of a wife just reunited with her husband after a prolonged absence.

If he'd given her any indication that's what he wanted, she probably would have, but his attitude had not been inviting. He'd been cool and formally polite from the moment he stepped into the room.

Heath ate the soup, part of the salad and half the cheeseburger, then sighed and put his napkin on the table. "That was very good," he said, "but after years of short rations I can only eat a little at a time." He picked up the rest of the burger and the french fries and wrapped them in the napkin. "I'll put these in the refrigerator and warm them in the microwave later."

He stood and walked into the bar area where there was a tiny refrigerator, then paused at the window and looked out.

Michaela still sat at the table, unsure of what to do now. He stood with his back to her, and she had no idea of what he was thinking.

She didn't have to wonder long. "Michaela, I had some time alone to think after I woke up, and I've decided to check into the hospital at Bethesda as the doctors have advised. I realize now that I need help."

She tried not to show her dismay, but walked over to stand beside him. "Heath, if this is about last night, because you yelled at me, I'm not blaming you. I've hurt you...."

"No." His tone was sharp and compelling. "You did nothing wrong. Intellectually I know that, but emotionally I don't think I can handle it yet. I need counseling."

"Of course you do, but can't you get it in Seattle? I know you're anxious to see Skipper and your parents—"

"Not yet," he interrupted. "I need time. Is Darren still registered at the hotel?"

She blinked at his sudden change of subject. "No, I don't think so. I talked to him on the phone earlier, and he decided to go back to Seattle as soon as he could book a flight."

Heath's eyes narrowed. "Was this his idea or yours?"

She fidgeted. It had been her idea, and she'd had a hard time convincing him to agree to her staying here alone with Heath. "Well...uh...it was my suggestion, but he realized that his being here only upsets you."

"It does upset me, but I'd hoped he hadn't left yet. I don't like the idea of your traveling alone."

She gasped. "Traveling? Me?"

He nodded. "Yes, Michaela. I want you to go back to Seattle. I don't know how long I'll be in the hospital here, and Skipper needs you. I'll have the navy guard get in touch with Lieutenant Newman and ask him to make all the arrangements."

His gaze sought and held hers. "Believe me, love, it's best that you do as I ask." His tone was flat and determined.

Chapter Five

Michaela stared at Heath, for a moment unable to speak. When she did it was little more than a whisper. "You . . . you're sending me away?"

An odd expression flitted across his face. It might have been regret, but it was gone so quickly that she couldn't tell. "There'll be no reason for you to stay. I'll be in the hospital, and if it's anything like it was in Wiesbaden, the days will be crammed with tests, counseling and debriefing sessions. It's not safe for you to be all alone in a strange city."

She was dismayed at how badly his rejection could hurt her. "Last night you said you needed me." Her pain sounded in her tone.

He jammed his hands into the pockets of his stiff new jeans and turned his face. "I did need you, Michaela. You sensed that need and stayed with me." His voice shook and he cleared his throat. "I couldn't have made it through the night without you."

His voice, thick with suppressed emotion, became choked up, making further talk impossible. For several long moments he stood with his head bowed until at last he spoke again. "I'm neither a child nor an invalid, and I'm not going to cling to you like one. I'm rested now and regaining the strength I lost because of the rotten prison food. By the time I get to Seattle I'll be my old self again."

"I . . . I like you just the way you are now." The words were out before she could bite them back.

"You do?" He couldn't hide his surprise.

She nodded. "I like being needed. You never did before."

He looked puzzled. "Never did what?"

"Never did need me. Oh, you wanted me. I guess you even loved me in your own way, but you never really needed me until last night."

With lightning speed his expression changed from puzzlement to indignation. "My God," he grated and clutched her by the upper arms. "How can you say such a thing? I obviously needed you a hell of a lot more than you ever needed me. You were quick enough to take my brother as a substitute."

The jab went straight through her heart. "That's not fair." She bristled with exasperation. "I thought you were dead."

His anger disappeared as quickly as it had appeared. "I know," he said quietly as he dropped his hands from her arms and turned away. "Are you in love with Darren, Mickey?"

She'd known he'd ask that question soon, but how could she answer it without being disloyal to the man who had been so good to her for so long?

"Darren has been a combination big brother and best friend to me all the time you've been gone," she began.

"You don't marry your big brother," Heath reminded her.

"No," she agreed, "but many marriages are based on friendship rather than passion. I hope you can understand the distinction when I say that I love Darren, but I'm not *in love* with him."

Heath's short laugh was not inspired by mirth. "Sorry, but the subtlety of that escapes me," he said heatedly.

"It wouldn't if you weren't so determined not to understand," she snapped, and was immediately sorry. It was imperative that she remember at all times that he was in a most precarious emotional state. But then, so was she.

She took a deep breath and gentled her tone. "All right, let me try to explain. I was shattered when I was told that you'd gone overboard during a skirmish in the Persian Gulf and drowned. You'd only been at sea for a few months and we weren't at war! You didn't even know that you were going to be a father. If it hadn't been for our families I don't know how I'd have gotten through that first year."

She crossed over to the couch and sat down. "Your dad handled all the legalities since he was a career military man and knew what had to be done, and Darren took over as big brother and best friend."

"Don't forget husband," Heath retorted.

Michaela's head jerked back and she glared up at him. "I won't dignify that remark with a comment," she said, "and I'm not going to continue to apologize for agreeing to marry him. You'd been gone for six years and I was legally free. I'm truly sorry that it's causing you so much anguish, but the navy told me I was a widow. Skip needed a man in his life, but that's not the only reason I was planning to remarry."

She paused to catch her breath, and watched as Heath dropped into the nearest chair. She hated to hurt him even more. If it were possible to lie and tell him she had no feelings for Darren and was only marrying him for Skip's sake she would, but she couldn't do that. If she and Heath were to have any future together it would have to be based on the absolute truth.

"I'm not passionately in love with Darren," she continued softly, "but I do care about him. He'd have been a good husband, and I didn't want to spend the rest of my life alone. I haven't lied to him. He knew that he'd never take your place in my heart."

For a long time Heath said nothing, and the silence was vexing. When he finally spoke all he said was, "I see," as he stood and headed for the door.

Michaela's tight nerves quivered. "Where are you going?"

"I just want to speak to the guard," he said.

He went out into the hall, and when he came back a few minutes later he crossed to the telephone, picked it up and dialed. Michaela fled to the bathroom so that he could have a private conversation.

When she returned Heath was watching the news on television. It was the same report she'd seen earlier featuring his every move from the time he'd appeared in the door of the plane until he and Michaela had disappeared into the limousine, and again at the hotel as they were escorted through the crowd to the elevator.

The narration covered his imprisonment and release briefly, but dwelled with exaggerated, and almost totally inaccurate, detail on the fact that the returning prisoner's wife was in the process of marrying his brother when notified that her husband was still alive. A play on the classic Tennyson story about Enoch Arden that was guaranteed to send audiences flocking to their sets.

Heath pushed the Off button on the remote control and patted the seat beside him on the couch in silent invitation. Michaela sat down.

"I talked to Lieutenant Newman," he told her, "and he's agreed to make arrangements for me to check into the hospital later this evening."

Michaela knew she'd failed him, and the knowledge was almost intolerable. They should be happily making plans to return home together for a reunion with Skip and the rest of his family.

She reached over and touched his hand. "Are you sure that's what you want to do?" Her voice broke and she swallowed.

Heath caught her hand in his. "It's what I have to do, honey, and don't blame yourself. I...I guess I'm not ready yet to face the real world and all its changes."

He hesitated, and Michaela could feel the tension mounting in him as his hand tightened on hers. "I've been totally isolated," he continued. "Not only was I locked up in a remote area of a strange country, but I didn't speak the language. It didn't do me any good to listen to a radio, or to the other prisoners and guards talking, because I couldn't understand what was being said."

His voice broke, and he swallowed as he fought to overcome his agitation. "I've been alone so much that open spaces and crowds scare the hell out of me."

There was no hint of self-pity in his tone. He was simply stating facts for her information, but her compassion was almost her undoing. She wanted to hold him, comfort him, but she instinctively knew that he wouldn't welcome her embrace. Why?

Last night when he'd needed her loving warmth and enthusiasm she'd been too shocked and dazed to supply it. Now that she'd regained her equilibrium and was not only willing but anxious to give him the support he required, he no longer wanted it. He didn't seem to be blaming her for disappointing him, but he was sending her away!

"Do I scare you, too, Heath?" she asked quietly.

He turned toward her, and his gaze searched her face as he lifted his hand to stroke his fingers through her hair. "You most of all," he admitted. "I've been living in a fantasy with you for so long that I lost track of reality."

His tone changed and became brisk. "I don't remember much about the first few months of my captivity. It's mostly a blur of pain and fear and despair, but when I finally adjusted and realized that it wasn't going to end soon I started fantasizing that you were with me."

He drew his hand back and looked away. "This will sound silly to you, but I created a world with just you and me in it. It was a haven I could retreat into when reality became unbearable."

His expression changed to a more dreamy, thoughtful look. "Time stood still in my little world and nothing changed. We were deeply in love and never quarreled. You never grew older, or more mature, and you always loved me, needed me, wanted me. I never let myself think of the years rolling by, or the changes that might be taking place back home. I only knew that someday I'd be free and we'd take up where we left off."

Without warning he stood and walked away from her, and when he spoke again his voice was harsh. "Only a fool would believe his fantasies. I was released so quickly and unexpectedly that I didn't have time to let go of them before I had to face the world as it is, and not as I wanted it to be. Now I need help. I can't trust myself to react rationally."

Michaela didn't attempt to speak. She knew she'd break down if she did. Heath had spent one-fifth of his young life in prison, although he'd committed no crime.

After a while the silence became oppressive, and Heath came back to the couch and sat down. He put his fingers under her quivering chin and raised her face to his. A tear had slipped out of the corner of her eye. He leaned over and, in a startlingly familiar and intimate gesture, licked it away.

"I don't want your pity, sweetheart. That's not why I'm telling you these things. Don't cry for me. I'm free now, and I have so much to look forward to. You've given me a gift that will brighten all the rest of my life, a son." He grinned mischievously. "How'd that happen, by the way? I thought we'd been taking precautions."

Michaela managed to grin back. "We had, but while we were separated I'd quit taking the pill. When you got your orders for sea duty and…uh…came to me, I started taking it again, but it must not have been effective yet."

He frowned. "Separated? Oh, you mean when I went on active duty?"

"Well, yes," she said hesitantly, puzzled by the question. "But we were separated before that."

Heath looked confused. "We were? Why?"

Good heavens, was there something wrong with his memory? How could he have forgotten that last violent quarrel? Even their uneasy reconciliation weeks later hadn't dimmed that recollection for her.

"Don't you remember the fight we had over your behavior after your college graduation?" she asked incredulously. The hurt he'd inflicted still had the power to rankle her. "You went out for a drink with the guys and didn't come home for three days. When you finally did, and I knew you weren't dead or injured, I packed my bags and went home to my parents."

Heath stared at her and his face became pale. "You left me?"

"You mean you honestly don't remember?" He shook his head. "We didn't see each other again for two months until you got your orders for sea duty. You had a week's leave before you shipped out, and you came to Phoenix and asked me to spend the time with you."

His expression was one of stunned disbelief. "Are you telling me that I let you go and didn't make any effort to get you back for two months?"

She bristled. "You had no choice about letting me go. I was furious and couldn't stand the sight of you, but you did spend a lot of time on the phone and writing letters trying to get me to come to San Diego where you were stationed."

"But you didn't?"

"No."

He seemed to be struggling to understand. "But surely one quarrel wasn't enough to break up a marriage."

He held up his hand when he saw her mutinous expression. "Now wait, if I went on a three-day binge then I deserved your wrath, but surely there was some way I could have earned your forgiveness."

Michaela felt a cold shiver slither down her spine. There was something very wrong. Didn't Heath remember anything about their brief marriage?

She bit back a sharp reply and asked instead. "Tell me, what is your impression of the time we spent together?"

He answered with hesitation. "It was a wonderful time. We were so much in love, and our nights were sheer ecstasy. You were the bride every man hopes for but seldom finds, virginal but willing and eager to learn.''

Michaela closed her eyes and let the remembered rapture wash over her for a moment before once more facing cold reality. ''I agree, our lovemaking was great, but we didn't spend all our time in bed. Can you tell me how we spent our days?''

''Well, sure,'' he said in a tone that indicated he was humoring her. ''We went to school. You also had a part-time job in the bookstore, and I was quarterback on the football team. We didn't see much of each other except at night.''

Well, at least he remembered that. ''You're right, we didn't. You were always at practice, or out of town with the team, or drinking beer with the guys at the nearest bar....''

''Are you saying that you resented my being on the team?'' He seemed genuinely perplexed.

''Damn right I did,'' she snapped, ''and I find it hard to believe that you don't remember the fights we had about it.''

He looked as if he were about to interrupt and she hurried to explain. ''It wasn't your being on the team that I resented. I was proud to be the wife of the university's star football player, but I very much objected to playing second fiddle to the game. I cut back on my classes and took a part-time job to help pay our expenses, and you lived and breathed football. All you wanted me for was convenient sex, and you better believe I was irate.''

Even as she spoke Michaela was appalled at how bitter she sounded. She'd had no idea that she still harbored this much rage over what she considered Heath's indifference and neglect after they were married.

One look at the bewilderment in his expression convinced her that he actually didn't have any recollection of the stormy side of their marriage. All he remembered was the fantastic lovemaking.

She'd never been with any other man, but even so she knew the chemistry between them was rare and powerful. He'd taken them to heights she'd never dreamed of and kept them there until they were wild with the need for release. Each time it came it shattered them both and put them together again as one.

Never, after the first night, had she been able to resist him, and in time this bewitchment she felt for him began to frighten her. No matter how violently they quarreled, he had only to take her in his arms, kiss her and touch her in the places he knew so well would turn her to flame, and she was his, body and soul.

She wasn't going to let that happen again. She was older now, and mature enough to understand that an obsession such as that was dangerous. She'd earned her independence and had no intention of giving it up. Never again would she be manipulated by a man, not even one she loved as much as she'd loved Heath in those days.

"Michaela, I honestly don't know what you're talking about," Heath said desperately. "I've been in love with you ever since you literally fell into my arms while climbing out of your second-story window at the dorm."

A relaxing warmth stole through her as the memory of their first meeting unfolded in her mind. "I wasn't climbing out," she said dreamily. "Remember, I was trying to climb in. I'd locked my key in the room, and my roommate, who had the only other one, had gone home for the weekend."

"So you always said," he teased, and the tension lines around his mouth and eyes disappeared. "But whatever the reason you were on that ladder, it's a good thing I was cutting across the lawn at the time. You missed a step and would have fallen if I hadn't caught you."

He was right, but in retrospect she knew it wasn't the fear of falling that had set her heart to pounding. It was that magnetism that had held her captive from the very first time he'd touched her.

"I did fall," she corrected him. "I fell in love with the handsome football hero who caught me, and he cast a spell over me that scrambled my good sense."

The lines around his mouth returned. "Are you saying you regret having married me?" His voice was laced with pain.

Without thinking she reached out and put her hand on his thigh. His muscles contracted, and she snatched her hand back.

He captured it and returned it to his leg, then gently held it there. "Don't inhibit your reactions. I like to have you touch me."

"I ... I didn't mean—" She floundered for words.

"I know you didn't, but that's no reason for you not to stroke me if you want to." She felt him shiver beneath her palm. "It's been so long since anyone touched me with tenderness...."

His voice trailed off, and he seemed lost in another time, but after a moment he continued. "I promise not to ravage you or expect more than you want to give."

She left her hand where he'd put it. As long as she was Heath's wife he wasn't going to have to go hungry for a gentle caress. "I know you won't. I just don't want to send you mixed signals."

"You don't." He stretched his leg in a silent invitation for her to stroke it and sighed contentedly. "You've made it plain how you feel."

With her thumb, she explored his knee. "I doubt that," she said emphatically, "since even *I* don't know how I feel. I didn't mean to imply that I regretted marrying you, but I do regret that we didn't take the time to get to know each other first. We were married just three weeks after we met, and now I can understand why our parents were so dead set against it. We should at least have waited until the end of the school year."

His hand on top of hers pressed lightly. "I couldn't wait, and neither could you." He was stating a sober truth. She'd been raised to believe that the vows came before the union was consummated, and they'd been frantic with their need for each other.

"I know," she said sadly, "but that's my point. A marriage shouldn't be based solely on physical attraction."

"Is that all you felt for me?"

She removed her hand from his knee. "No, Heath, it's not. I loved you so very much, but you were more concerned with making love than with building a future with me."

He leaned forward to put his elbows on his thighs and hold his chin on his linked fingers. "That's just not true, Michaela. I'm sorry if it seemed that way to you, but I don't understand why. We were happy. I remember how eagerly you fixed up that dingy little apartment we rented. You made frilly curtains, crocheted colorful scarves to cover the scarred tops of the cheap tables, and dragged me all over Tempe to garage sales." He chuckled. "The sheer joy that radiated from you each time you found a treasure among all the junk made the searching worthwhile."

A bittersweet nostalgia crept over her as he led her back to the early days when their marriage was still very new and filled with delight. But all too soon the bloom had faded and Heath became restless.

"Do you also remember that I spent most of my time in that apartment alone waiting for you to come home from a game, or a practice, or a night out with your teammates? We moved in together, but you never gave up your bachelor status. The only reason you studied at all was so you could keep your grades up high enough to play football and basketball."

Heath shook his head in bewilderment. "I don't know how we could have such different memories of the same time." He paused as though searching for an answer. "Maybe something happened to my mind in that prison, but I was never aware of any problems with amnesia." Another pause. "I know I've deliberately blocked out some of the things that occurred while I was there, but not anything that happened before I was captured."

He looked so perplexed that Michaela chided herself. When she'd realized that he had such selective memories of their time together, she should have been more careful in her response. He'd been back less than twenty-four hours, and in that time she'd managed to thoroughly disillusion him. No wonder he wanted to get away from her.

She put her hand on his back and rubbed gently. "Don't worry about it. Now that you're home it will all come back. The past has little to do with the way we are now. After all these years apart we're two different people. We have to get to know each other again, and maybe this time we'll be more thorough."

He flexed his shoulders to accommodate her massaging palms. "One thing I do remember for sure is that you used to massage me like this to loosen the kinks after a game. It felt almost as good then as it does now."

Michaela remembered, too, and used both her hands to knead the tight muscles across his back. "Why don't you stretch out there on the couch so I can do it properly?"

He rubbed his face in his hands. "I'm afraid I'll go to sleep," he said wearily.

"Don't fight it, Heath." She stood to give him room to move about. "You need the rest."

"I slept for over twelve hours," he muttered as he positioned himself full-length on his stomach with one cheek resting on his crossed arms. "I shouldn't be so tired."

"You've had six years of physical and emotional abuse." She sat back down on the edge of the sofa. "It's remarkable that you've come through it as well as you have, but it'll take a long time to get your strength back."

"I feel like such a weakling," he protested dispiritedly.

The compassion that welled within her overcame her hesitation, and she leaned down and kissed his exposed temple while her thumbs explored his nape. "You're the strongest man I've ever known," she murmured against his ear. "I think that's why I loved you even after I could no longer live with you. You always fought for what you wanted. You'd never have survived this long ordeal if you hadn't. A lesser man would have given up, so don't ever again tell me you're anything other than amazing because I won't believe it."

She rubbed her cheek against his and felt a telltale dampness there. "Oh, my love." Her voice was thick with unshed tears of her own. "It will be all right." She brushed an unruly lock of black hair off his forehead. "You're back, and that's all that matters. We'll work out our problems even though it may take a little while."

She kissed him again and straightened to her task. He hadn't offered to remove his shirt, and she didn't ask him to as she commenced the technique they'd perfected together to relieve his screaming muscles after a punishing game.

Heath was asleep within minutes and was still sleeping when a knock on the door brought him wide awake and to a sitting position. His expression was one of alarm, but Michaela was no longer surprised by his skittishness. She walked to the door and opened it to admit Lieutenant Newman, who had come to escort Heath to the hospital at Bethesda, Maryland.

Newman smiled as he glanced from Michaela to Heath, who had come briskly to his feet. "Relax, Heath," he said genially. "Am I too early?"

Heath looked at his watch. "No, sir, I'm afraid I fell asleep. I'll be ready in a minute."

He shot Michaela an apologetic glance and hurried toward the bedroom.

"Please sit down," Michaela said, and took a seat so Newman would, too. "I'm sorry, I should have wakened him, but he needs the rest so badly."

Newman settled in a chair opposite her. "Of course he does, and there's no hurry." He fidgeted for a moment then came to the point. "Is everything all right, Mrs. Tanner? Are you agreeable to his going into the hospital for psychological evaluation?"

"I'm agreeable to anything that will help Heath," she answered, "but I have no intention of going back to Seattle until he can go with me."

Newman looked startled. "But he asked me to make arrangements for you to catch a flight tomorrow morning. It's all taken care of."

She shook her head. "I'm sorry that you've been inconvenienced. Heath didn't tell me you were making those plans so soon, but it doesn't change anything. I think it's better if we don't tell him right now, though. Let him get settled in the hospital first. Will the navy arrange a place for me to stay?''

"Certainly. You can stay on here if you like. The suite's been reserved through the rest of the week."

Michaela looked around her at the luxurious setting, then answered with a tinge of regret. "That's very generous, but actually I'd prefer to be closer to the hospital. Just a room somewhere would be fine."

Newman thought for a moment. "They may be able to put you up in dependent housing. Let me check into it. When would you want to move?"

"As soon as possible, tomorrow morning if it can be arranged. Oh, and one more thing. Do I qualify for counseling, too? I need help in dealing with this."

"Of course you're entitled to counseling," he said. "I'm sorry if nobody thought to tell you that. Would you like me to set up an appointment with one of the psychologists?"

She smiled. "Yes, please. You're being most helpful, and I do appreciate it."

Just then the sound of the bedroom door opening brought the conversation to a close. "Remember," warned Michaela, "don't say anything about this to Heath tonight."

Newman merely nodded as Heath walked into the room. He'd changed into his uniform and was carrying his suitcase. "Sorry to keep you waiting," he said, "but I'm ready to go now."

Michaela didn't see any need for him to be so impatient to leave, but she didn't want to argue. "Just let me get my purse and I'll be right with you."

She started across the room, but a firm "no" from Heath stopped her. "I don't want you to go to the hospital with me," he said. "We'll say goodbye here."

The sharp pain of banishment swept over her, and she turned slowly to face him. "But I—"

The lieutenant's voice, sounding embarrassed, broke in. "Look, I need to talk to the guard. I'll wait for you in the hall." He made a quick exit, shutting the door behind him.

Michaela was only vaguely aware of the intrusion as her gaze held Heath's. "Why are you distancing yourself from me like this? How can we get to know each other again if you shut me out?" It was a cry of frustration.

He put his hand on her arm. "It's better this way, Mickey. I'm not up to a public goodbye. Arrangements have been made for you to fly back to Seattle tomorrow morning. Lieutenant Newman will give you all the details."

She didn't tell him that she already knew about the plans, but when she tried to protest that she didn't want to leave him he seemed to draw more deeply into himself.

"Please don't do this to me," he said, and she could hear the strain in his tone. "Don't make it more difficult than it already is. Just go home to Skipper and your parents. I'll join you as soon as I can."

All the fight drained out of her. She knew it was useless to argue, and it would only upset him. Her shoulders slumped in defeat, and she looked away. "All right. If that's the way you want it, I won't go to the hospital with you."

She had no intention of promising that she'd leave him and go back to Seattle.

He gave her arm a tight squeeze. "That's my girl," he said gently. "Say hello to Mom and Dad for me, and tell our son that his daddy is eagerly looking forward to seeing him.''

His voice broke, and he picked up his suitcase and strode across the room and out the door.

Michaela stood alone, her eyes unseeing as her mind played one phrase over and over.

He didn't even hug me or kiss me goodbye. He didn't even hug me or kiss me goodbye. . . .

Chapter Six

Several hours later, in the quiet darkness of the huge hospital, Heath twisted and turned in his bed trying to shut off the tormenting thoughts that ran like an out of control movie in his mind.

Last night he'd had Michaela in his bed, in his arms, for the first time in over six years, and all he could do was sleep. Now he was alone in a different bed, and his whole body ached for her.

What in hell was the matter with him? Twenty-four hours ago he'd been nearly delirious with the anticipation of finally being reunited with his wife. Now he had left her and was sending her clear across the country from him.

Why? Why couldn't he just take what she so generously offered and ignore the fact that she belonged to his brother?

The thought sent a shaft of rage tearing through him, but even as he shook with it he knew he was being unreasonable. Damn, why hadn't he been prepared for the possibility that Michaela had found someone else? Surely he wouldn't have wanted her to mourn for him forever!

Maybe that was the problem. He'd known he was alive and would someday return, and he'd apparently refused to face the likelihood that his shipmates had every reason to believe he'd drowned. It had been dark and there was no other ship in the area. They had no way of knowing about the small boat that had eventually picked him up and taken him to shore, where he was turned over to the local authorities.

If his intention was to punish Michaela then it had sure as hell backfired. He'd been hurting with need ever since he'd walked away from her. He'd wanted so badly to take her in his arms and kiss her goodbye, but he hadn't dared. If he had, he'd never have been able to let her go.

Maybe it was himself he was punishing by sending her back to Seattle and Darren. If it had been anyone else but his big brother she'd taken up with it might not have been so shattering, but he'd always looked up to Darren. There was ten years' difference in their ages, and Darren had seemed more like a second father than a brother.

They'd always been close, so why had his brother betrayed him? Darren was good-looking, bright and well-heeled, he could have any woman he wanted. Why did he have to choose his own brother's wife?

Now Heath couldn't trust either of them. Michaela said she wasn't in love with Darren, that she'd never slept with him. Was she telling the truth or merely saying what she knew he wanted to hear? The thought of his wife and his brother entwined in each other's arms was driving him crazy!

Michaela gazed around the pretty bedroom that was to be hers for the length of her stay and liked what she saw.

The late morning sun streamed through the crisp white curtains at the window and spilled across the blue spread that covered the brass bed. It was a feminine room with white-and-gold French provincial furniture that had belonged to her host and hostess's daughter before her recent marriage.

It was Monday morning, the start of a new week. The stupefying weekend was behind her, and, in spite of having slept little the night before, she felt relaxed and happy. It had finally sunk into her shocked mind that her husband, whom she'd loved not wisely but too well, was alive and reasonably healthy!

The problems arising from the miracle of his return could be dealt with later, but for now she was overcome with thanks that he wasn't dead.

She opened her suitcase and started to unpack. Things were running more smoothly today. Early this morning Lieutenant Newman had called the hotel to tell her that the Protestant chaplain and his wife had invited her to stay with them on the grounds of the medical center while Heath was in in the hospital.

It was a godsend, since the news media was still hot on her trail and she could be sheltered from them more easily on navy property. She shuddered as she remembered being hustled out of a back entrance of the hotel into a waiting car for her trip to the base. Eventually both she and Heath would have to talk to the reporters, but not yet. Neither of them was ready for that kind of pressure.

Her host and hostess, Lieutenant Commander Joseph and Irene Preston, were a middle-aged couple who welcomed her cheerfully and volunteered to act as her guides until she found her way around.

Arrangements had been made for Michaela to make long distance phone calls at navy expense, and when she finished unpacking she picked up the phone and dialed her apartment in Seattle. Her mother answered, and after ascertaining that Skipper was making a quick recovery from chicken pox, Michaela brought Lila up to date on what had been happening.

"Then you and Heath won't be coming home for a while?" Lila asked, disappointment evident in her tone.

"I'm afraid not, Mom. I haven't any idea how long. Heath doesn't know yet that I didn't take that flight this morning. He'll probably be pretty mad when he finds out, but I just can't leave him. I have an appointment after lunch with a Lieutenant Vivian Young, a psychologist who'll be counseling me. Is it going to be awfully inconvenient for you to stay on there and take care of Skip?"

"Of course not," Lila said emphatically. "We love doing it, and Heath's parents will be staying on, too, I'm sure. They're so anxious to see him, and they enjoy Skipper as much as we do. Everything's fine here, dear. You just take care of your husband and don't worry about your son. He's standing right here anxiously waiting to talk to you, so I'll turn the phone over to him."

"Hi, Mom," Skip said excitedly. "When are you coming home?"

"Not for a few more days, darling. Your daddy will be in the hospital for a while."

There was a pause, then, "Why don't you come home and leave him there? Uncle Darren came back last night. He brought me a football and a cap that says Washington Redskins on it. It's neat!"

Again she felt the chill of apprehension and wished Darren hadn't been so thoughtful. It wasn't fair to Heath for him to continue to act like a father to Skip. "I'm sure it is, and it was nice of Uncle Darren to bring it to you, but I can't leave Daddy all alone in the hospital.''

"Why not?'' he asked with a child's simple logic. "There's lots of people in the hospital to take care of him. They got doctors, 'n' nurses, 'n' candy stripers....''

Ah, yes, he knows all about hospitals, Michaela thought. *He's spent quite a bit of time in them during his young life.*

"But that's not the same as having someone you love with you,'' she explained.

"*He* doesn't love us, Uncle Darren does,'' Skip retorted.

Michaela sighed with frustration. "Oh, Skip, of course Daddy loves us. It isn't his fault that he was away for so long. He's very anxious to come home and see you, but he's sick right now and needs to be in the hospital.''

"*He's* not my daddy, Uncle Darren is. You promised,'' he repeated stubbornly, and Michaela knew it was time to tell him goodbye and hang up before she became impatient and said something to make him even more resentful.

Dinner that evening was at six o'clock, but, although both Lieutenant and Mrs. Preston made her feel right at home, Michaela ate little. The chaplain was driving her to the hospital to see Heath as soon as the meal was over, and she was tense and anxious about her reception.

What would she do if he insisted that she go home? She didn't want to make things more difficult for him, but she couldn't believe that he really wanted her to leave. He'd needed her with him badly that first night, even after he knew about her involvement with Darren. What had happened to change his mind?

Dr. Vivian Young, her counselor, was a compassionate and supportive person, and Michaela had been relaxed and open with her at their first session that afternoon, but even she couldn't tell Michaela how to handle this problem. She didn't know either Heath or Michaela well enough yet to form an opinion other than to advise her not to upset her husband unduly until they'd had a chance to evaluate his emotional condition.

"Michaela, aren't you going to finish your dinner?" Irene Preston asked.

Michaela was snapped out of her reverie. "Oh, I'm sorry. I'm afraid I'm not very hungry."

"I'm not surprised," Irene said, and her tone was soft with understanding. "You're under a lot of strain." She looked at her tall, distinguished husband. "Joseph, why don't you take her over to the hospital now? They're undoubtedly through with dinner, and Ensign Tanner will be free to have visitors."

Joseph smiled at Michaela. "Are you ready?"

She nodded. "Yes, as ready as I'll ever be. I'll get my purse."

The hospital was only a short distance from the Preston's house, and Joseph pulled into one of the parking spaces reserved for the chaplains. "I have some patients to see here," he said. "If it will make it easier for you, I'll go with you to see Heath."

It was tempting, but she knew it would just delay the inevitable. "Thank you, I appreciate your thoughtfulness, but I have to do this by myself. Just pray for me that he won't be too angry."

Joseph smiled. "I'll do that, but I suspect that your presence will do a great deal for your husband." He looked at his watch. "I'll be here for a couple of hours, so let's meet in the lobby at nine o'clock. If you need more time, I'll wait for you."

The hospital was huge, and when she inquired at the information desk she was given a map and instructions on how to find Heath, along with her visitor's pass. Also she was advised to inquire at the nurses' station before going into the room.

After an elevator ride and what seemed like miles of corridor, Michaela arrived in the area she sought and stopped at the desk. She introduced herself and asked to see her husband.

The nurse checked her files then pointed to her right. "If you'd like to wait in the lounge at the end of the hall, I'll inform Ensign Tanner that you're here."

Michaela hesitated. "Could you just tell him he has a visitor and not mention that it's his wife? He thinks I'm in Seattle."

The nurse frowned. "All right, but his visitors are carefully screened. If he refuses to see an anonymous one, I can't force him to."

"If that happens, then by all means tell him it's Michaela," she said, and walked on.

She was relieved to find the small cozy room empty. She wanted to see Heath alone. Her stomach churned, and the explanations she'd prepared for disobeying his wishes had been erased from her mind without a trace. Did the wives of men who were declared missing in action go through this when their husbands returned home, or was she the only one who repeatedly messed up?

Nervously she retreated to one end of the rectangular room and stood fidgeting until she heard footsteps coming down the hall. Then she squared her shoulders and lifted her head. If he was angry she'd just have to make him understand that she'd learned to make her own decisions and no longer took orders.

When Heath came through the open doorway Michaela had a few seconds to observe him before he saw her. He was dressed in jeans, a T-shirt and slippers, and he looked irritated. Oh dear, had the nurse told him she was here?

He turned toward her, and his eyes widened as his face mirrored his surprise. He hadn't known she was the visitor!

For a moment he just stood there, his jaw slack and his gaze roaming hungrily over her. Then he held out his arms and murmured just one word in a tone that was both tender and joyous. "Michaela."

All her anxiety disappeared and she was in his arms, holding him and snuggling against him as he clung to her.

"Oh, my God, Michaela." His tone was a cross between a moan and a prayer as he buried his face in her hair.

For a long time they stood clasped in each other's arms, savoring the chaste intimacy of their embrace. Now that she was no longer held together by the tension that had plagued her for the past three days, she felt like a rag doll that was losing its stuffing. Her legs trembled and her knees threatened to give way. She wasn't sure she could stand alone if Heath should release her.

She needn't have worried, Heath had no intention of letting her go. He'd spent a hellish night remembering how she felt snuggled against him, and his longing for her had been almost unbearable. The only thing that made it better today was the fact that he'd been too busy with tests, debriefing and counseling to think about anything else.

He moved his head to trail kisses down her cheek to the sensitive hollow at the side of her throat, and she tightened her arms around him. She was so soft, and so warm, and the illusive scent she used was titillating as hell. It wasn't the same one she'd used in college; this one was more haunting, more expensive.

Had Darren bought it for her?

The tormenting suspicion was like a knife in the gut, and his muscles tightened with jealousy, fierce and painful. Damn! Where had that idea come from? He'd resolved to put all speculation about his brother and his wife behind him and make every effort to win her back, but how could he when unwanted thoughts kept popping up out of nowhere?

Come to think of it, what was she doing here anyway? Why wasn't she in Seattle where he'd arranged for her to go?

He straightened and with an effort put her away from him. "Why are you still here, Michaela?" His tone was harsher than he'd intended, but he couldn't seem to control it. "I asked you to go back to Seattle and you said you would, so why didn't you?"

Michaela had been so relieved when Heath welcomed her with such loving tenderness that she was totally unprepared when he suddenly stiffened and pushed her away. How could he shift moods so quickly?

She was still trembling and leaned against the wall to steady herself and try to collect her thoughts. "You didn't ask me to go back to Seattle, you told me to, and I didn't say I would. You just went ahead and made arrangements without consulting me and assumed that I'd jump to do your bidding."

His expression was stormy. "Why not, I always made the decisions before?" he snapped.

"That's because I was eighteen and too awed by my big macho football hero to know better." Her temper was heating up. "I'm twenty-five now, and I've been on my own for a long time. I do my own thinking and make my own decisions.''

He turned away and ran his fingers through his hair. ''What made you decide I wouldn't be upset if you ignored my wishes rather than tell me what you wanted to do?'' he asked gruffly.

The last thing Michaela wanted was to quarrel with him, but she had to make him understand that she was an independent woman who wouldn't be treated like a child. She didn't need a father; she had one. What she wanted was a husband who would regard her as an equal.

''I...I hoped you'd be glad I'd stayed once you had time to think it over,'' she said quietly.

He turned back and looked at her, and she could see the anger drain from him. He reached for her, and she went back into his embrace. '' 'Glad' just doesn't cut it, sweetheart,'' he murmured into her ear. ''Try gratified, elated, jubilant! I missed you so much that I'd just about decided to check out of here and catch the red-eye flight to Seattle. I couldn't have stood another night like the last one.''

She rubbed her cheek against his chest. ''Then why did you try to send me away?'' she asked, totally confused.

He sighed. ''Because I'm an idiot. I hate being so dependent on you; it's not fair to either of us. Intellectually I know that you've built a new life for yourself, one that doesn't include me—''

She started to protest, but he put his finger to her mouth. ''No, let me finish. There's nothing wrong with that. It proves that you're a strong woman, one who cared enough about my little son to pull yourself together and be both a mother and a father to him.''

He moved his finger and kissed her gently on the lips. ''I'm proud of you. You've come a long way from the teenage student I left behind, but I seem to have not only stood still all those years, but regressed. Now you're strong and I'm the dependent one. I don't like it one bit.''

He released her and moved away.

Michaela could understand his dilemma. The Heath she'd married had been a self-contained man—strong, independent, arrogant, and almost impossible to live with. He hadn't wanted help when the going got rough. He'd been too tough to need anybody, certainly not a woman, not even her.

She followed him and put her hand on his arm. ''Heath, you've been out of prison less than a week. What did you expect, for heaven's sake? It will take months to get your health back to normal, and you're bound to be emotionally drained after what you've been through.'' She tugged on his arm. ''Come over and sit down with me. We need to talk.''

They settled themselves comfortably on the vinyl couch, and Heath put his arm around her and drew her close. There was still no sexual tension between them, but the warmth and contentment that radiated from one to the other was even more binding. Michaela put her arms around his narrow waist and leaned against his chest.

''Tell me about your day,'' she suggested. ''Did you talk to a counselor?''

''Yes, a Dr. Knox. He's an older man, probably late fifties, and was a prisoner in Korea for a while, so he knows something of what I've been through. Today was just a get-acquainted session, we'll probably get more done tomorrow. I'm scheduled for an hour with him every day through Friday.''

He nuzzled the throbbing pulse at her temple. ''But now I want to hear about you. How did you talk Lieutenant

Newman out of putting you on the flight to Seattle this morning?''

Michaela sighed. Obviously that still rankled him, so they'd better discuss it and get it behind them.

"Simple," she said. "I told him I wasn't leaving until you were able to come with me. He couldn't very well wrestle me onto the plane and strap me in a seat."

She heard the sarcasm in her tone and softened it. "Actually he was most helpful. He found me a place to stay here on the grounds and made arrangements for me to get counseling, too."

She told him about Lieutenant and Mrs. Preston and her first session with Dr. Young. "She got her Ph.D. from Yale, and can't be more than thirty. We spent the time getting acquainted today, too, and I'm to see her again Wednesday." She kissed his chest through the white T-shirt. "I hope she can tell me how to help you."

He tightened his arms around her. "You don't need anyone to tell you how to help me, sweetheart," he said tenderly. "Just being here for me and letting me hold you like this is what I need more than anything. If you'll be patient with me until I learn to adjust to this new and bewildering world, then we can decide about our future."

That last sentence sounded ominous, and she raised her head to look at him. "Decide our future? What's to decide? I don't understand."

He kissed the tip of her nose. "Later," he said, then changed the subject. "Have you heard from Seattle today? How's Skipper?"

Still uneasy, she put her head back on his chest and followed his lead. "I talked to Mother and to Skip. Both sets of parents are staying on until we get home, and Skip is feeling much better. He's giving Mom a bad time about wanting to get out of bed."

Heath chuckled. "How much longer will that be?"

"Oh, probably about a week."

"A week!" She felt him tense and silently cursed herself for not thinking before she spoke. "Why would he have to stay in bed for a week with chicken pox?"

Michaela tried not to let her own tension show. "Oh, well, he was pretty sick, a high temperature and all."

She didn't want to tell him about his son's heart condition tonight. She knew that if she did, he'd worry and not sleep well, but she made a mental vow to give him all the facts tomorrow.

Heath relaxed again and ruffled her hair playfully. "You're not one of those overprotective mothers, are you?"

She knew he was teasing, but he'd come so close to the truth that for a minute she almost defended herself. Instead, she swallowed and tried for an equally playful tone. "Of course not," she said primly. "Just because I still sterilize all his dishes and make him wear long underwear all summer doesn't mean—"

"Michaela, you wouldn't..." He sounded horrified.

She looked up and grinned, and he moved his hands to her ribs and tickled gently. "You little minx," he growled as she squealed with laughter and squirmed to get away from him. "Just wait, I'll get you yet."

He stopped tickling and took her face in his hands. "In fact, I think you owe me a forfeit," he said gently. "I'll settle for a kiss."

He didn't swoop down on her or make any move to claim his prize, but hovered just inches above her mouth and captured her gaze with his shimmering brown eyes. A small bud of desire slowly opened low in the pit of her stomach and sent tiny petals of need floating outward in every direction until all her attention was focused on his mouth.

She raised her hands and framed them on either side of his head. "It would be my pleasure," she whispered unsteadily and guided him downward.

His lips touched hers, moved a fraction of an inch away, then touched them again. His breath was fresh and sweet on her skin, and she stroked his temples as the tip of her tongue fondled and tasted him.

Gradually he applied more pressure and covered her mouth with his own. It had all the sweetness of a first kiss but without the awkwardness. She'd had no idea Heath could be so gentle but still so fervent. The silent magic of communication between lovers told her how badly he needed this long-awaited kiss from her, but he made no move to deepen it or to touch her intimately.

Michaela was both grateful and disappointed. She doubted that she was ready yet for the total commitment of making love with him, but as her lips moved under his, her breasts and thighs ached for his caress. She remembered all too vividly how quickly he'd always been able to arouse her with his eager mouth and his talented fingers. When at last he raised his head, breaking the contact, she moaned a protest and pulled it down again.

He didn't resist but cuddled her closer and nibbled on her earlobe, then trailed gentle love bites along her throat that sent tiny shivers spiraling down her spine.

When he spoke his voice was unsteady. "Easy, love. Let's take it slow and easy. I don't want to scare you again."

"I'm not afraid of you," she assured him and nuzzled his shoulder.

"I think you are," he said, "and if you're not, you should be. My control is still pretty tenuous. Don't start something you might not want to finish, because I may not be able to stop.''

Michaela knew he was right, but she wasn't sure she wanted him to stop. She was beginning to feel right at home in his arms, and he was stirring up feelings she'd thought she'd never enjoy again. That was good, but intimacy was only part of their problem. Their coupling had been mind-blowing before, but they'd been incompatible in almost every other way.

She'd married Heath without knowing him, and that had been a mistake. Now she was getting a second chance to try to make a go of it, but the Heath who had returned to her was a different man, a stranger. The overpowering physical attraction was still there between them, but this time she knew better than to expect it to be enough.

He needed her now, but once he'd adjusted to being a free man again, would he revert back to the self-centered macho male who expected her to walk in his shadow? She intended to find out before she went up in smoke with him and started that addiction all over again.

She settled her head back on his chest. ''I'm sorry,'' she said. ''I don't mean to blow hot and cold.''

He stroked her cheek. ''I like the hot part. Any time you want to go on from there just say so and I'll be happy to oblige.''

Reluctantly he straightened and put her away from him, then changed the subject. ''The media is pressuring the State Department and the navy to persuade me to hold a news conference. They're not going to let up and give us some space until I do, so I've agreed to schedule it for tomorrow morning. Would you be willing to appear with me?''

Fear twisted her stomach. ''Oh, Heath, I don't know... I've never done that sort of thing. I wouldn't know what to say, and they're bound to ask about my...my interrupted wedding...."

Heath winced, and his expression turned grim. "Your plans to marry Darren," he muttered. "No, that's one thing I've refused to talk about whether you're there or not. I've told Newman to let the reporters know that I won't answer any questions about my private life, only about my imprisonment."

She wanted to say no, to beg him not to insist, but she couldn't let him down again. She looked up and met his gaze. "Do you want me to?"

He nodded. "I'd like to have you with me. I'm also getting my long-delayed promotion to lieutenant, so it won't all be unpleasant, but if you'd rather not I'll understand."

She took a deep breath and smiled to camouflage her reluctance. "Congratulations, darling, and if you want me there, then of course I'll come. What time?"

Michaela was up early the next morning to dress and prepare for the ten o'clock interview. Irene Preston was invaluable. A former model, she wasn't the stereotypical minister's wife. At age fifty-three she was still beautiful, but in a more quiet, sedate manner. Although she'd toned down her wardrobe and use of makeup since her marriage, she'd retained her keen interest in the world of high fashion and was always available to the young officers' wives who needed help in improving their image.

Michaela sought her expertise, and they set about choosing something for Michaela to wear from the few outfits she'd brought with her. Her bags had originally been packed for a cruise in the Alaskan waters, and this one included mostly slacks and tops. She hadn't had the time or the wits about her to repack before coming to

Washington, and she'd left the suitcase containing dresses and evening wear at home.

"If I'd known about this earlier, I could have gone out and bought a new dress," she lamented as they laid out pants and tops on the bed.

"You don't need anything new," Irene said cheerfully. "This set will be perfect." She held up a pair of dove-gray slacks and a color-coordinated silk blouse. "This color photographs well and is a perfect complement to your beautiful red hair."

She put the clothes down and moved to inspect Michaela's makeup that had been set out neatly on top of the vanity. "I see you've already learned to match your makeup to your hair, so all you have to do is put it on a little heavier than usual. Not much, but those TV lights drain the color."

While Michaela dressed and fixed her face, Irene gave her tips on how to walk, stand and sit. "Fit your bottom to the back of the chair, then lean forward slightly, it gives a more graceful line, and if you're asked questions take your time and think before you answer. It's so easy to say something you don't mean, or that can be taken the wrong way, when you're confused and frightened."

"Oh, thanks a lot," Michaela moaned. "I really needed to hear that."

Irene laughed. "You'll do just fine. In fact, I suspect that you're going to be the new all-American heroine for the next few days."

Michaela grimaced. "Keep it up, lady, and I'm going to crawl under the bed and never come out," she quipped, only partly teasing as she tried to apply lipstick with a shaking hand.

"Seriously, my dear," Irene said, "Americans are fascinated by romance, and the news media have made you and Heath into classic lovers. Your story has all the drama of a bestseller or a hit movie: tragedy, mystery, return from the 'dead,' a child, even another man.''

"There's no 'other man,' Michaela snapped. ''I'd never have become involved with Darren if I'd known Heath was alive.''

Irene put her hand on Michaela's shoulder. ''Of course you wouldn't, but nevertheless, he *is* in the picture and you and your husband are going to be badgered about him.''

Michaela shook her head firmly. ''No. Heath has made it plain that he won't answer questions about that.''

"I understand, but that doesn't mean the questions won't be asked. If not today then later. All three of you will have to deal with it. Prepare yourself, Michaela, and try to get Heath to discuss it with you. From what you've told me, I think he's holding a lot of rage and resentment in. If he doesn't let it out through nonviolent channels, such as counseling or talking it over with you, it's apt to explode from him at a time or place that could do a great deal of damage.''

Her troubled glance caught Michaela's in the mirror. ''I've seen that happen, and believe me, the results can be irreparable.''

The news conference was held in the hospital auditorium, and even from the lounge, where Heath, Michaela, Lieutenant Newman, Eli Fisher from the State Department, the hospital spokesman and a navy captain who was in charge of naval public relations were waiting to make their entrance, it was evident that the place was packed with reporters and photographers.

The butterflies in Michaela's stomach had escalated from upsetting to nauseating, and she hoped she wouldn't do something embarrassing like break into tears or toss her breakfast. On the other hand, Heath, except for being a little pale, looked cool, calm and at ease. His beige uniform was spotless and without a crease, and he sat quietly beside her while she squirmed.

They were holding hands, and it was only when she became aware of the pain in hers that she realized he was squeezing it so hard it hurt. More important, she knew he wasn't even aware that he was doing it! During his imprisonment he'd become expert at hiding his churning emotions behind a bland exterior.

Michaela vowed that hereafter she'd probe more deeply before she formed opinions about his feelings.

At exactly ten o'clock, Lieutenant Newman ushered them into the auditorium and the promotion ceremony began. The captain made a little speech commending Heath for his bravery and conduct under intolerable conditions, then pinned one of the double bars on Heath's shoulder. He handed the other bars to Michaela and, with trembling hands, she pinned them to his other shoulder, then kissed him. Dozens of cameras clicked in unison, but she didn't care. She was proud of her courageous husband, and she wanted him to know it.

When the applause died down they were all seated on straight chairs behind a table on the dais. Each participant had a microphone, and the captain took charge by introducing the members of the panel. There was applause again when Heath and Michaela were presented, and Michaela hoped their goodwill would keep them from asking hurtful or embarrassing questions.

Reading from a prepared statement, the captain recalled the skirmish six years before and explained why the navy had every reason to believe that Lieutenant Tanner had drowned. It seemed perfectly logical, and no one challenged the assumption.

He told of the stunning shock the navy and State Department had received on learning, less than two weeks ago, that Lieutenant Tanner was alive and imprisoned in a hostile foreign country.

"I can't go into detail about the negotiations to free him," the captain concluded, "but last Wednesday he was released to a representative of the Secretary of State, and the rest you already know. Now, you've been briefed on the way this interview will be conducted, so if you have a question please hold up your hand and we'll call on you one at a time."

Every hand in the place, except those occupied with cameras, went up, and Michaela had the sinking feeling that she and Heath were innocent lambs being thrown to ravenous news hounds.

Heath took the brunt of the questioning, and his answers were unhurried, thoughtful, and for the most part seemed satisfactory to the reporters. When asked if he'd been beaten or otherwise mistreated, he said, "yes," but when encouraged to elaborate he declined with a firm, "Sorry, I can't talk about it."

Once the subject of his incarceration had been thoroughly explored, someone asked about Skipper. Michaela felt Heath tense beside her, but outwardly he remained at ease as he described his surprise and jubilation upon learning that he had a son.

Another journalist asked what Skip's reaction was to the father he'd thought was dead, and Michaela saw Heath's jaw clamp and his fists clench. She quickly intervened by answering. "Skipper has the chicken pox and was unable to come to Washington with me, so he hasn't seen his daddy yet, but he's excited and waiting eagerly for us to come home."

"Do you know how long that will be?" someone else shouted, and was given a noncommittal reply by the hospital spokesman.

In an effort to reassure him, Michaela put her hand over Heath's clenched fist where it lay on the table. He looked at her with gratitude, then turned his fist over and clasped her hand tightly in his.

There were a couple more questions about the possibility of other American prisoners who were being secretly held that were answered by Quimby, and then the inevitable happened. A representative from one of the tabloids raised his hand and was called on.

"Mrs. Tanner," he began, "it's a fact that your little boy thinks of your husband's brother, Darren Tanner, as his dad. Isn't this going to cause a great deal of heartbreak for the child when he's forced to accept a stranger as his real father?"

Michaela gasped, and Heath blanched. She was sitting close enough to him to feel his body tense as his fists clenched. A muscle in his jaw twitched from the pressure he was applying in an effort to maintain control as he stood and sent his chair crashing to the floor.

The room quieted to a deadly stillness as he stared at the offending reporter. When Heath finally spoke his voice was hoarse with rage.

"You dirty rotten son of a bitch," he said in a tone that was icy enough to freeze hell, then turned and strode out of the room with a quiet but unmistakable dignity.

For a moment the eerie silence continued. The air vibrated with the hostility of the audience toward the man who had asked the question, but Michaela didn't wait to see what happened next.

She got up quickly and ran after her husband.

Chapter Seven

The following morning, Wednesday, Michaela nervously paced the floor of the small but comfortable office while Dr. Vivian Young sat behind the desk and toyed with a pencil. The clock on the wall read 9:08.

"It was a terrifying scene," Michaela said. "I've never seen Heath in such a cold murderous rage. Not that the stupid reporter didn't deserve it, but I hate to think what would have happened if Heath had gone for him instead of walking out."

"What did Heath do after he left the room?" Dr. Young asked.

"I don't know," she said, and there was desperation in her tone. "By the time I got out into the hall he was nowhere in sight. When I tried to find him I was stopped and told I'd have to wait in the waiting room."

Her voice broke and she turned to look directly at Dr. Young. "I haven't seen him since, and I'm frantic with worry. Nobody will tell me anything."

The psychologist frowned. "Why haven't you seen him?"

Michaela gestured angrily with her hands. "They won't let me. They say he doesn't want to see me. They wouldn't even let Lieutenant Preston see him."

Dr. Young picked up the phone on her desk and gestured to a chair. "Sit down and try to relax, and I'll find out what's going on."

Michaela sat, and Dr. Young dialed, then turned her swivel chair so that her back was to Michaela.

The psychologist talked quietly into the phone. Her end of the conversation was conducted in a combination of naval jargon and medical shorthand that to the uninitiated was more confusing than informative.

When she finished she turned back to face Michaela. Her tone was compassionate but firm. "I talked to Dr. Knox, your husband's psychiatrist, and he confirmed what the hospital staff told you. Heath doesn't want to see you."

Michaela knew her distress must have shown on her face as Dr. Young continued, "It's not just you, he doesn't want to see anybody. That's why they wouldn't let the chaplain in, either. I'm sure he's understandably upset."

"But all I want is to help him," Michaela pleaded.

"Then don't pressure him. Let him work through this problem at his own pace." Dr. Young leaned back in her chair. "Why don't you tell me about the relationship between your son and his uncle. Is there apt to be a conflict?"

They talked for the rest of Michaela's scheduled hour, and when she left the office she felt less threatened and confused. The counselor had made her see that for six years Heath had been isolated, if not physically, certainly mentally and emotionally. Now he was surrounded by people, all pulling him in a different direction, and it was threatening to him. His survival instincts had been sharply honed and were triggered by such small things as a sound or a touch. He hadn't yet learned how to deal with them in a nonthreatening atmosphere.

During a pause in the conversation, Heath glanced at his watch. It was 10:14 on Wednesday morning, and he was sitting in Dr. Knox's rather austere office at the medical center.

It was one of those uncomfortable pauses with each waiting for the other to bring up a topic. Finally Dr. Knox spoke. "When are you going to see your wife?"

Heath shrugged. "I doubt that she wants to see me."

"Of course she does. She's upset because you don't want her with you. She's worried about you."

Heath jerked to attention. "Have you been talking to Michaela?"

Knox shook his head. "No, but I've had indirect contact through her counselor, Lieutenant Young."

"And she actually thinks I don't want her with me?" His tone was incredulous.

Knox shrugged. "What else could she think?" He paused. "I gather that's not your reason for rejecting her?"

"Rejecting her?" Heath glared at the counselor. "I'm not rejecting her. I'd give anything to have her here beside me right now. She's the one who rejected me."

The psychiatrist's face was impassive. "Oh? Did she tell you she didn't want to be married to you anymore?"

"No, of course not. She wouldn't do that. She'd stay with me whether she wanted to or not."

"Then why do you say she rejected you?"

"She was in the process of marrying my brother when she got word that I was on my way home." The bitterness was thick in his voice.

"And you see that as rejection?" Dr. Knox sat forward in his chair. "Aren't you being a little unreasonable? She'd been alone for six years after you were declared dead—"

"Dammit, I wasn't dead!" Heath roared, and bolted out of his chair. "Everyone just seems to ignore that fact. I may have been in hell, but I was very much alive."

He started to pace. "The only thing that kept me going was the certainty that Michaela would be waiting for me when I finally got out. Hell, she wasn't waiting for me." The bitterness escalated. "Not only was she carrying on with my brother, but she'd let my son think Darren was his father!"

"Are you sure of that?" Dr. Knox asked. "Did Michaela confirm that she'd told Skipper Darren was his father?"

Heath glared. "She didn't need to. The reporter—"

"Why aren't you even giving your wife a chance to deny or explain? Why are you willing to take the word of a reporter who deliberately broke the rules of conduct set up for the interview?"

The very reasonableness of the other man's questions only enraged Heath further. "Because I can't get a straight answer out of her," he snapped. "When I asked her if she's in love with Darren, she says things like 'I love him but I'm not *in love with* him' and 'He'd have been a good husband, and I didn't want to spend my life alone.'"

He threw up his hands in frustration. "Why in hell didn't she want to spend her life alone? I would have if anything had happened to her."

"How do you know that?"

Heath was in no mood for logic. "Because I love her, I don't want anyone else! Dammit, whose side are you on, anyway?"

Dr. Knox straightened in his chair and looked directly at Heath. "I'm not on anyone's side. There's no right or wrong to this dilemma, Heath. I'm just trying to make you look at both sides before you come to any conclusions or make irrevocable decisions that you'll have to live with for the rest of your life."

Heath dropped back down in the chair and rubbed his face with his hands. "Sorry," he said wearily. "I guess I'm not making much sense. I had no idea that coming home would be so difficult. All I ever thought of was how great it would be to have Michaela with me again. I never got beyond that."

Knox relaxed once more, too. "That's not unusual under the circumstances. Don't worry about it, but you have to understand that your wife and family haven't done anything wrong, either. They did what all healthy, well-adjusted people do when they lose a loved one. They work through the anguish and then make an effort to adapt to the loss and pick up their lives again. To make the most of what's left."

It was later that evening that Michaela walked the several blocks from the Preston home to the hospital. The sun was still shining, but a light breeze had come up and the humid temperature had dropped to almost bearable.

As she approached her destination her anxiety increased. Heath's counselor's secretary had called earlier to tell her that her husband would like to see her at her convenience after dinner. She couldn't help but feel a little agitated. How many women had to be given an appointment in order to see their own husbands?

Why hadn't Heath called her instead of asking a stranger to do it? Had Dr. Knox persuaded him to see her, or had it been what he wanted?

She seemed to exist in a constant state of confusion, and it was taking its toll on her nerves and her self-assurance.

The hospital was swarming with people as she made her way to the elevator and up to his floor. Were all these people navy personnel and their dependents? Probably so. That should have made her feel more secure, but instead it alienated her even more. Heath had been 'killed' so soon after he went on active duty that she'd never had the chance to be a navy wife.

She presented her visitor's pass at the nursing station. "Lieutenant Tanner is expecting you," the nurse said and gave her directions on how to get to his room.

Heath was sitting in the one easy chair in the private room reading a newspaper when she appeared in the open doorway. He looked up with a start, then tossed the paper aside and stood.

There was no welcoming smile. Instead, he looked apprehensive. "Hello, Michaela," he said uneasily.

The muscles in her stomach knotted. "How are you, Heath?" Her tone was cool and impersonal.

For a moment they just stood there awkwardly, then he motioned. "Come on in. Sit down."

He offered her the unupholstered chair. She was too jumpy to sit still, but neither did she want to appear argumentative, so she seated herself as he walked to the window and stood looking out.

He had his back to her, but she'd seen his strained expression and the shadows of fatigue under his eyes. He was dressed in light blue slacks and a blue plaid, short-sleeved shirt, and from the back he looked young. It was his face that had aged beyond his years. It had been ravaged by hunger, mistreatment, fear and loneliness, but there was an appealing vulnerability about him that she found even more attractive than his former youthful cockiness.

She was casting around in her mind trying to think of something to say when he spoke. "I'm sorry, Michaela," he said quietly. "I didn't intend to go off the deep end and embarrass you."

"You didn't embarrass me," she said calmly. "Frankly, I was hoping you'd go after the bastard."

That time he did turn around, and his expression was one of surprise. "You were?"

She grinned and stood up. "Right at first I was, yes. He deserved the beating you'd have given him, but I was glad when you walked out instead."

An expression of relief softened his face and he reached out to gather her to him. She melted into his embrace and put her arms around his waist. "Have you any idea how much I love you?" he murmured as he cradled her close. "No matter what I do or say, don't ever doubt my love for you."

He lowered his head and nuzzled the side of her neck. "Dr. Knox said you thought I was rejecting you, but nothing could have been further from the truth." His breath was warm against her ear. "It's just that sometimes when a thing like that reporter's implication is thrown at me, I can't cope with it. My good sense deserts me, and I strike out at whoever it is that's turning the knife in my gut."

He leaned against the windowsill and widened his stance so that he could pull her closer between his legs. A pulse leaped deep in the core of her womanhood when the lower part of her abdomen collided with the evidence of his arousal.

She felt the shiver that rocked him as his hands held her buttocks and pressed her more firmly into him, and she fought to keep her body from breaking its restraints and rubbing against him.

"Oh, God, that feels so good," he whispered brokenly.

"Yes, oh yes, it does," she gasped softly as her arms tightened around him, bringing her even closer.

She raised her head just as he lowered his and their mouths met, and clung, and parted to allow the intimate invasion of tongues. Heath closed his thighs urgently around her hips and her self-control shattered as she moved against him in the restless rhythm of loving.

The liquid heat that poured through Michaela melted everything but her burning need for this man who had returned to her a stranger, but who ignited fires in her that no one but her husband ever had.

Forgotten were all her good intentions to wait until they knew each other better before they made love. She wanted him, now, right here, this minute, and her involuntary moan told him so.

For a moment he clutched at her as though trying to hang on to some semblance of sanity, then his muscles slowly relaxed and he put her away from him.

Her head spun, and her whole body throbbed as she sagged against the wall.

Never had she been so thoroughly banished.

"Wh-why?" was the only word in her vocabulary, and it was a cry of anguish.

Heath didn't answer immediately. When she managed to focus on him, she saw that he was still propped against the windowsill, but he was bent slightly forward and his arms were wrapped tightly around his chest. His features were twisted in a grimace, and her first thought was that he was in pain.

"Heath?" she said anxiously and reached out to him.

He shied away from her. "No, don't touch me." His voice was ragged, and he took a deep shuddering breath. "I'll be all right, just give me a minute."

It was only then that she realized he was hurting all right, but it was the agony of sexual frustration. She could sympathize because the same malady was tormenting her.

"Why did you stop?" she asked, still dazed and disoriented.

He straightened up and looked at her. "I may have spent years in a cage, but I'm not an animal," he said harshly. "This is hardly the place, or the time."

She followed his glance around the room, and her frustration was replaced by a wave of shame and embarrassment. The hospital room had a door that not only didn't lock but wasn't even closed!

Michaela had spent quite a bit of time in hospitals with Skipper, and she knew that nurses, doctors, technicians and an assortment of other personnel were always popping in and out of the rooms. How could she have been so careless?

She felt the hot blush that brightened her cheeks, and closed her eyes. "Oh, no!" she groaned. "I didn't even think..."

"Neither did I, sweetheart, but I'm not going to say I'm sorry." Most of the strain had gone out of his voice, and she opened her eyes to see that he was smiling. "It was great while it lasted," he continued. "I've waited so long to feel you turn to flame in my arms again. At least now I know you can still respond to me."

She felt another wave of heat, but this time it wasn't embarrassment. "Didn't I always?" she asked shakily.

His smile disappeared. "Not lately." He touched her moist lips with his finger, then reached down to take her hand. "Come on," he said, and pushed himself away from the window. "We'd better get out of here. Let's go for a walk."

They strolled through the hospital and out onto the grounds. Even at eight o'clock in the evening the humid heat was a shock to Michaela after the air-conditioned coolness of the building.

The East Cost humidity had come as an uncomfortable surprise to her. She'd been born and raised in Phoenix, which was hot but dry, and now lived in Seattle, which was wet but cool. The oppressive muggy weather of the nation's capital was hard to get used to.

The sun had set, and the rolling green lawn and stately old trees gave the illusion of coolness, even though Michaela felt trickles of perspiration in the cleft between her breasts. As they ambled along, hand in hand, stopping occasionally to sniff a rose or admire a flower garden, they talked of the events of the past two days.

Heath seemed relaxed, but Michaela was uneasily aware of a thin line of tension in him she was almost sure wasn't a result of the aborted intimacy that had taken place in his room. When they came to a secluded spot in a clump of lush, green bushes beneath an elm tree, they sat down on the soft grass.

She reclined against the thick tree trunk with her legs stretched out and crossed at the ankles in front of her. He pulled his knees up and rested his arms on them. The tension she'd been vaguely apprehensive about was more pronounced now, and he looked straight ahead of him as he spoke. "Michaela, is it true what that reporter said? Does Skipper think Darren is his father?"

The question seemed to explode inside her, and she understood why she'd been uneasy. Although they'd been discussing the ill-fated news conference and its repercussions, they'd skirted gingerly around the central problem. Neither of them had mentioned the reporter's snide questions.

She didn't answer immediately, but took time to gather her scattered thoughts first. "No, Heath. Skipper knows Darren isn't his real father. I've always told him that his daddy was a sailor who was killed during a battle at sea before he was born. He has the picture of you in your uniform, and he keeps it on his dresser."

Heath turned his head to look at her. "Then the reporter was lying? He just said that hoping I'd make a scene that could be splashed across the front page of his yellow rag?"

Now Michaela looked away. She couldn't avoid the subject any longer. She had to tell Heath all the facts about Skip and his relationship with Darren. Would she be able to make him understand?

"Well...not exactly," she said carefully, then turned back to look at him. "Darren has always been a very concerned and loving uncle to his only nephew. You see, there's something I haven't told you about Skipper. He was born with an abnormal opening between the upper right and left chamber of his heart. It's called ventricular septal defect."

The blood drained from Heath's face. "Oh, my God," he groaned.

"It's not immediately life threatening," she hurried to assure him, "and it can be corrected, but it does limit his activity."

"How much?"

"Well, he can't play ball, or ride a bike, or... Oh, you know, none of the rough or tumble stuff." She saw the anguish in Heath's eyes, and hastened to assure him. "He doesn't seem to mind. I read to him a lot, and he likes to watch the children's programs on television. He plays well by himself."

Heath shivered and ran his fingers through his hair. "If it can be corrected, then why hasn't it been?"

She felt a twinge of conscience that was immediately followed by a rush of defensive anger. "He's just a baby," she said, "and correcting it requires major heart surgery. There's no hurry."

Heath didn't look convinced. "He's five years old and will be starting school in the fall. What does his doctor say?"

"I just told you," she snapped, then was sorry for her peevishness. Heath had a right to ask questions.

"Why didn't you tell me about this before?" he persisted.

She sighed. "I would have. I intended to, but you were so happy when you learned you had a son that I didn't want to dim your pleasure. Then I had to tell you about my...my plans to marry Darren...." Her voice broke. "Oh, Heath, when that upset you so, I just couldn't hit you with even more distressing news. Since then, things have been so...so turbulent...between us that I could never find the proper time."

"The proper time was when you first told me about Skip," he said angrily. "You had no right to keep anything pertaining to him a secret from me. I'm his dad. Are you going to tell me you thought you were doing me a favor by letting that reporter inform me on national television that you've let my son think my brother is his father?" His voice shook with indignation.

Michaela blanched. He was right. How could she have botched things so?

"I told you, Skip knows Darren's not his real father!"

Heath picked up a stone and threw it with such force that it landed out of sight. "Then you'd damn well better explain why that reporter thinks he doesn't." His tone warned her that he wouldn't stand for more evasions. "He may have twisted the facts to make a better story, but you can be sure there was some basis of truth in his statement."

Michaela's patience was severely strained. "I've been trying to explain. If you'd just be quiet for a few minutes and listen. When I learned that my baby had a congenital heart defect, I was terrified. I hardly dared let him out of my sight for fear he'd stop breathing, and when the doctor said he'd have to have surgery I simply couldn't allow it. He was so tiny. Only five and a half pounds at birth, and I'd already lost you. I couldn't take a chance on losing him, too. Especially after the doctor said the surgery could be postponed."

Heath tried to say something, but she hurried on. "Darren and your parents were wonderful. They understood my feelings so well because of their experience with you." She paused. "Why didn't you ever tell me you'd had heart problems as a child?"

He looked disgusted. "Because that's all in the past, and I didn't want to dredge it up. I had rheumatic fever, which temporarily weakened my heart. I got over it, but not until my family had made my life miserable by treating me like an invalid for most of my childhood."

Her eyes widened. "But they were worried about you!"

"They smothered me with their concern." His tone was harsh. "They'd have made a real cripple of me if a doctor hadn't finally intervened, but I don't want to talk about that. I want you to tell me how Darren fits into this."

She didn't know what to say. How could she tell him that his brother "fit into this," as he put it, exactly as

Heath would have if he'd been there? As a concerned and loving father. Darren had comforted her when she fell apart, and seen to it that Skip received the best available medical care even when he'd had to pay for part of it himself. He'd been the only daddy the little boy had ever known, but she couldn't tear Heath apart by telling him that in blunt terms. Still, she had to prepare him for the very real possibility that Skipper would be antagonistic toward him at first.

"If you remember, I'd never met Darren up to the time you shipped out," she began. "He was working in Seattle even then, but was in England on extended travel duty, so wasn't able to attend our wedding or your graduation."

Heath nodded. "I'm not suffering from amnesia, Michaela. Of course I remember."

She hated his patronizing attitude, and it was on the tip of her tongue to tell him that his memory so far had been mighty selective, but she swallowed back the words and continued as though he hadn't interrupted. "Darren flew back to Arizona immediately when he learned you'd been lost at sea and presumed drowned. When you were declared dead a few days later, he couldn't have been kinder or more helpful. As you can imagine, your mother was in a state of collapse, and your dad wasn't in much better shape."

"And you?" Heath asked. "What shape were you in, Mickey?"

She wasn't going to let him bait her. "I've already told you how the news of your death affected me. Also, I was in the early stages of pregnancy, and there were signs that the shock might cause me to lose the baby. The doctor made me stay in bed for a week. If it hadn't been for your brother I don't know what we'd have done."

Heath looked stricken. "Is that what caused the baby's heart defect?"

Her impatience with him subsided at the twinge of guilt in his tone. She reached over and put her hand on his shoulder. "I asked the doctor the same question. He said there's no possible way of knowing, but that about one baby in a hundred is born with an abnormality of the cardiovascular system.

"Don't ever blame yourself. I went through that, wondering if it was something I did or didn't do that caused it, but the doctor finally made me understand that it's just one of those things that happen. It's not something you can blame anyone for, and it probably wouldn't happen again if we were to have more children."

Heath reached up and put his hand over hers. "Go on," he said bleakly. "What happened after that?"

"I had to have something to keep me busy, so I continued on at school and finished the first semester of my sophomore year. I didn't enroll for the spring semester since the baby was due in April. It's a good thing I didn't because I spent all my time with Skipper for months after he was born." Her voice dropped to a whisper of remembered agony. "He was so frail and tiny."

Heath squeezed her hand, and she continued. "Again Darren was the rock that your parents and I clung to for strength. He took a two-month leave from work and came to Phoenix to make sure that Skip got the best possible medical care."

She smiled as memories crowded her mind. "He's a very 'take care' kind of person, and he seemed to know exactly how to cut through red tape and get things done in the quickest possible time. We owe him more than we can ever repay, Heath. Possibly even our son's life."

Heath nodded but didn't look at her. "Yes, we do, but I should have been there to take care of you and the baby. I've missed so much...."

Michaela put her arm around his shoulders. "I understand how you feel, but be grateful that you weren't dead like we thought. Don't waste time regretting the things you couldn't have changed."

She rubbed her cheek against his back. "Skipper thrived even with his heart condition, and in the fall I was able to leave him with your mother while I went back to school. When I graduated two and a half years later, Darren arranged for me to be interviewed for a job where he worked in Seattle, and when I got the position, Skip and I moved up there. Until then your dad had been the father figure in Skip's young life, and afterward Darren took over the role."

She felt Heath flinch beneath her cheek, and he buried his face in his crossed arms atop his knees. She kissed his back through the cotton shirt and put her arms around his waist. "I know it hurts to have missed your son's first five years, but it might help to know that there were never any other men, except family, in his life or mine."

Heath didn't move or speak, but she could feel his refusal to release his misery. She wished he'd let go and cry, let the tears and the sobs pour out, and with them the pain, but she knew he wouldn't. The only way she could offer comfort was to hold him, and be there for him when he needed her.

Unfortunately, too often, as now, she was the cause of his distress.

After a few minutes he shifted position and put one leg down so he could pull Michaela across it and support her with the raised one. She snuggled against him with her head on his shoulder and could feel his strong, steady heartbeat. He was too thin, and undernourished, but it didn't seem to have affected his strength much. When he held her, it was with a leashed power that made her long to unleash it.

He put his hand under her chin and raised her face to his. She reached up and kissed him chastely, then captured his lower lip and sucked gently.

He caught his breath, but didn't move as her tongue slid across his teeth and coaxed them open to allow her entry. His tongue met hers and caressed it, sending shivers of longing down her spine as he shifted again and lowered them to the ground. She opened her mouth and he plunged and retreated then plunged again, each time more deeply as he groaned and rolled them over so that he lay partially on top of her with one leg between both of hers.

Her arms tightened around him and held him so close that his swollen hardness was taut against the firm flesh of her thigh, making her throb with desire. His free hand roamed over her other slacks-clad thigh and hip, then up to cup her breast through her blouse before returning downward again.

When they finally broke the fiery kiss it was to gulp in great drafts of air, and to try to regain some of the control that had evaporated in the flame. They were both breathing heavily and trembling as they lay entwined in each other's arms.

Heath pillowed his face between Michaela's breasts, and she could feel the massive effort he was making to relax. When he finally spoke it was with a note of pleading. "Michaela, I want to go home to Seattle with you." His lips nuzzled at the soft rise they'd settled against. "I can't stand living apart from you any longer. Even…even if we don't share a bed, I want you in the same house with me."

His voice wavered, and he paused for a moment before continuing. "I want to see my son, and my parents, but most of all I don't ever want to say goodbye to you again after tonight."

She cradled his head against her and threaded her fingers through his hair. "Of course I'll take you home, love," she said huskily. "And when I do, we'll share everything, including the bed."

He tightened his arms around her, and she leaned down to place a kiss in his thick black hair. "Will tomorrow be soon enough?"

Chapter Eight

Heath and Michaela weren't able to make arrangements to leave Washington, D.C., quite as quickly as they'd hoped, and it was Saturday morning before Heath was checked out of the hospital and cleared by the navy for sixty days of immediate leave.

The amount of paperwork was staggering, complicated by the fact that his enlistment had been up two years before, and his present status was uncertain. No one was suggesting that he decide immediately whether or not he wanted to reenlist. He had almost six months of leave accrued in which to make up his mind, but meanwhile his situation was unique and everything was thrown into a state of confusion.

Complicating matters was the fact that he was a world-class military celebrity and therefore required to travel with his navy and State Department escorts. To these had been added a couple of husky shore patrol guards. Michaela wondered if she and Heath would ever have any privacy.

Because of the swarms of reporters, photographers and admirers that perpetually waited outside the gates of the medical center hoping for a chance to interview Heath, especially since the spectacular ending of the first news conference, he, Michaela and their party were taken by helicopter directly from the hospital to a nearby naval air base. There they were put aboard a plane and, after a nonstop flight, were now approaching the naval air station in Seattle.

The same one she and Darren had flown out of exactly a week ago.

Michaela's world had been turned topsy-turvy in the course of the past seven days. Never again would she be complacent about anything! She was starting to settle down, though, and adjust more easily to the many changes.

As she watched the seaport city built on hills and around lakes come into view, she was glad she and Heath wouldn't have to confront the problem of Heath's attitude toward his older brother right away. Both had made daily phone calls to their parents; Heath's were staying at Darren's apartment, and Michaela's were at her apartment with Skip, so they were aware that Darren was out of the country on a hastily arranged tour of duty for his job.

Michaela felt a stab of guilt. She'd hardly thought of Darren once he'd returned to Seattle, and he deserved better than that. He'd always deserved more than she could give him, and she'd tried to tell him so, but he wouldn't listen.

Sometimes she'd wondered if it weren't his strong sense of responsibility for his brother's widow and his small nephew that drew him to her rather than the deep, passionate type of love a man should feel for his wife. If that were true, then maybe now he'd feel free to search for a woman he could love in that way. Michaela hoped so. Darren was very dear to her, and she wanted him to be happy.

Heath had been restless all during the flight, and for the past hour he was either squirming in his seat or pacing up and down the aisle. Michaela realized the anticipation of seeing his parents again after six years, and meeting the son he had not known about, must be agony.

She'd suggested a tranquilizer, but he'd refused. He wouldn't drink or smoke, either. "I was forced to withdraw cold turkey from both those vices after I was captured," he explained, "and I'm not going to make the mistake of taking them up again."

Now, as the pilot's voice boomed through the cabin telling them that the temperature was sixty-nine degrees in Seattle and to fasten their seat belts for landing, Heath returned to his seat beside her and buckled himself in.

Michaela put her arm through his and hugged it. "Just a few more minutes, honey. I know your parents are as eager as you are. I'm only sorry Skipper isn't well enough yet to come to the airport."

Heath shook his head. "I'm glad he won't be here," he said. "We'll be mobbed by media people, and we both know what that's like. All the commotion would scare him. Besides, I want my first meeting with him to be in private. Just family. I couldn't bear to have the whole world looking on."

"That's true," she agreed, "but I wish the navy hadn't felt it was necessary to allow the reporters and photographers into the area." Her tone held disapproval. "They didn't have to."

He leaned over and kissed her cheek. "It's all right, sweetheart. I agreed to this." His knuckles caressed her other cheek. "There's no compelling reason not to, and hopefully if they get to photograph us here they won't bother us too much at the apartment."

He cupped her chin with his palm and raised her face to his. "Give me a kiss for luck," he murmured huskily just before his mouth found hers.

Heath had been right. When the plane landed they were mobbed. Not only by the media but by hundreds of curious well-wishers who worked on the base. It was a chilly gray day in the Pacific Northwest, and the ground around the plane was jammed as they stepped out the door.

They were preceded down the steps by the shore patrol guards and the official escorts, but when Heath and Michaela appeared at the top there was a roar of welcome and thunderous applause. Michaela's first impulse was to turn and run back into the plane, but Heath's arm around her kept her at his side as he smiled and waved. They paused for a moment, then hurried on down where more shore patrolmen cleared the way for them through the crowd.

They'd only gone a few yards when Heath spotted his parents. He grabbed Michaela's hand and started running.

His mother got to him first and he threw his arms around her, then his father, and finally he hugged them both together in an emotional three-way embrace. Tears of joy streamed down Alice's plump face as she murmured brokenly, "Heath. Oh, my boy...my boy..."

His father, Army Colonel Uriah Tanner, Retired, fought a losing battle to control his emotions, and for the first time ever, Heath saw his undemonstrative parent cry.

Michaela retreated a few steps to give them as much privacy as possible in the midst of bedlam.

Heath was grateful that there'd been no public announcement made of his arrival in Seattle, so there were no formal ceremonies or news conferences, although he did answer some of the questions shouted at him as they made their way to the waiting limousine.

On the ride to Michaela's apartment in the Bellevue district he sat between his mother and father. It was great to see them again, but he couldn't keep his gaze from seeking Michaela who sat across from them. She was his anchor, his link to both the past and the future, and now that he was cut loose from the restraints of the navy and the State Department for the next two months he couldn't bear to let her out of his sight.

For years he'd dreamed of returning to his family, but it was different then he'd expected. Certainly this was an exhilarating homecoming for him, but it was also a difficult one.

He had no home to return to.

Both his wife and his parents had moved from the familiar places where he'd lived with them in Phoenix. He'd never been in the Pacific Northwest before, but now he was going "home" to Michaela's Seattle apartment where he'd never lived and wasn't even sure he was welcome.

Was this what she really wanted, or was she just doing her duty as his wife? He broke out in a cold sweat. How was he supposed to find out? Now that he was back, Michaela would never admit it if she wanted Darren. And he couldn't question Darren because his brother had put himself out of reach.

Heath did his best to push aside his doubts and keep up a cheerful conversation, but when the limo pulled up in front of a large two-story house in a well-kept older neighborhood he again felt the clutch of panic that was becoming all too familiar.

At last he was going to see his son!

The father in him wanted to jump out of the car and run to the house to claim his child. The coward in him opted for hiding in the limo and postponing the ordeal for as long as possible.

What kind of reception would he get from the little boy? It was pretty obvious that Skip had come to think of Darren as a father, whether Michaela had encouraged it or not. Would he resent the stranger in the navy uniform who arrived on the scene five years late?

The driver helped Alice and Michaela from the car, then Heath motioned his father to follow. He was the last to exit, and Michaela was waiting just outside the door for him. He put his arms around her and drew her close. It was like gulping air into oxygen-starved lungs.

How did she always know when he desperately needed her?

He held her for only a moment. His parents were waiting, and he didn't want to come across as a lovesick teenager, but if he ever managed to get her alone it would be sheer heaven, even if all she'd let him do was hold her.

She put her hand in his, and he grasped it as they walked toward the house. The front door opened and Michaela's parents rushed out and down the steps to greet him. There was a short delay while they hugged and kissed him and shed tears of happiness.

"Skipper is napping," Michaela's mother, Lila, said as she wiped her eyes, "but he'll be waking any minute. We know you're eager to see him, and you don't need a crowd around when you do, so George and I are going to spend tonight at Darren's apartment with Alice and Uriah. We'd like you to bring Skip and come for dinner this evening so we can all be together for a while before George and I leave tomorrow to go back home.''

Heath was relieved when Michaela didn't protest their parents' plan to give them time alone with their son. After helping the Burdetts stash their luggage in the trunk of the limousine, they agreed to a six o'clock dinnertime and waved as the driver drove away with the two couples.

When the car was out of sight Heath put his arm around Michaela and looked down at her. ''Now, how about introducing me to our son?'' he said, and heard the wariness in his tone.

She put her arm around his waist and hugged him. ''It'll be all right, darling,'' she said quietly. ''Just remember that he's very young and try not to expect too much too soon. Once he gets to know you he'll adore you.''

As they climbed the steps to the big old-fashioned porch, Heath wished he were as certain of that as Michaela seemed to be.

Michaela had told him she lived on the first floor of a two-story house that had been converted into two flats. It was painted dark green with white trim, and surrounded by giant shade trees and lush flowering bushes. There were two front doors, one large and ornate, the other, off to the side, was smaller and newer and was the entrance to the stairway and the upper story.

They entered into a hallway with a wide arch on the right that opened onto a spacious living room. A door on the left was ajar and Heath could see a bedroom beyond. A few steps further on Michaela stopped in front of a closed door, and Heath noticed a bathroom across the hall and the kitchen at the end.

Michaela opened the door quietly and looked into the room, then entered and motioned Heath to follow. It was obviously Skipper's bedroom, and was furnished with

maple bunk beds and a matching chest of drawers. There
was a child-size table and two chairs in one corner, and a
large, gaily decorated wooden toy box on wheels in another. Framed on the walls were Norman Rockwell prints
depicting small boys in various difficulties, and a big,
garish circus poster hung above the chest.

Heath took this all in quickly before he let his hungry
gaze drop to the sleeping figure on the bottom bunk. The
little boy was smaller than he'd expected, but then what did
he know about kids? The child lay on his side with a red
blanket drawn up under his arms, and his black hair curled
damply, disheveled from twisting in his sleep. Thick black
eyelashes touched against alabaster skin, and Heath could
see that Skip's complexion, which still held traces of the
chicken pox, wasn't rosy but pale and had a faint bluish
tinge around the eyes and the mouth.

A tightness in Heath's chest made it difficult for him to
breathe. *My son*, he thought with amazement. *Blood of
my blood. A miracle I neither asked for nor knew about.*

He was vaguely aware of Michaela standing just behind
him as he hunkered down beside the low bed and stroked
the little head with his fingers. It was wet with perspiration, although the room was cool. Was that normal? Or
was it, like the blueness, caused by insufficient oxygen?

He ran one finger down the soft warm cheek. A tiny
muscle twitched at the corner of the mouth, and Heath
snatched his hand away. He didn't want to wake the boy.

For a minute he just watched the sleeping youngster
while his thoughts rambled....

*He looks like me. There's hardly anything of Michaela
in him except maybe his small bone structure....*

*I'm a father! Son of a gun, that's the last thing I'd
expected. How does a father act? What does he talk about
to his small child...?*

Do I dare kiss him? No, better not. I'm a stranger to him....

Hell, I'm a stranger to everybody.

Heath put his hand over the small one lying on the blanket. It was cool, and so little. Why was his hand cool when his cheek was warm?

Disregarding his earlier decision, Heath leaned down and kissed the exposed temple. A wave of emotion rocked him as his lips touched the tender skin.

My little son...

He smells so clean. Like soap and baby powder, and maybe a hint of peppermint candy.

Heath rose up and gazed down at the child.

He looks like a sleeping angel, but I hope there's a bit of devil in him, too. Boys need to be tough these days if they're going to survive as men. It's a rough world out there and getting worse.

A strong protective urge gnawed at Heath.

My son's got to be taught to take care of himself. He may someday be in the same situation I was where there's nothing to rely on but his own strength....

He must not be unprepared!

As though sensing the intrusion of others into his room, Skipper straightened his legs out and rolled onto his back. His eyelids fluttered, then opened to reveal wide brown eyes flecked with green. The same color eyes that looked back at Heath every morning from his mirror.

The expression on Skip's face changed from blank to surprise. "Who're you?" he asked, then glanced up and shouted joyously, "Mom, you're home!"

Heath moved quickly away as the little boy jumped to his feet on the bed and threw himself into his mother's arms.

Michaela hugged and kissed him, then held him away from her. "Let me look at you," she said happily. "My, your chicken pox are almost gone. How do you feel?"

"Fine," he said and promptly dismissed the subject of his illness. "What did you bring me?"

Heath laughed at the question. How typical. He could have been listening to himself twenty-four years ago.

Now that Skip was no longer covered by the blanket, Heath could see that he was wearing a blue-striped T-shirt and white knit briefs. His legs and arms were well rounded and sturdy, although still lightly disfigured with drying pustules, and his body was slender but not skinny.

Heath watched as Michaela again hugged the child and teasingly chided him for being more interested in a present than in her return home. The love that radiated between the two cast a bright glow over the whole room.

It must be a dream. It had to be. A man didn't climb out of hell and into heaven in a week. Any minute now he'd wake up and find himself still trapped in that sweltering prison cage.

The thought made him shudder. Never again would he take happiness for granted! It was too fragile to be treated casually. He'd been given a second chance with Michaela, and a small son as a bonus. This time he was going to hang on to what he had.

Michaela turned to him and put her hand on his arm while still holding Skipper around the waist. "Skip, honey," she said, "this man is your daddy. He's been a prisoner of war in another country for a long time, but now he's come back to us."

"Prisoner of war" wasn't exactly accurate since the United States wasn't at war, but Heath supposed it was easier for a five-year-old to understand than "political prisoner."

Heath was suddenly struck mute. What does a man say when he's first introduced to his young son? *How do you do. Nice to meet you?* or maybe *Hi, guy, whatja think of the game Saturday? How about them Mariners?* Neither hardly seemed appropriate. Why hadn't he anticipated this moment and been prepared?

Skipper must have been having the same trouble because he just stood there on the side of the bed with his arms around his mother's neck and silently stared at the intruder. It was obvious to Heath that he wasn't going to get a warm welcome from his only child.

Well, he was the adult; it was up to him to make this relationship work. With a desperate need to do something he stuck out his hand and said the first thing that came to mind. "Hello, Skipper. I'm sorry you've been sick."

He cringed at the impersonal sound of his words. *Nice going, Tanner, you jerk. That ought to really bowl him over.*

The big brown eyes continued to stare for a moment, then Skip hid his face in his mother's shoulder. Heath felt the rejection like a knife to the heart.

"Skipper Tanner," Michaela scolded, "where are your manners? You know—"

"No, Michaela, don't," Heath interrupted. "Don't punish him. I'm a stranger and he's shy, aren't you son?"

"I'm not your son," Skip muttered against his mother's shoulder.

"Skipper!" Michaela's tone was one of outrage.

Heath felt sick. He knew zilch about child psychology, but one thing he remembered from his own sheltered childhood was that forcing an adult on an unwilling kid never worked.

"Please, honey," he began, anxious to forestall further scolding, "give him time to get used to me. Maybe it would be better if I go out in the other room while you get him dressed."

Michaela's tortured eyes met his over the child's head. "I'm sorry," she whispered.

He reached out and cupped her cheek. "Don't be. It's not your fault. It's not anyone's fault. We shouldn't have expected him to accept me right off the bat. Don't fuss at him. It will only make things worse."

Michaela watched as Heath walked dejectedly out of the room and shut the door, then she turned to confront her son. "Skipper," she said sharply, "there's one thing I want to make clear to you right now. I won't tolerate your rudeness. Your father is a good man who has had a lot of bad things happen to him. He didn't even know about you until he came back to this country, and he's so happy to have a little boy."

Skip looked mutinous. "I don't want him. I want Uncle Darren."

For one of the few times in his young life Michaela was truly angry with her son, but she knew Heath was right. If she forced the issue it would only make the child more resentful.

"Honey, I know this is scary and upsetting for you," she said carefully, "but both of your grandmas and grandpas have told you all about what's happened. I'm sure Uncle Darren has, too, so please be nice to this man even though you don't know him yet. He loves you very much."

"How can he love me when he doesn't even know me?" Skip retorted, and Michaela had to admit that to a child that was a logical point.

"Because you're his son and you're a part of him, just as he's a part of you," she explained, feeling her way along as she spoke. "I know you don't understand that, but trust me, he loves you, and it hurts him when you say you don't want him for a father."

Skipper looked away, but showed little sign of remorse. Searching for a way to get through to him, Michaela took his face between her hands and turned it toward her. "Skip," she said, and held his glance with her own. "When you hurt him you hurt me, too, and I don't think you want to do that."

A pink flush covered the little face. "Awww, Mom," he drawled in a mixture of impatience and disbelief. "Okay, I'll try, but I'll always like Uncle Darren better."

He pulled away from her and jumped off the bed. "I gotta go to the bathroom," he muttered, and scampered out of the room and across the hall.

Michaela sighed and took a clean pair of jeans out of a drawer. This was going to be even more difficult than she'd anticipated.

If only Heath could have come back before she and Darren started preparing Skipper to accept Darren as his father! Could the damage to Skip's relationship with Heath ever be undone?

The atmosphere for the next hour was tense and uncomfortable. Heath changed out of his uniform and into jeans and a colorful sweatshirt. He made no further overtures toward Skipper, and Skip ignored him. Michaela tried too hard to make everything seem normal until she noticed that Heath looked exhausted.

In her anxiety to make things right between father and son, she'd forgotten that Heath had only been dismissed from the hospital that morning, and then had been flown clear across the country to a highly emotional reunion with his son and parents. Also, it was three hours earlier in

Seattle than the eastern standard time with which they'd started the day.

No wonder he looked tired.

Michaela ached for him, and chided herself for losing sight of her husband's weakened physical condition. If only he would complain, or tell her when his strength was giving out, but he never would. He still felt that it was unmanly to be in less than top form both physically and emotionally.

Skip was sitting on the floor in the living room watching an old western movie on television, and Heath sat in a well-worn leather-upholstered chair watching his son and trying not to fall asleep. Michaela walked quietly across the room and knelt beside the chair. Heath's head was bowed and he was dozing, but when she touched his leg he came instantly awake and clasped the arms of the chair as though bracing himself for a blow.

"I'm sorry, darling," Michaela said remorsefully as he brought her into focus. "I didn't mean to disturb you, but you'd be so much more comfortable if you'd lie down on the bed and take a proper nap."

He smiled and reached out to put his hands under her arms and coax her onto his lap, then relaxed as she cuddled against him. "No," he said, "I'm the one who's sorry. I don't want to sleep. I hate it when I run out of energy so easily."

This was the first time he'd held her on his lap since he'd come back, and she tingled with the intimacy. She kissed the side of his neck. "I know, but it takes time to overcome the abuse your body's taken and get your strength back again. It'll happen faster if you obey the distress signals your system sends and rest when you feel tired."

She slipped her hand inside the loose neck of his sweatshirt and caressed his bare shoulder as she murmured, "Will you let me put you to bed?"

He tightened his arms around her. "Sweetheart, you can put me to bed anytime, you don't even have to ask." He spoke against her ear in little more than a whisper.

With a glance at Skippy, who was totally absorbed in the movie on the television screen, she spoke softly. "I'm afraid I can't join you right now, but Skip goes to bed early and then we'll have all night...."

His breath caught, and his hand roamed over the silken fabric of her skirt where it lay against her leg. "Are you sure?" he asked huskily.

"I'm sure," she whispered and tugged at his earlobe with her teeth.

He wrapped her in his embrace. "I love you."

"I love you, too," she answered, very much aware that it was the first time she'd said those words to him in over six years. Her tone was thick with emotion.

Again he caught his breath, and when at last he spoke his voice trembled. "Don't say that unless you mean it."

"I mean every word of it," she assured him. "I still don't know whether it's a blessing or a curse, but I've always loved you and I want to be your wife again, in every way."

He groaned softly, and for a moment they just sat there holding each other as they savored the strong sensual pull that radiated between them.

It was Heath who finally moved to slide her off his lap. "Is your offer to put me to bed still good?" he asked with a crooked grin.

"Sure is," she teased. "I want you all rested up for tonight."

* * *

When Michaela wakened Heath three hours later, he barely remembered his head hitting the pillow before he'd fallen asleep. He remembered what she'd said to him just before that, though, and he captured the hand that was shaking him awake and pulled her down to lie beside him on the bed.

"Did you mean what you promised?" he asked as he rolled over to hold her full-length against him.

She didn't insult either of them by pretending not to know what he was talking about. "Yes, I meant it," she answered tenderly. "All of it, from 'I love you' to 'I want to be your wife again.'"

He closed his eyes and breathed a little prayer of thanksgiving in an effort to control his runaway emotions. He was dangerously close to breaking down and sobbing with relief, and that would never do. Not only would his wife lose respect for him, but it would be a miserable example for his son.

When he could finally speak he strove for lightness. "Do you... That is, do you think we have time for a little practice session? Just to see if we still remember how?"

Amusement supplemented the love-light in her eyes, and a tiny smile tilted her mouth. "I guarantee you we both remember how," she said pertly, "and if we start practicing now we won't get out of bed before morning. How would you explain that to our parents and our son?"

He felt a chuckle rise in his throat. "I'm afraid I'd be long past caring what they thought," he said and rolled away from her to sit on the other side of the bed. "Now get out of here and leave me to my cold shower before I change my mind."

The dinner with their parents was a pleasant interlude, and there was much catching up on events that had happened over the years. Heath spoke only briefly of his imprisonment, but was avidly interested in everything that had happened to his family and friends. They discussed everything but Darren and Michaela's relationship. By mutual unspoken consent, that subject was taboo.

There were a few tense moments when Heath's dad, a dedicated military career man, asked his son if he was going to reenlist in the navy. "The navy financed your college education through the ROTC program, but you only actually served a few months," he concluded. "You really do owe them—"

"Owe them!" Heath roared as he came to his feet, his eyes blazing with fury. "I lost six years of my life in a filthy, rat-infested prison for the navy. I don't owe them a damned thing!"

Uriah's features twisted with shock, and it was obvious that he hadn't thought through what he'd said and how it would sound to a man who had just lived through six years of hell.

Terrified of what Heath might do, Michaela jumped up and clutched at his arm as she spoke soothingly to him. Alice maneuvered her husband in a like manner, and Michaela's parents remained seated and didn't interfere. Both men apologized, and the subject of Heath's future with the navy was dropped.

By ten o'clock, Skipper was nodding off in his Grandpa Tanner's lap, and Heath announced that it was time to go home and put him to bed. His father nodded his understanding. "You're right, the little guy needs his rest, and I'm sure you do, too. You'll have a lot of settling in to do, and your mother and I have been away from our own home much longer than we'd anticipated. Since George and Lila are returning to Phoenix tomorrow, we've decided to leave, too."

Heath tried to protest but his father was adamant. "We're already booked on the seven o'clock flight in the morning, but we hope you and Michaela and the boy will come to Palm Beach to visit us soon."

It took another half hour to get through all the good-bye's and the loving hugs and kisses, so it was after eleven before Heath and Michaela got back to the apartment and put an already sleeping Skip to bed.

As they shut his door behind them and walked up the hall to their own bedroom, Heath put his arm around Michaela and hugged her to him. For days she'd been looking forward to being alone with him, but now that she was she felt like a virginal bride.

It had been so long since they'd made love, and Heath was a different person now. What would he expect of her? Would he understand that she was shy and more than a little concerned about her ability to please him?

Her heart pounded as they entered the bedroom and Heath closed and locked the door. She knew he wasn't locking her in; he just didn't want Skipper to come wandering in at an inappropriate time, but she fought the strong urge to unlock it again.

He put his other arm around her, and she lifted her head to look at him. He searched her face and frowned. "Are you afraid of me, Michaela?"

She knew her uneasiness must be written all over her face, and she didn't want anything to spoil this night for him.

She put both her arms around his neck and raised on tiptoe to kiss him lovingly on the mouth. "Not afraid, darling, just a case of first-night jitters. It's been such a long time."

"Tell me about it," he moaned and held her close. "What can I do to make it easier for you?"

Again she was struck by how different he was now than on their wedding night. She'd been a true virgin then and even more shy and fearful, but he'd just laughed at her and taken her anyway. Not that he'd hurt her or been rough. Actually he'd aroused her skillfully, and by the time he'd entered her she'd been cooperating all the way. He was a marvelous lover, but tonight he was more concerned for her than for his own long-unmet needs.

No wonder she loved him so much.

"Would…would you mind if I take a shower first?" she asked timidly. "I've been wearing these clothes since early this morning, and I feel grimy."

He kissed her eyelids. "Go ahead. I took one after I woke up from my nap. Take all the time you need. I'm not going anywhere."

He released her and she took a robe from the closet, unlocked the door and headed for the bathroom.

Heath stood in the middle of the room for a long time staring after her. He was already aroused, but he always was when he held Michaela in his arms. She brought him to attention in record time, even when she wasn't trying to.

He finally turned and walked around trying to take his mind off the ache in his groin. If she changed her mind now he didn't think he could stand it, and that thought scared the hell out of him. His reactions were trigger-sharp and he couldn't always control them.

He thought of the scene with his father just a few hours before and began to pace. The old man hadn't meant any criticism by his thoughtless statement, and Heath had known it, but still he'd lashed out before he could stop himself. He'd hurt his father, frightened Michaela and upset his mother, and that had never been his intention.

He'd die before he'd force Michaela into anything she didn't want to do, but what if one of those rages took over and . . .

No! That wouldn't happen. Couldn't happen. He wouldn't let it happen!

Absently he unbuttoned his shirt and pulled it out of his slacks. The plumbing in this house was old and noisy, and he could hear the water running in the shower. A picture of Michaela standing nude under the cascading stream flashed in his mind, and he saw a misty vision of full high breasts topped with rosy nipples, a tiny waist he could span with his two hands, and gently flaring hips. . . .

His body tightened so sharply that it actually hurt, and he swore angrily as he made an effort to turn his thoughts in a different direction.

Slipping out of his shirt, he hung it over a chair then sat down to untie his shoes and remove them and his socks. The sound of the shower stopped, and the silence was louder than the noise had been.

She'd be coming back any minute. He stood and unfastened his slacks, then stepped out of them and his white briefs before climbing into bed and pulling the sheet up to his waist to spare them both embarrassment. She wasn't the only one having first-night jitters.

He heard the bathroom door open and her footsteps in the hall bringing her to him. Then the bedroom door opened and she stood before him in a shimmering white satin robe that he recognized as the one she'd worn on their wedding night almost eight years before. Her strawberry blond hair tumbled around her shoulders, and she was the most desirable woman he'd ever seen.

Their gazes clung as she walked to the bed, then stopped. He swallowed and licked his dry lips as he balanced himself on one elbow and held the other arm out to her, palm up.

"Take off your robe, sweetheart," he said, his voice hoarse with emotion, "and come to bed."

Chapter Nine

Heath watched, hypnotized, as Michaela untied the sash and let the robe fall open, giving him a glimpse of the small, perfect body that for so many years he'd seen only in his dreams.

His heart hammered with such ferocity that it seemed to drum in his ears and make his head spin. He clutched the sheet and took a deep breath in an effort to calm down as she slowly slid the robe off her shoulders and let it drop to the floor.

Her nude body was tinged a delicate pink with embarrassment, and even though she'd carried his child for nine months, her belly and breasts were still as firm and unblemished as they'd been the last time he'd made love to her. He'd never seen anything so erotic in his life, and he'd never loved her more.

Temporarily deprived of movement or speech, Heath let his gaze follow her as she sat on the side of the bed and reached up to pull the cord of the low-hanging swag lamp that was draped by a chain from the ceiling. That broke his trance, and he found his voice. "No, don't turn it off. I want to look at you."

She swiveled gracefully to put her legs on the bed, then lowered herself into his waiting arms.

She was warm and damp from the shower, and he fought the almost overpowering desire to crush her to him. Lust could come later when she was more comfortable with him. Now he was going to make love to her. Slow, tender, gut-wrenching love, the kind that is eternal.

He brushed a steam-curled tendril of hair away from her forehead and gently kissed her naturally rosy lips. "Mmmm, you smell like lilacs," he murmured as he turned his attention to her throat.

She snuggled against him and stroked the back of his head, sending shivers down his spine. "It's soap and splash cologne." The words were mundane, but her tone was low and sexy.

He trailed tiny love bites down to the rise of her breast, and her hands moved to the nape of his neck. He'd often wondered how such small hands could make him feel good all over no matter where she happened to be touching him.

He cupped the side of her breast with his hand and took the hard-tipped nipple in his mouth. It was larger and darker now than it used to be, and it tasted of forbidden delights. He envied his baby son who had actually drawn nourishment from her. No wonder the child thrived so well in spite of his heart condition. A bonding such as that was spiritual.

He ran his tongue around the pebbly surface and suckled, all the while keeping a tight rein on himself so as not to startle or hurt her. He was determined to pleasure her as much as she was pleasuring him, but she was moving sensuously, and each time she arched against him it became more agonizing to hold back.

He let his hand roam to the indentation of her waist, then over the curve of her hip to rest on her thigh. She moaned and clutched at his shoulders, and his exhilaration was complete. She wasn't just accommodating him, she was responding, completely and without reserve.

He raised his head and found her mouth. It was sweet, and fresh, and as hungrily demanding as his. His sanity gave way to the elation she stirred in him with her touch, her scent, the little involuntary noises that issued from deep in her throat, and the tantalizing rhythm of her body that nearly drove him wild.

For a short while he was aware only of the fire that threatened to consume him, and it took all his concentration to control his passion long enough to ask a vital question.

"Michaela, are you protected?"

She twined her legs with his and eagerly sought his mouth again as she rasped. "Yes, I'm on the pill. Oh please... don't make me wait any longer."

He rolled over to finally end the torment and join his body with hers when her words rebounded in his head. *I'm on the pill... I'm on the pill... I'm on the pill.*

With sickening suddenness the desire drained from him, leaving him limp and cold.

Of course she was on the pill. She'd been within minutes of marrying his brother and she'd been taking the pill to protect her from conceiving *Darren's* child too soon!

Michaela felt the tension abruptly ebb from Heath's body, but she was too aroused to realize the significance of it as she dug her fingers into his shoulders in anticipation of the union he'd made her so desperately ready for.

It didn't come. Not the way she'd expected. Instead he moved his fingers up the inside of her thigh and into the damp throbbing core of her.

She gasped and stiffened, trying to hold on until he joined her. "Heath," she moaned. "I can't wait...."

"It's all right," he said. "Just let it happen." His finger probed further.

She shuddered with need, but still managed a semblance of restraint. He was sending her over the edge without him, but that's not the way she wanted their first time together in so long to be.

"I want you with me."

He nuzzled the side of her neck. "Shhh..." he murmured against her ear. "I want to do this for you. Let go, sweetheart, and enjoy."

She had no choice. She'd reached the end of her endurance, and his wanton probing shattered her control as she cried his name and soared.

It was a bittersweet release, and almost before Michaela had touched earth again Heath rolled away from her and got out of bed. She reached for him, but he had his back to her and was putting on his slacks.

Still too fuzzy to understand what was going on she sat up and drew the sheet around her. "Heath, what's the matter? What happened?"

He zipped his pants and reached for his shirt. "You're not that innocent, Michaela," he growled impatiently. "You know what happened. I couldn't complete it."

She was snatched back to reality fast. Of course. She should have realized....

"But why?" It was a cry of bewilderment. "There was no problem at the beginning. Did I do or say something to upset you?'' She pulled the sheet higher. ''If so, I'm sorry. I have no idea—''

''It's not your fault,'' he snapped, and his tone was heavy with pain and self-disgust. ''I should be apologizing to you. It's my problem, and I'm the one who has to deal with it.''

He finished buttoning his shirt and slid his feet into his shoes without bothering to put on his socks, then strode out of the room.

Frightened, Michaela jumped out of bed and grabbed her robe off the floor. She was putting it on as she rushed into the hallway just as Heath disappeared out the front door without even stopping to put on a jacket.

She hurriedly tied her sash, but by the time she had unlocked the door and raced onto the porch, he was out of sight.

Her first instinct was to run after him, but she wasn't dressed and she couldn't leave Skip alone in the middle of the night. Besides, Heath couldn't go far; he didn't have the keys to her car.

She shivered in the damp, cold breeze that blew of Puget Sound and nearby Lake Washington, and rubbed her arms through the slippery satin fabric as she turned and went back into the house.

Returning to the bedroom, she put on a nightgown and a heavier robe, shoved her cold feet into a pair of fur-lined slippers, and went into the living room. It had taken her a long time to get used to the weather in Seattle. It was cool and rainy all year round, and even in July it was sometimes uncomfortably chilly in the house at night.

She sat on the couch and prepared to wait for Heath to return. She could understand his frustration, but why had he walked out without a word? He'd insisted that he didn't blame her for his ... his ... his what? Clinically it would probably be considered impotence, although everything was working fine right up to the last minute.

She ran her hands through her disheveled hair. What had happened? It wasn't something she said, because they'd both been too aroused to think, let alone talk. He did ask if she was protected, but he was the one concerned about it, and she'd reassured him. That wouldn't have upset him.

The minutes ticked by and became hours as she fretted and fumed. Fretted because he was humiliated and miserable, and wandering around a strange city on a cold wet night without even a sweater. Fumed because he'd left her alone with no word of where he was going or when he was coming back. His strength was still limited. He could at least call and let her know he was all right.

When he hadn't returned by dawn she was so distraught that she started to notify the police, but put the phone down after dialing the first three digits. There was nothing they could do. Heath was a grown man who could come and go as he pleased without his wife's permission, and if word got out that the country's military hero was unstable or having marital problems so soon the media would have a field day.

At seven o'clock Skipper was still sleeping soundly, and Michaela was in the bedroom frantically searching through Heath's possessions for the phone number where his navy escort, Lieutenant Newman, could be reached. She was past caring about the publicity or invasion of privacy; Heath was out there somewhere alone, and upset, and maybe even sick by now. She needed help to find him.

The ring of the telephone on the nightstand beside her made her jump, and she quickly grabbed for it. It was Heath, and her relief was so great that her knees gave way and she sank down to sit on the side of the bed.

"Heath! My God, where are you?" she heard the hysteria in her voice, but couldn't tone it down. "Are you all right? I've been going out of my mind!"

"I'm sorry, sweetheart," he said contritely, "I didn't mean to worry you. I'm in the emergency area of the naval hospital...."

Michaela sucked in her breath. "The hospital! Oh Heath, what happened? I knew I should have gotten help!"

"No, no, Mickey, I'm all right. I'm neither sick nor hurt, but I did get lost and tired. I didn't remember your address, and you're not in the phone book, so I hailed a cab and had the driver bring me here. When they found out I'd just been released from Bethesda, they insisted on checking me over again, and they just finished. They also got in touch with Lieutenant Newman, and he's here with me. He had your number."

"But you must be exhausted. Do you want me to come and get you? Skip's still asleep, but I can wake him—"

"No, honey, listen to me," he interrupted. "Don't do that. I ... I'm going to check in here for a few days."

He sounded uncertain of her reaction, and well he might. After a long night of pacing the floor, terrified that he may have been mugged, or hit by a car, or possibly run out of strength and collapsed, she was in no mood to hear that all the time he'd been checking into yet another navy hospital.

"You're what?" she asked, and her tone betrayed her exasperation.

"Michaela, I know you're upset, but—"

She forced herself to remain calm. "Heath, are you ill?"

"No. I promise you, I'm fine," he said reassuringly.

"Are you injured?"

There was a slight pause. "No."

"Are you disoriented in any way?" Her voice became chillier with each question.

"Honey, please, let me explain...." He sounded desperate.

"Are you disoriented?" she repeated patiently.

He sighed. "No."

She clenched the phone and drew a deep breath in an effort to control her mounting anger. "Then I want you to listen to me, Heath. I'm sorry things went wrong last night. I understand how devastating something like that can be for a man, but running away from the problem isn't going to solve anything."

"Dammit, I'm not running away."

"Yes, you are," she retorted. "You shut yourself up in a hospital the first time it happened, and now you're trying to do it again."

"Michaela, that's not true!" He was practically yelling into the phone.

She ignored his protest. "The morning after you came back to me I was willing to agree to anything you thought would make the transition from prison to freedom easier. You moved into the hospital, and I asked for counseling, too, in an effort to understand how to help. I learned some valuable things during that week, and one of them is that I'm no longer willing to assume all the blame for our difficulties."

"I don't blame you—"

"Then why are you moving out and leaving me?"

He groaned, and she could feel his pain and frustration. A wave of guilt washed over her. Was she being too hard on him? After all, she had no conception of what he'd suffered during his confinement. It might take years for the effects of that experience to wear off.

"I'm not leaving you," he said. "You're my life, my reason for surviving. It's because I can't stand the thought of losing you that I'm willing to go back into the hospital...."

His voice broke, and her anger melted as her love for him swept away everything but her intense desire to reassure him.

While she struggled with the tears in her throat which made speech impossible, Heath continued in a tone that was ragged with torment. "I just need more time, Mickey."

"Heath, my darling," she murmured, hoping he'd recognize the love that throbbed in her voice, "you can have all the time you want, but it doesn't have to be in a hospital. Make appointments for counseling as often as the doctors feel is necessary, but that's only an hour a day at the most. I'm sure the navy will even arrange transportation if you don't feel up to driving back and forth."

There was a long pause at the other end before he answered. "Honey, it's not only the counseling. I don't want a recurrence of what happened last night."

Michaela put her hand over the mouthpiece so he wouldn't hear the sob that unleashed her pent-up tears. "I understand that," she said, struggling to hold back another sob. "I know how shattering it was for you, but it's something we have to work out together. It's not your fault, or mine, but it'll take both of us to overcome it."

Once more she covered the mouthpiece and sobbed while Heath struggled with his own emotions. When he spoke again it was in a brisk, businesslike tone. "All right, Michaela, if that's what you really want, then I'll come home, but I have to arrange for appointments with a counselor first. Hopefully I can have the first session this morning, so don't worry about picking me up. I'll take a cab."

Even though Michaela kept busy, the morning hours seemed to crawl by. The low hanging clouds of yesterday had disappeared, and the sun shone brightly while the temperature climbed from chilly to warm. She dressed in her new jeans and blouse and tried to forget they were bought for a honeymoon with Darren. As soon as possible she'd return the trousseau nightgowns and lingerie to the department stores where she'd bought them, but everyday items like slacks and dresses shouldn't cause a problem.

Skip woke about nine, and she gave him his breakfast and let him go out in the backyard to play with the little girl from next door. The Ziegler family had only recently moved into the house to the south, and since Michaela worked and Skipper went to the child care center, she knew the parents only slightly. Skip and four-year-old Yvonne had become good friends, though, and enjoyed playing together on weekends and holidays.

Michaela observed but didn't comment on the fact that Skipper didn't ask about Heath or even seem to notice that he wasn't there. She sighed and glanced at her watch again.

As she rearranged drawers to make room for Heath's clothes her apprehension grew. When he'd given in and agreed to come home, he'd sounded so cool and unemotional, as though he were only doing it under duress.

What was wrong with him? Didn't he want to live with her? Was he using his sexual problem as an excuse for keeping her at a distance?

But that didn't make sense. His need for her, even discounting sex, was very real. That first night he'd pleaded with her to stay with him even though there was no chance that they'd make love.

But the next morning he'd checked into the hospital, and they hadn't been alone together since until last night.

He'd never had trouble before. He'd been exceedingly virile during their short time together, and she still turned him on. There was no question about that, so why was he reluctant to face her and discuss it with her?

Heath finally arrived while Michaela was in the kitchen fixing lunch. She was so on edge and tuned for the sound of the taxi that she heard it as it pulled up in front of the house.

She dropped the tomato and the knife she was slicing it with on the counter, then rinsed her hands under the faucet and wiped them on the gingham apron as she hurried up the hall to unlock the front door.

How should she greet him? Should she throw herself in his arms or let him make the first move? Did he need reassurance that she was no longer angry, or was he upset with her now?

She opened the door and unlocked the screen door as he was coming up the porch stairs. One glance at his face and her wide smile faded. He looked tired and drawn and miserable.

She stood aside to let him enter, and he walked past without touching her, then turned and met her gaze. His brown eyes were dull as was his voice when he spoke. "I'm sorry, Michaela. So very sorry."

She leaned wearily back against the wall. "Sorry for what, Heath?"

A flicker of surprise crossed his face. "For being a dud in bed last night," he said crudely. "For walking out and letting you worry about me."

If she could spare him the further humiliation of talking about this she would, and gladly, but they'd never correct the problem if they kept skirting around it.

"I accept your apology for worrying me," she said carefully, feeling her way through the mine field of words and nuances, "but you don't owe me one for the...the other..." she finished, embarrassed in spite of her resolve not to be.

He blinked, and a wry grin touched the corners of his mouth. "It's kind of you to try to be delicate, but the truth is that I failed you in the most mortifying way possible."

The grin was gone and with it the momentary lightening of his mood.

"Mortifying for you, but not for me," she said, anxious that he understand. "Our lovemaking was good for me. No, more than good, it was exquisite."

He looked stunned. "It couldn't have been. I didn't—"

She reached out and put her hand on his arm. "It's not what you *didn't* do, darling, but what you *did* do for me. You took the time and the patience to make sure I reached completion even though you must have been shattered by your own body's treachery."

Some of the grimness in his expression dissolved, but he still wasn't convinced. "It's sweet of you to want to spare my feelings, but—"

Michaela shook her head. "I'm not sparing your feelings, nor am I exaggerating to make you feel better. I'm simply telling you how I felt."

She put her arm through his and led him toward the kitchen. "Let me tell you something about women. To us, lovemaking is touching, kissing, caressing with the man of our choice. The whispered endearments, the caring enough to be considerate, the closeness of just being held. It doesn't have to end in the act of sexual intercourse every time to be satisfactory."

Heath looked dubious and she chuckled. "Your expression adds credence to that I'm going to say next. To most men, lovemaking means taking their partner to bed and having sex that isn't complete until he's reached a mind-blowing orgasm."

"Now just a damn minute—"

Michaela interrupted. "Don't snarl at me until you've heard me out. I admit that I protested when you didn't . . . uh . . . join with me. . . ."

Another wave of embarrassment made her tongue stumble, and she'd resorted to being "delicate" again. Darn, why couldn't she just come right out and say what she meant without the euphemisms?

She hurried on before he could cut in. "But it was only because I wanted you to feel the same exhilaration I was feeling. My satisfaction was complete, and I . . . I love you for making it so."

He reached for her then and took her into his arms, but although she raised her face expectantly, he didn't kiss her. Instead, he guided her head to rest against his chest and cradled it there with his hand. Without her high heels she barely came to his shoulder.

"What did I ever do to deserve you?" he murmured thickly.

"You married me," she answered simply.

Michaela knew that wasn't the answer today's woman was supposed to give a man; it implied that he'd done her a favor. But she realized that Heath would know what she meant. When they'd first fallen in love, he'd suggested they live together, but that was something Michaela wasn't prepared to do and she told him so.

After that he'd kept a tight reign on their making out, and two weeks later he asked her to marry him. Not once did he try to change her mind, or seduce her, or belittle her for her moral standard. He'd respected her decision and later decided she was the woman he wanted to spend his life with.

He hadn't been the perfect husband, but neither had she been the model wife. They'd both been so young and immature, but they'd loved each other passionately.

They still did, so surely they could resolve their problems if they just worked at it together.

The opening and closing of the door from the laundry room to the backyard alerted them, and they moved apart as Skip came into the kitchen, followed by a little girl with tangled blond hair and big blue eyes.

"Hey, Mom, when are we gonna eat? I'm—"

He stopped talking and blinked when he saw his father, but Heath smiled. "Hello, Skipper. I think your mother has lunch about ready. Why don't you wash up while I set the table?"

For a moment more Skip stared, then, much to Michaela's relief, he nodded agreeably. "Okay," he said, "can Yvonne eat with us?"

"If it's all right with her mother," Michaela answered. "I'll call while you introduce Yvonne to your dad."

Skip glared at Michaela, but when she stared right back in a clash of wills, he finally broke the stalemate by looking away. "This is my...my mom's friend," he muttered without glancing at either Yvonne or Heath.

Michaela cringed at his deliberate rebellion, but Heath spoke before she could mete out punishment. "Hello, Yvonne," he said calmly and smiled at the child. "I'm Heath Tanner, and I'm Skipper's father. Do you live near here?"

It was obvious that Heath had everything under control so Michaela reached for the phone. She made a note to deal with her son's continued rudeness later.

The meal consisted of bacon, lettuce and tomato sandwiches, potato chips, and fresh peaches and cream. In a touchingly thoughtful gesture, Michaela's mother had stocked the refrigerator so that her daughter wouldn't have to rush out to buy groceries before she could feed her family.

Yvonne, who had three considerably older brothers, was bright, friendly and knowledgeable beyond her four years. She kept them all entertained with a running commentary of anecdotes about her family, most of them personal enough that her parents would have been horrified had they known their daughter was broadcasting them around the neighborhood.

By the time lunch was over Michaela was practically nodding in her plate. She'd slept only in snatches the night before while waiting for Heath to come back, and now she could hardly keep her eyes open.

After giving the children permission to play in Skip's room until his nap time, she got wearily to her feet intending to clear the table, but Heath stopped her. "You look like you're about to collapse," he said as he took both of her hands in his. "You didn't get much sleep last night, did you?"

She shook her head, too tired to make light of it. "No, I was up all night waiting for you to come home."

He put his arm around her shoulder and turned her toward the hall. "You go to bed. I'll do the dishes." His tone was tender and protective.

"I . . . I have to put Skipper down for his nap."

He prodded her into walking with him. "I can do that, too, but isn't he a little old for afternoon naps?"

Resentment flared and Michaela bristled. Was he criticizing the way she raised her son? "No, he's not," she snapped. "He gets up early and he tires easily. He doesn't have the stamina that other little boys have."

Heath frowned. "Because of his heart condition?"

"Yes. I shouldn't have to explain that to you. You must know what it's like."

"I do," he said sadly. *And I don't want my son to go through what I did because of it,* he thought, but he'd heard the edge in Michaela's voice and didn't want to argue with her.

Later, when his list of sins wasn't so grievous, he'd take on the subject of Skipper's health.

She relaxed against him as they headed for the bedroom. "You look just as tired as I feel," she protested. "Will you rest, too?"

"I am and I will," he promised. "Just as soon as I clean up the kitchen and put Skip down to nap. What do I do with Yvonne?"

Michaela chuckled. "Send her home. She lives right next door and runs back and forth all the time."

He led her into the room and sat her down on the bed, then knelt in front of her and removed her shoes.

"Heath, you don't have to do that," she exclaimed.

"I want to," he said soberly. "Now lie down and and don't be afraid to sleep soundly. I'll stretch out on the couch in the living room so I'll be sure to hear Skipper if he wakes up before you do."

She snuggled down into a ball and closed her eyes, waiting for him to lean over and kiss her, but he didn't.

Instead, the bedroom door closed behind him and she was left alone.

It was hours before she woke, and then only because of a loud crash coming from the direction of the kitchen. She sprang to a sitting position on the bed, still half asleep.

Skipper! What had happened. Had he dropped something or had something dropped on him?

She jumped to her feet and ran down the hall toward the sound of raised voices. "Don't move!" It was Heath issuing orders. "You'll step on that glass and cut yourself. Just stand there while I sweep it up."

"But the fish'll die," came the plaintive reply.

Michaela reached the kitchen to find Heath and Skipper standing in the middle of the floor surrounded by broken glass and water, with Skip's two goldfish flopping helplessly in the mess.

Heath looked up and saw Michaela. "Sorry we woke you, honey," he said, then hunkered down and reached for the fish. "I'll put them in the sink and run water in it," he told Skip, and proceeded to do as he promised while his son stood barefoot on the wet floor without moving.

Michaela was also barefoot, but she made her way gingerly across the linoleum until she could pick up Skip and carry him to the far side of the room.

"Careful," Heath warned, "don't get those little splinters in your feet. They're the devil to find and get out."

"What happened?" she asked as she sat the child down on the sturdy oak table.

"We were gonna clean the fish bowl," Skip said, "but it was slippery and I...I dropped it." He looked away from her, knowing he'd done something wrong.

Michaela sighed. "I've told you never to pick that bowl up and try to carry it when it's full of water, haven't I?" She wasn't sure whether she should have been scolding Skip or Heath. Heath should have been watching him more closely.

"It was my fault, Mickey," Heath explained as he finished fixing the sink for the fish to swim in and started sweeping up broken glass. "He wanted to bring it to me, and I...well, I'm not very knowledgeable about little boys. I should have known it was too cumbersome and heavy for him. I'm sorry."

Her glance wandered to Skip's feet swinging from the side of the table. "Why is he barefoot?" she asked.

Heath shrugged. "I just assumed he went barefoot during the summer. I always did when I was a kid."

She tried not to let her annoyance show. "You grew up in the hotter parts of the country. It's cool and wet in Seattle, even in the summer, and Skip mustn't catch cold. It affects his respiratory system and could go into pneumonia."

Heath looked thoroughly chastized as he swept pieces of glass into the dustpan, and Michaela felt like a shrew. It hadn't been her intention to scold him, but she had to make him understand that his son wasn't as robust as other children his age and needed to be protected from his own exhuberance.

She lifted Skip and started to carry him across the room. "I'll put his shoes and socks on him while you finish up there."

Heath put the broom down and met her at the kitchen door. "He's too heavy for you to carry, Michaela," he said, and put his hands under the child's arms. "Let me have him. I'll take him into his room."

Before she could protest, he'd lifted Skipper into his arms. She was amazed when Skip offered no resistance but let his father take him away from her without a peep.

The goldfish survived, and Heath and Skipper transferred them into a new clean bowl while Michaela warmed a chicken and rice casserole she had in the freezer and served it with fresh string beans, hot rolls and chocolate pudding for dinner.

As a means of saving time, she'd gotten into the routine of fixing a large casserole once or twice a week and freezing half of it so it could be heated in the microwave for another meal. She also made her own TV dinners with leftover stewed chicken or slices of roast beef and vegetables.

Take-out foods were a rarity in Michaela's meal plans. She was determined that Skipper would have balanced meals with all the nutrients he needed, and none of the additives that he didn't.

After dinner she read to Skip until his bedtime, and Heath watched the news on television. He was addicted to news in any form in his quest to catch up on everything that had happened while he'd been shut away with no English-speaking radios or English-language reading material.

It gave Michaela a new and powerful appreciation of her freedom to almost any information she cared to pursue. Never again would she take it for granted!

By nine o'clock the dinner dishes were done, Skip was tucked into bed and asleep, and the air in the living room was thick with tension as Heath and Michaela sat at either end of the couch with two cushion widths between them. The silence was chilling, but their attempts at conversation were even more so.

They'd exhausted the subjects of the weather, the news, Skip's goldfish, and whether or not their parents had arrived at their respective homes on schedule. Everything but the most important subject of all.

What was going to happen when it came time to go to bed?

Chapter Ten

Fifteen minutes later Heath stifled a yawn, then another, and Michaela decided she'd better bring the subject of going to bed out in the open.

"You didn't get much of a nap this afternoon, did you?" she asked. "What time did Skipper wake up?"

Heath looked sheepish. "Sorry. Guess I am tired. I didn't sleep last night, either, but I got in a couple of hours this afternoon while Skip slept."

She stretched. "I'm having trouble keeping my eyes open, too, so why don't we make an early night of it?"

He squirmed uneasily. "Okay, but...uh...there's something we have to talk about first."

A wave of apprehension swept through her. Oh dear, now what? Why couldn't they just go to bed and let whatever happened happen. Nothing could be as bad as the anxiety and suspense they'd been enduring all evening.

Heath looked away from her and hurried on as though anxious to get it over with. "Honey, I . . . I think it would be better if I bunk out here on the couch for a few nights."

Michaela could feel the blood drain from her face. He didn't want to sleep with her anymore!

He stood and walked to the bookcase, putting more distance between them. He was erecting a barrier as solid as if he were using bricks and cement.

"I couldn't leave you alone if we shared a bed," he continued, "and I can't face another last-minute failure right now."

She could understand his frustration, but surely isolating himself from her would only make things worse. "Did the new psychiatrist you talked to today say we shouldn't sleep together?" She didn't want to argue against any medical advice he'd been given.

He shook his head. "No. Those shrinks don't give advice." His tone was sarcastic. "All they do is ask questions." Raising his voice, he mimicked, "And how do you feel about it, Heath?"

He snorted in disgust. "No matter what I tell them, all they say is, 'And how do you feel about it, Heath?' Hell, how I feel about it isn't the point. What I want to know is what to *do* about it."

Michaela had had experiences like that with her counselor, too, but she'd taken several semesters of psychology in college and knew that the way a patient feels about a given experience is important information if that patient is to understand why he or she reacts in a certain way.

He was standing with his back to her, and she got up and walked over to put her arm through his. He squeezed it against his side, but didn't touch her otherwise.

"I'll go along with whatever you want," she said, unwilling to force the issue, "but we've been apart for a long time. It's important for us to learn to be comfortable with each other again." She smiled. "Maybe all you need is a little practice."

She expected him to smile with her, but instead he seemed to draw back within himself. "If we were talking about a game of golf, I'd agree," he said, "but this sort of thing is more than I can cope with. I hate to sound like a broken record, but I really do need more time to come to terms with it."

Michaela heard the anguished uncertainty in his tone, and she withdrew her arm and stepped back. Her heart bled for him. She would have give anything if there were some way she could comfort him, convince him that it was a temporary condition that affected thousands, maybe millions, of men at any given time, but her efforts had been in vain. The only thing she could do now was to allow him the dignity of wrestling with the dilemma in his own way.

She tried to keep her disappointment out of her voice. "All right, if you feel that having separate rooms for a while is best, I won't argue, but you're not going to sleep on the couch. I shudder to think about what you've been using for a bed all these years, but as long as I'm your wife you're going to have a comfortable mattress. You take the bedroom and I'll commandeer the other bunk in Skipper's room.

For the next week Michaela and Heath lived more like brother and sister then husband and wife. Along with Skipper they ate together, shopped together and played together, but Heath never touched her, or held her, or kissed her. She knew he wanted to. Several times a day he went for an abrupt walk, or took Skip to a nearby playground when the sensual tension became too uncomfortable.

She wanted him, too, and she ached for his embrace; his hands caressing her; his mouth moving over hers with an insistent hunger; but she understood his distaste for becoming aroused only to have to ignore it. The same thing kept happening to her.

The nights were the worst. During Heath's long absence she'd gotten used to sleeping alone again. But now, knowing Heath was just down the hall, the nights were torment. It kindled perfectly natural desires and caused erotic dreams that made her restless and disturbed her sleep.

Heath wasn't resting well, either. Not only could she see the dark shadows under his eyes and the lines of weariness on his pale face, but many times when she was wishing for the blessed oblivion of sleep to put her out of her misery she heard him pacing the floor in his room on the other side of the wall that separated them.

On other nights she'd wakened suddenly with the sound of a shrilly cry of pain, or terror, ringing in her ears. The first time she decided it was just her imagination and went back to sleep. The second night she got out of bed and turned on the light to make sure Skip was all right. He slept soundly and everything was still, but this time she wasn't so willing to believe she'd been dreaming it.

The third night it happened, she had a nagging suspicion that it might be Heath. Again she got out of bed, but this time she left the lights off and walked up the hallway to where he slept.

She stood outside the door and listened, but, although she heard him turn over on the bed, there was no cry or other sound of distress. She debated whether or not to go in and make sure he was all right, but when all remained quiet she decided against it and went back to Skipper's room.

The following night was Saturday, a week since they'd come home to Seattle and since the one time they'd made love. If Heath remembered the "anniversary" he didn't say so, and Michaela climbed into her lonely narrow bed feeling resentful and abandoned.

Did he expect them to go on like this forever? It had been seven days since he'd touched her. They would never solve the problem this way, and the tension was tearing them both apart.

Did he discuss it with his psychiatrist? He'd had three sessions this week and was scheduled for two a week through July, but he didn't talk about them with her and she didn't want to pry by asking.

They seemed to be growing further apart each day, and without Heath's cooperation there was nothing she could do about it. The only positive side was the gradual melting of Skipper's resentment of his father. He still refused to call Heath "Daddy" or "Dad," instead referring to him as "he," "him" or "Mom's friend," but Heath was spending a lot of time with his son and Skip had loosened up and was much friendlier.

Which left Michaela out in the cold without either a husband or a son.

Muttering an oath, she pounded her pillow and chastised herself silently so as not to wake Skip in the top bunk. She hated sniveling, self-pitying women who took on the role of martyr rather than do something about whatever was bothering them, and it was time she quit feeling sorry for herself and let Heath know that her patience was about exhausted.

Tomorrow she'd have it out with him. It couldn't make things much worse, and maybe she could get him to agree to try sleeping together again. Once she'd reached that decision she was able to relax and doze off.

Hours later she was jolted out of a deep sleep by the phantom cry again. By this time she'd decided it was a mild form of nightmare she was having and rolled over and shut her eyes.

She'd just started to relax when it came again, but now she was awake and there was no doubt that the sound was real. Raising herself up on her elbow, she listened intently, but as before all was silent.

It had to be Heath. Skip was snoozing peacefully just above her, and the sound had definitely come from inside the house.

While she was still trying to decide what to do, an agonized scream split the air. Michaela landed on her feet in the middle of the room and took off running up the hall. She burst through the door and flipped the light switch to find Heath sitting in the middle of the bed fighting the covers that entangled him. He was breathing heavily, his bare chest heaving as another unearthly yell was torn from it.

Her only thought was to get to him as quickly as possible, but when she reached the bed one flailing fist grazed her shoulder and knocked her off balance.

It was obvious that he was still asleep, and this time she was more cautious. She reached over the bed to grab his leg and shake it. "Heath! Heath, it's Michaela," she said loudly. "Wake up, darling, it's just a bad dream!"

He continued to struggle with the sheet and blanket, which had been pulled from under the mattress and wrapped loosely around him. In his somnambulistic state, he no doubt thought it was his captors binding him in order to inflict more of their punishment.

Again she shook him and called his name, at the same time hoping Skip wouldn't waken and come to see what was going on.

"Heath! Sweetheart, wake up. It's all right. You're safe. No one's going to torment you."

The threshing of his arms and legs slowed, and she carefully climbed up onto the bed and put her arms around him. "Wake up, darling, it's all right," she crooned soothingly. "You're home with me now, and no one's going to chain you up ever again."

He clutched her to him in a bone-crushing embrace. His breath was still coming in gasps, and he was trembling uncontrollably. "Michaela! Oh God, Michaela." His voice was gravelly with a combination of horror and relief.

"Yes, love," she answered as he buried his face in her shoulder. "I'm here. You're safe at home. It was all a bad dream."

She held him, and stroked him, and repeated the reassuring phrases, punctuating them with kisses on the glistening damp skin of his neck and shoulders.

Gradually he became calmer and loosened his hold on her slightly. She drew a deep breath to fill her oxygen-starved lungs, then winced as she realized that her ribs were sore from the strength of his grip.

He raised his head and their gazes meshed and held. "I...I didn't mean to be rough," he said anxiously. "Did I hurt you?"

He seemed to be probing the very shadows of her soul, and daring her to delve into the secrets she would find in his if she cared enough to search. She shook her head, careful not to break eye contact. He'd hate himself if he thought he'd injured her. "No, but you were holding me so tightly that it was a little hard to breathe." Her voice wasn't much more than a whisper as the powerful magnetism between them had the same effect.

With a groan he lowered his mouth to cover hers, and the electricity that radiated from one to the other detonated in a fiery conflagration of need. Wrapped in each other's arms, they fell backward on the bed and rolled over so that he was partially on top of her with his groin pressed against her hip, and one of his legs between both of hers.

His hand roamed hungrily over her breast and pushed aside the silky low-cut bodice that covered it. Her lips parted to allow his exploration, and their tongues dueled and danced to the fierce drumming of their heartbeats.

Heath was totally nude, and Michaela could feel the swollen hardness of his manhood as he pressed urgently against the firm flesh of her thigh. She was drunk with the power she had to inflame him, but his power over her was just as strong. She whimpered with need as his hand left her breast and traveled downward to her inner thigh.

Once more the nightgown intruded, and she heard a ripping sound as the delicate fabric tore, exposing her peach-hued flesh to his eager palm.

He wrenched his mouth from hers and bent down to the throbbing breast his hand had been caressing. This time his tongue teased her nipple, sending pinpricks of flame racing to her already-overheated core.

She clutched at his shoulders and rolled her head from side to side as he started the suckling that sent waves of desire coursing through her. She loved the intimacy of his bare body pressed against hers and let her hands roam over his broad back, his narrow waist, and down to the spot at the base of his spine that she knew from earlier experience was erogenous.

As she rubbed the slight indentation, his muscles tightened and he shivered as he quickly moved into position over her. "I can't...hold back...." He panted and thrust into her.

For a fraction of a minute it hurt, as it had on their wedding night, but the discomfort was forgotten in the sheer ecstasy that followed. He'd lost all control and his thrusts were quick and deep. She wrapped her legs around his hips and welcomed them with cries of rapture.

This time there was no one-sided bittersweet release but a mutual explosion that went on and on until they finally collapsed, exhausted and more than a little awed.

One of their problems had been resolved. There was absolutely nothing wrong with Heath's sexual prowess!

They slept, then woke to a slower, more romantic, loving and slept again. When Michaela opened her eyes to find sun streaming into the room, she felt sated and relaxed and well loved.

She rolled over to cuddle against Heath and found the other side of the bed empty. A glance at her watch told her that it was almost eleven o'clock. Good heavens, how come Skipper hadn't wakened her?

Before she could gather her wits about her and get out of bed the door opened and Heath appeared carrying a tray of food. He was dressed and looked as sated and relaxed and well loved as she felt!

A broad smile lit his whole face. "Good morning, Mrs. Tanner," he said happily. "I brought sustenance to replace the energy we used up last night so we can start depleting it again."

For the first time since she'd told him about her aborted marriage to his brother, he looked completely happy. She held up her arms to him and grinned. "And a bonnie good morning to you, Mr. Tanner. Come, man, don't just stand there, put the damn tray down and kiss me."

He practically dropped it on the floor in his haste to comply. He was still damp from the shower, and he smelled of soap and shaving lotion and musky male. His lips were warm and eager, and he held her as though afraid she might yet slip away from him.

He lowered her down on the bed, and for a while they were lost to everything but the wonder of just being together in an uninhibited embrace.

"Why didn't you wake me before you got up?" she asked contentedly, a few moments later.

He chuckled as he ran his hand over her bare back. "It was a temptation, believe me. You were curled around me without a stitch on, and I was...uh...ready and more than willing...when I heard our son calling for his mommy."

He nibbled playfully at her neck and made her giggle. "Having a kid around the house does have its drawbacks at times, doesn't it?"

"It's just another of the many things you'll have to adjust to, sweetheart," she said softly. "I'm sorry I behaved so badly last week when you wanted to check into the hospital. I should have been more understanding, but by the time you finally called I was going crazy with worry wondering if you'd gotten lost, or mugged, or hit by a car...."

He put his fingers to her lips to still her. "Don't apologize to me, Michaela," he said sternly. "I was a selfish, unthinking bastard, but that night we were finally on the verge of making love, when you told me you were taking the pill. All I could think of was that you'd been taking it to protect yourself from bearing Darren's child, not mine. I...I just lost the ability."

She kissed his fingers and moved his hand to cup her cheek. "I wish I could have spared you that, but I think you're coping amazingly well. Much better than I am."

He trailed his hand slowly down her throat until it settled on her breast. The fires she'd thought had been extinguished began to flicker. "We both have a lot of coping to do," he said with a sigh. "It's bound to be difficult at times, but you were right to insist that I come home instead of checking into the hospital. You said I was running away, and I realize now that I was. It was easier than facing the problem and admitting that such a thing could happen to me."

She rose and brushed her lips across his. "That particular difficulty more or less solved itself, with the help of the nightmare."

He nibbled at her teasing mouth. "Yes, thank God." He shuddered. "I never thought I'd be grateful for those grotesque dreams."

She wrapped her arms protectively around him. "You've been having them a lot lately, haven't you?"

He looked at her quizzically. "How do you know that?"

She told him about hearing him cry out in the night and thinking it was either a dream or Skip. "It wasn't until last night that I realized it was you." Her tone was filled with remorse. "I would have come to you the very first time if I'd known. You shouldn't ever have to suffer through something like that alone."

He nuzzled her bare breast. "I won't again, will I?" He raised his head to look at her. "You will sleep with me from now on, won't you?"

She pushed his head back down and held it between her breasts. "If you think I was determined when I objected to your going into the hospital, just wait till you try to send me back to sleep in Skip's room...." A sudden thought made her gasp. "Oh good heavens, where is Skip?"

The bedroom door was open and she was not only curled up intimately with Heath, but she didn't have anything on!

Heath lifted his head and chuckled. "It's okay, honey. Yvonne's mother has taken Yvonne and Skipper to Madrona Park for a picnic. She assured me that it's only about a mile away on the shore of Lake Washington.''

Michaela frowned. ''I know where it is, but did you tell her not to let him run or play rough? Did you put a sweater on him? It's chilly down there with the breeze coming off the lake....''

''Michaela.'' There was a hint of impatience in Heath's tone. ''Skip will be fine. Mrs. Ziegler already knows that he's not to be too active, and she promised to bring him home at two o'clock for his nap. Both he and Yvonne wore sweaters, and I contributed three of the apples we bought the other day at Pike Place public market and the rest of the cookies you made yesterday to the picnic.''

He ran his fingertips over her forehead and smiled. ''Now stop glowering at me and relax. We have the house all to ourselves for the next two and a half hours.'' His eyebrows rose suggestively. ''I don't suppose you have any recommendations for making use of that time?''

She knew she'd overreacted, but where her little boy's precarious health was concerned it was difficult not to. She'd have to be careful about that from now on, though. After all, Heath wasn't going to let anything happen to the son he'd only recently discovered he had.

She grinned and put her hands on his chest to begin unfastening the buttons of his shirt. ''Oh, I think if I put my mind to it I can come up with something,'' she assured him solemnly as she reached for the clasp of his jeans and pulled it apart.

The next few days were like a second honeymoon, except now they had Skipper and were a family. Since Heath had never been in the Seattle area before, they did all the tourist things: cruised Elliott Bay and the port of Seattle; lunched at the restaurant atop the 605-foot Space Needle;

watched through underwater viewing windows as hordes of salmon swam up the ladders at the Chittenden Locks; and took an overnight guided tour of Mount Rainier National Park, the tallest volcanic mountain in the lower forty-eight states.

The company Michaela worked for had given her a four-week leave of absence on top of the two weeks' vacation time she'd already taken to be with her hostage husband, and Heath had months of leave accumulated, so there was no pressure on either of them. Their days were busy with sightseeing and getting to know each other again, and their nights were spent happily trying to appease the insatiable passion that had been suppressed for so many agonizing years.

Heath and Skip settled into a friendly, buddy-type relationship. Skip still refused to call Heath "Dad" and glowered when Heath called him "son," but Michaela had recently noticed that her bright little boy had discovered that Heath was more lenient with him than she was. He started asking Heath for permission when he wanted to do something that his mother might not approve of.

Fortunately Heath always checked with her before giving an answer, but it still irritated her. Skipper had been her sole responsibility all his young life, and they'd becom. very close. She didn't like sharing him. Not even with his f ither.

Tl.at discovery made her feel selfish and mean-spirited, but she couldn't control the resentment that flared when Skip sought out Heath instead of her.

On Wednesday morning of the third week after Heath and Michaela had returned to Seattle, they were up early getting themselves and Skipper ready to board the cata-maran boat, *Victoria Clipper,* for a one-day trip to Victoria, British Columbia. The sky was overcast and the breeze off the bay was chilly as Michaela dressed Skip in jeans, a long-sleeved shirt and a heavy pullover sweater.

"Aw, gee, Mom, I don't need all these clothes," he complained as he tied the high-topped canvas shoes he wore over heavy socks.

"Yes, you do, honey," Michaela assured him as she rummaged through his drawer for a knitted cap. "It's cold on the water in the early mornings. Daddy's wearing a heavy sweater and so am I. Now hurry, we don't want to miss the boat."

She turned to see Heath standing in the doorway. He, too, was wearing jeans, but with them he wore a short-sleeved T-shirt and there was no sweater in sight.

"See, *he's* not wearing a sweater and cap," Skip said accusingly.

Heath looked bewildered, and she hurried to give him a clue so he wouldn't say the wrong thing. "But he's going to, aren't you dear?" She accented the last three words.

Heath blinked. "Well, I...uh...oh yeah, sure I am." He didn't sound enthusiastic.

Michaela gave the child some last-minute instructions then left the room with Heath right behind her. "Hey, what was all that about?" he asked. "I hadn't planned on wearing a sweater. It's not all that cold."

She turned and glared at him. "Maybe not for you, but I told you I have to make sure Skip doesn't get a respiratory infection. It puts too much of a strain on his heart. It will save a lot of fuss if you just put on a sweater."

Heath's mouth tightened with annoyance and he muttered, "Yes, Mama," as he headed for the closet.

The red, white and blue *Victoria Clipper* was one of the world's largest catamarans, a vessel propelled on top of the water by two water jets, with a passenger capacity of three hundred and a service speed of slightly over thirty knots. Heath, Michaela and Skipper settled into the comfortable upholstered seats near the glass wall at the front that provided a wide-angle view.

Michaela had taken this two-and-a-half-hour trip north before. Once with Darren when she'd first moved to Seattle, and again with her parents during one of their visits. Both of those times it had been sunny and the scenery along the Sound's coastline had been spectacular, but on this morning there was a light drizzle that gradually fogged-up the windows, making it difficult to see out.

For a time Skip was restless and bored, but when the attendants came around with snacks and announced there were ice cream bars and soft drinks for sale at the small shop in the back, he perked up.

By the time they reached the Strait of Juan de Fuca, the clouds were left behind, the sun was out, and they could see the San Juan Islands, a group of small, individually named islands discovered by Spanish explorers, to the far east.

Thirty minutes later they entered the inner harbor at the quaint port city of Victoria, the capital of the province of British Columbia, situated on Vancouver Island.

As always when she came here Michaela's gaze sought out the stately old ivy-covered Empress Hotel that looked like part French château and part English manor. She pointed it out to Heath as the *Clipper* slowly moved toward its dock. "It was named in honor of Queen Victoria, you know," she said excitedly. "I was here last year with Mom and Dad, and we had afternoon tea there. It was fabulous. I never saw such an array of sweets and finger sandwiches."

Heath was holding Skipper on his lap in preparation for carrying him off the boat. "I'll bet that appealed to Skip, didn't it, Slugger." He gave the child a playful hug.

Michaela saw that she'd managed to talk herself into a trap. "Oh, Skipper didn't go with us," she said, hoping that would end the subject.

"I stayed with Uncle Darren," Skip said, eager to be included. "We went to the mu . . . mu . . ."

"Children's museum," Michaela supplied with a sinking heart.

"Yeah. That place. It was neat. We got to touch stuff and pick it up. I got to draw a picture, and they let me keep the crayons. Uncle Darren put the picture on his wall right where everyone could see it."

Heath didn't say anything or interrupt, but his expression changed from open and carefree to the tight, closed look he always got when his brother was mentioned.

There was an awkward, uncomfortable silence as they got off the boat and went through customs, then climbed the hill and crossed the street to catch their sightseeing bus in front of the Empress Hotel. When Skip saw the red-and-cream vehicles lined up his squeal of delight broke the tension. "Hey, look! They got an upstairs!"

They were indeed double-decker buses, and when they'd located the one going to the Butchart Gardens, Skip insisted they sit on top. They had an excellent view of the lush green countryside during the fourteen-mile drive along the winding road that twisted through gentle hills among western red cedar and Douglas fir trees.

The tour guide gave a brief history of the world-famous fifty-acre gardens as he skillfully drove the big bus toward the one-hundred-thirty-acre estate of Mr. and Mrs. Robert Butchart. "Mr. Butchart, a pioneer in the cement manufacturing business, bought the land because the limestone deposits on it made it an excellent site for his cement plant,'' the guide said. "The fields, forests and sheltered ocean waters also made it an attractive site for his family home, and as soon as they moved in, his wife, Jenny, an artist, started planting flowers.

"As time went by, a series of individual gardens began to surround the home, but the limestone quarry was an eyesore between the residence and the plant." The guide chuckled. "You can imagine how frustrating that would be to a wealthy woman who was both a fine artist and a landscape artist, as well as a gardener.

"Well, after fifteen years the quarry was abandoned,'' he continued, "and Jenny envisioned a garden in the desolation. It was a gigantic undertaking, but in a few short years the huge hole in the ground became the spectacular, world renowned Sunken Garden.

"Tales of the Butcharts' fabulous gardens spread, and now people come from all over the world to see them."

When they reached their destination Michaela could understand why. The flowers, bushes and trees were breathtaking, the colors so unbelievably brilliant that they almost seemed to glow. She wished she knew what the army of gardeners used in the soil to make the blossoms so gigantic, especially the begonias, geraniums and roses.

They had lunch at the Greenhouse restaurant, an actual greenhouse remodeled into a gardenlike room with cafeteria service, and spent the afternoon touring the grounds. Michaela relaxed her vigilance with Skipper and let him enjoy roaming around and darting in and out. He wasn't getting his usual nap, but she knew he'd sleep all the way back to Seattle on the boat.

The weather had become uncomfortably warm, and they'd shed their sweaters and left them in the bus, but Skip still complained about his heavy shirt. It was almost time for them to meet the other tour passengers back at the bus, and they were walking faster than usual in order to see the Sunken Garden the guide had told them about.

When they came through the trees to the rim of the canyon Michaela gasped. It truly was a magnificent sight. Not only the floor but the sides as well were covered with rolling lawn, colorful blossoms, lush bushes and towering trees that had transformed the former chunks of rock and stagnant puddles into a wonderland of nature.

Heath put his arm around Michaela as they stood side by side, drinking in the awesome beauty before them. She felt Skip's hand slip out of hers as Heath began to speak. "I'd forgotten there were places like this in the world," he said shakily. "I'd gotten so used to the hot barren desert, the filth, the wind and the grinding poverty—" His voice broke and he pressed her closer. "Oh, Michaela, don't ever take scenes like this for granted. In just the blink of an eye it could be lost to you forever...."

She turned and put her arms around him. "Don't think about it, darling," she said soothingly. "Just enjoy what we have now, and try to let go of the past. I know it's difficult, but I'll help if you'll just tell me how."

For a few moments they stood there in each other's arms, unaware of the people who passed by and smiled. It was Michaela who finally drew back. "I hate to be a killjoy, but we'd better get to the bus or they'll go off without us." She looked around. "Where's Skipper?"

Her gaze quickly scanned the nearby area, and the contentment that had engulfed her drained away. There was no sign of him on their side of the rim.

"Skipper," she shouted. "Come here. It's time to leave."

People turned to look at her, but there was no answer.

"Skipper!" This time it was Heath, and his voice carried better than hers. "Answer me. Where are you?"

Still no reply; but a teenaged boy in jeans approached them. "Hey, mister, are you lookin' for a kid about so high with black hair?"

"Yes," Heath said anxiously. "Have you seen him?"

The boy nodded. "Yeah, just a few minutes ago. He was goin' down the hill while I was comin' up."

He pointed to the steeply terraced side of the canyon where steps had been built from the floor to the rim. "See," he said, "there he is. Is he the one you're callin'?"

Relief flooded through Michaela as she saw that it was indeed Skip standing at the bottom of the steps looking up, but it was short-lived. It was fifty feet from the top to the floor of the quarry! She'd never have allowed him to go down all those stairs, it was far too much exertion, but climbing up would be much more.

She grabbed the wooden rail and leaned over. Skip was looking up at her. "Stay where you are," she called as loudly as she could. "We'll come and get you."

Apparently he misunderstood her because he started climbing up the stairs!

She clutched Heath's arms. "Heath, he can't climb back up. It'll kill him!"

"Dear Lord," Heath murmured and took off, running down the steep embankment.

A panic-stricken Michaela was behind him, but she couldn't keep up with his long steps. Skip continued to climb as fast as his little legs would carry him, and even though both Heath and Michaela called to him to stop he just picked up speed.

Heath was within a few feet of him when Skip suddenly stopped, put his hands to his chest and crumpled onto the grassy slope.

Michaela watched wide-eyed with horror as the small body rolled over, and over, and over, until it was stopped by a cluster of flowering bushes on the flat bottom of the wonderland into which he'd tumbled.

Chapter Eleven

It seemed an eternity before the paramedics arrived. Michaela spent the time crouched on the ground beside the unconscious form of her little son, holding his hand while the nurse from the first aid station administered oxygen.

As soon as the people in charge had learned that Skip was a heart patient, they'd arranged for a medivac helicopter to pick him up and fly him to the hospital in Victoria. They'd been advised not to move him, and while they waited, Heath stood beside Michaela and Skipper and answered questions for the accident report.

Finally Michaela heard the distinctive sound of the chopper approaching, and some of her terror receded. Skip's pulse was erratic, but he was breathing easier with the oxygen. The nurse assured her that the tumble down the hill had caused no major injuries, only contusions and abrasions that looked worse than they really were.

Even through the haze of shock and anxiety, Michaela was impressed with the way the pilot managed to set the small aircraft down in the canyon without doing too much damage to the flower beds. She stood in the circle of Heath's arms while the paramedics examined the child, but when they followed the stretcher to the plane with the intention of riding with him one of the men stopped her.

"Sorry, folks," he said, "but there's only room for the two of us and the stretcher. The manager of the gardens is making arrangements for someone to drive you to the hospital. If you'll just sign these papers giving permission for the patient to be treated..."

The idea that she not stay with Skipper was unthinkable, and she started to protest when Heath intervened. "They know what they're doing, honey. It's vital that they transport Skip to the hospital as quickly as possible. Don't hold them up by arguing."

Her whole being revolted against being separated from her stricken son, but she could see that there was no room and knew Heath was right. The important thing was to get Skip to the hospital! She took the papers and signed them.

A car and driver were waiting, and nobody paid attention to speed limits as the powerful Chrysler hurled along the winding road toward the city. Michaela huddled in the corner of the back seat, miserable and overcome with guilt.

"I should have insisted that he hold on to my hand," she said to no one in particular. "I should have watched him more closely."

Heath, sitting beside her, was battling his own misery and guilt. He hadn't really believed that his son was as delicate as Michaela insisted he was, and there were times when he'd been impatient with her for being over-protective. What an arrogant jerk he'd been assuming that he knew more about Skip's condition after a few days than the mother who'd raised him for the five years of his life.

Well, he was paying for his conceit now. He should have been thanking God that she was so conscientious instead of accusing her of coddling the child. If anything happened to him...

No! He wasn't even going to think such a thing. Skipper would be all right. He was a tough little guy in spite of his disability.

Heath cringed at the word. *Disability.* It was an ugly word. One he'd grown to hate after his bout with rheumatic fever left him with a damaged heart. It was the only word his parents ever used to describe him during those long years of preadolescence. Not "good," or "handsome," or "smart." Not even "naughty," or "lazy," or "dumb," just "disabled."

Our son is disabled, you know.... Heath can't go swimming because of his disability.... No, you can't take gym, Heath, you have a disability excuse.

Did Skipper feel the same awful frustration that had tormented him when told he couldn't do all the rough and tumble things the other little boys did. Maybe not yet. Skip was still very young, and he'd been born with the problem, whereas Heath had been seven years old when he'd been stricken. He had known the joy of running and jumping and playing contact sports before it was taken away from him.

At the hospital, Heath and Michaela were ushered into a treatment room where Skipper's still little form lay on a bed with several medics surrounding him. Michaela had been through this before with her son, but not for such a dramatic reason. It never got easier.

The doctor beckoned to them, and they approached the bed to find that Skip had his eyes open and was conscious.

A wave of relief left Michaela dizzy as she clutched his small hand. They'd removed his shirt, and although his face was cut and bruised, his clothes had protected the rest of his body except for a few black-and-blue areas.

"Hey, Mom, how'd I get in the hospital?" he asked through split and swollen lips. "And where have you been?" His voice was weak and his breathing labored.

Michaela leaned over and kissed him. "You fell down the hill and hurt yourself," she said softly, then managed a smile. "You were brought here by a helicopter like the ones you've seen on television."

His dark eyes widened. "No kiddin'? A copter?"

She stroked a lock of hair off his dirty forehead. "No kiddin'," she assured him, "but there wasn't room in it for daddy and me, so a nice man from the gardens drove us here in his car."

Skip shifted his gaze to Heath, who was standing behind Michaela, then back to her. "Where's Uncle Darren? Why isn't he here?"

She couldn't see Heath, but she winced for the pain his young son's words must have caused him. "Don't you remember, honey, Uncle Darren's gone to Japan on business, but Daddy's here. You haven't said hello to him yet."

Again Skip looked at Heath. "Hello," he said briefly, then returned his attention to his mother. "Could you call Uncle Darren and tell him to come and see me?"

Michaela bit her lip to keep from scolding the child who had no idea he was being rude. "He's halfway around the world from us, honey," she said gently. "It would take him a long time to get back."

Again she leaned down and kissed him. "I have to talk to the doctor now, so you lie still and I'll be back in a few minutes. Okay?"

The youngster hesitated for a moment then nodded. "Okay, but hurry."

She blinked to hold back the tears that were stinging her eyes. "I will, sweetheart. I promise."

Heath and Michaela followed the doctor to the other side of the room, where they were out of the way of the nurse and technicians. "Your little boy seems to have come through this without any serious damage," he said encouragingly, "but with his heart condition he'll need to be monitored closely for a few days. If you'd like to take him to the hosptial in Seattle and his own cardiologist, I'm sure the move won't hurt him, but it must be made in a medically equipped plane. It will be expensive, and I'm not sure that your insurance will pay for it—"

"The expense is no problem," Heath interrupted. "Do you have such a plane available?"

"That's the other problem," the doctor answered. "We only have the one, and I doubt if the authorities will agree to having it out of the area for that length of time. We can check the child in here at this hospital. We have some excellent specialists on staff—"

Again Heath cut in. "Let me see what I can arrange first. Is there a telephone I can use?"

Michaela wondered what he had in mind as she waited beside Skip while Heath was making the call. He was gone for over half an hour. The medical people had finished working on Skipper and he was dozing when Heath finally returned.

"I called Lieutenant Newman and told him what we needed," he told her. "It took a little doing, but he finally arranged for a navy medivac copter to pick Skip up and take him back to the hospital in Seattle. This copter's bigger and there's room in it for us, too, but it'll be a couple of hours or so before it can get cleared and up here. This hospital's been notified and they're making arrangements for a transfer to the one in Seattle.''

He looked down at his sleeping son. ''How's Skip? The doctor says he'll need the oxygen for a while.''

''Yes,'' Michaela said. ''I have equipment at home, too, but they usually keep him in the hospital for a day or two where he can be monitored closely.''

Heath looked at her. ''You mean this has happened before?'' he seemed incredulous.

''Oh, yes. Well, not just this way, but he sometimes blacks out and needs oxygen when he overexerts himself. It's difficult to keep a youngster quiet all the time.''

He still stared at her. ''My God, Michaela, why didn't you—'' He bit off his words in midsentence and looked away from her.

''Why didn't I what?'' she asked, bewildered by his odd attitude.

''Nothing,'' he said gruffly. ''It's not important right now. The doctor says we're to come to the desk. They have more papers for us to sign, and they want to go over with us the treatment they've given Skipper.''

The rest of the night was a blur of waiting for the helicopter, then crowding into it along with the stretcher that held their son, and the hour-long flight to the big hospital in Seattle where Skipper was a familiar patient.

Dr. Carl Oliver, Skip's heart specialist, met them when they arrived and had him admitted, then went over the reports from Victoria and eventually got back to Heath and Michaela to tell them to go home. ''Your boy's doing fine and can probably be discharged in forty-eight hours, but you two look like you're about to collapse. Get a good night's sleep and come back in the morning. We'll call if there's any change.''

He smiled, patted Michaela and shook hands with Heath. ''It's a real pleasure to meet you, Lieutenant Tanner,'' he said. ''Hope you're recovering well from your ordeal.''

''I am, thank you, Doctor, and I can't begin to thank you enough for the care you've given my son all this time. It's obvious that he thinks of you as a friend and isn't afraid.''

''He's a great kid,'' the middle-aged doctor said jovially, ''and we get along just fine. Now get some rest and I'll see you both tomorrow.''

They took a cab home and went to bed, where Michaela snuggled into Heath's arms and fell asleep within minutes.

It wasn't quite that easy for Heath. Although his body relaxed with hers, his mind continued running, like a movie in his head replaying the scene of Skip struggling to breathe just before he collapsed then rolled endlessly down the steep canyon stairs.

Michaela said Skip had had these spells before. Why hadn't she had the surgery performed that would have corrected the problem? Was he too young? Heath was no medic, but even before he was captured they'd been doing surgery on newborn babies, so that didn't seem likely.

Was there something she hadn't told him yet? Another medical problem that complicated things? But if that were so, there wouldn't be any reason for her not to confide in him. She must know that he'd have to find out sooner or later.

Again the picture of the small chest heaving to take in oxygen. Dammit, why had the child remained an invalid for five years if his heart could be made whole?

He forced himself to clear his mind so he could sleep, but he knew he wouldn't really rest until he had some answers.

Tomorrow he was going to have a talk with Dr. Oliver. If there was any chance that his son could live a normal life, Heath was going to see to it that he had it.

When Heath and Michaela arrived at the hospital early the next morning, Skip was wide awake and wanted to go home. His face was scraped, swollen and discolored, but he was breathing normally and full of questions about the rides in the helicopter. Except for the discomfort of his injuries he considered the whole experience to have been an exciting adventure.

Dr. Oliver arrived about nine-thirty and checked Skipper over. "This young man has an amazing constitution," he said with a wide smile as he removed the stethoscope from his ears. "According to his chart he slept well through the night, and you can see by the monitor that his heart is back to its normal rhythm."

"Can I go home now?" Skip asked hopefully.

The doctor ruffled his hair. "Don't be in such a hurry. We want to keep you around for a while longer. Besides, you haven't seen the new fish we have in the playroom aquarium. One is red and the other's blue."

Skip bounced on the bed. "Oh, boy. Can I go down there?"

"Sure can. Soon as your mom gets you dressed, but you have to promise that you'll take a nap before lunch and another before dinner."

The doctor turned toward Heath and Michaela. "We can talk in the hall," he said in a lowered voice, and they followed him out.

"We're going to keep him for another twenty-four hours," the doctor explained as they stood just outside the room. "He's done fine as long as he's in bed, but we want to see how his heart reacts to normal activity. We'll let him wander around the halls and play with the other ambulatory children in the playroom. If he remains stable, and I'm pretty sure he will, then you can take him home tomorrow morning."

Before either of them could answer, Skipper's voice calling his mother interrupted them. "Hey, Mom, where are my jeans?"

"I brought you clean clothes," she called back. "Just a minute and I'll get them for you."

She turned and smiled at the doctor. "Obviously his energy hasn't been depleted a bit. Thanks, Doctor. We'll see you tomorrow."

She walked back into the room, but Heath remained behind. "Dr. Oliver," he said when Michaela was out of earshot. "I need to talk to you about my son's condition. I'd like a full report from birth up to this latest incident. Would it be possible for me to see you in your office sometime today?"

The doctor hesitated. "Unless someone cancels, I'm fully booked, but why don't we have lunch together? Do you like Italian?"

Heath grinned. "Love it."

Dr. Oliver chuckled. "Good. So do I. There's a small family-run restaurant called Dicicco's just down the street from my office. The food's home-cooked and delicious. Can you meet me there about twelve-thirty?"

Heath took a cab to the restaurant and arrived about ten minutes early. The doctor had made a reservation and Heath had just been seated at their table in a secluded corner with a cup of coffee and an appetizer tray when he arrived.

"Don't get up," he said as Heath started to rise. "Hope you haven't been waiting long."

"I just got here," he replied as Dr. Oliver seated himself and picked up the menu.

There was a little small talk while they scanned the menu, but after giving the waitress their orders the doctor took some papers out of the briefcase he'd brought along. "Suppose you tell me how much you already know about Skipper's heart problems and we'll go on from there," he said.

Heath recounted what Michaela had told him. "As I understand it," he concluded, "children like him used to be called 'blue babies' because of the bluish cast to their skin due to insufficient oxygen. They didn't live much past infancy."

The doctor nodded. "That's right. It's only been in the last thirty years that we've been able to perform cardiac surgery on infants. Now we seldom lose a tiny patient."

"That's what I want to talk to you about," Heath said. "If ventricular septal defect can be corrected, why hasn't Skipper had the surgery? Michaela says he's too young, but you've indicated that it's possible even on newborns."

Dr. Oliver frowned. "It is, and the pediatrician who cared for him in Arizona advised having it done shortly after they diagnosed the problem."

"Then why wasn't it?"

The other man hesitated. "I wasn't there. I think you should talk to Michaela about that."

Heath wasn't going to be put off. "I have, but she won't give me a straight answer."

"I see," the doctor said. "All I can tell you is that when she moved to Seattle and first brought him to me I also advised it, but she refused. She said she'd been told that it could be put off, so she was going to wait until he was older."

Heath couldn't believe that a mother as dedicated as Michaela would withhold vital medical treatment from her child.

"But why?" he asked. "Michaela would lay down her life for Skipper. Is the surgery dangerous? Is there something you're not telling me?"

Before the other man could reply, the waitress arrived with their lunch, and it was several minutes before they took up the conversation again. "You asked why Michaela is so reluctant to have her son's heart condition corrected," Dr. Oliver said. "It's because she's terrified that he might not survive the surgery, and apparently other members of the family are also fearful."

Heath's stomach muscles contracted, and he put down his fork. "Then it is dangerous?"

"Any surgery's a risk," the doctor answered, "and working on the heart is riskier than most, but you have to weigh that risk against the consequences if the condition is left uncorrected. Your son is in excellent health otherwise, and he's a happy, secure little fellow, which is also important. I've discussed his case with several of my colleagues, and they agree with me that Skipper is a good candidate for surgery."

Heath's eyes narrowed. "Have you told Michaela that recently?"

"Yes, I have," the doctor answered reluctantly.

"And she still refused?"

Oliver shifted uncomfortably in his seat. "Yes, but look, I really wish you'd talk to her about this instead of me—"

"I intend to," Heath assured him, "but I need to know exactly what I'm talking about. Is this operation really necessary?"

The doctor looked directly at Heath and his tone was grave. "Understand one thing, Heath. Without the corrective surgery, Skipper's going to die. He'll become progressively weaker, and the tips of his fingers and toes will club, which means they'll become bulbous, and the nails will curve. If he lives to adulthood, which is unlikely, he'll be an invalid."

He shook his head sadly. "The risk of having the surgery is minimal compared to the risk of not having it, and the sooner, the better."

Heath didn't tell Michaela about his talk with the doctor, and the following day they took Skipper home, as well and as whole as he ever was under the circumstances.

All weekend Heath silently agonized over how to convince her that their son needed surgery immediately without sounding judgmental and dictatorial. He'd noticed that any comments or suggestions he'd made concerning Skipper's health had caused her to bristle.

After a near-disasterous start a month ago, they'd finally established a warm and loving relationship, and the thought of disrupting that, or smashing it altogether, made him physically ill. If it were only a matter of her being overprotective he'd let it ride for a while and then lead into it slowly. But without meaning to, she was not only putting Skip's health in jeopardy, but also his life. For her sake as well as the child's he couldn't allow that.

He let the matter ride until Monday, but when Emily Zeigler took Yvonne and Skip to a Disney matinee he knew that he'd never have a better opportunity to talk to Michaela alone and it couldn't be put off any longer.

After waving goodbye to the movie-goers from the front porch, he put his arm around her as they walked back into the house. "Honey, there's something I need to talk to you about," he said, hoping his tone didn't betray his anxiety. "Why don't we sit in the living room where we can be comfortable?"

She gave him a puzzled look, but let him guide her to the sofa where he sat down beside her. He leaned back and tried to relax. "I . . . I had lunch with Dr. Oliver the day Skipper was in the hospital."

Michaela blinked with surprise. "You did? Why didn't you tell me?" Her eyes widened and she sat upright. "Is something the matter with Skip? Was there damage you're not telling me about?"

"Skipper's condition is exactly what the doctor told you it was," he said quickly, hoping to calm her. "He's survived this incident with no aftereffects, but next time he might not be so lucky."

Her fists clenched in her lap. "I'll see to it that there will never be a next time," she said, her jaw set with determination. "Hereafter we'll stay off hilltops, and I'll insist that he hold my hand at all times."

Heath felt a wave of compassion for the little boy whose well-meaning mother was so determined to bind him to her with chains of caution. "It's not more supervision he needs, Mickey," he said carefully. "He needs surgery to repair the hole in his heart so he can live a normal life."

The blood drained from her face. "Is that what you sneaked around behind my back to talk to the doctor about?" she demanded indignantly.

His patience began to slip. "I didn't 'sneak around,' I simply made an appointment to talk to my son's doctor about his health."

"You could have asked me."

"I did, love," he answered, "but I wanted more facts than you could, or would, give me."

"Are you accusing me of withholding information?" she asked angrily. "I've told you everything I know."

He sighed. "You didn't tell me that at least twice cardiologists have advised you that Skipper should have immediate surgery."

She gasped and stuck our her chin. "That's not true. They told me it could be postponed until he was older."

"Could be, but shouldn't be." Heath was fighting to hold on to his own temper. "Most babies with ventricular septal defect have surgery shortly after birth. Why didn't Skipper?"

"Because I was afraid he would die!" Michaela's voice had risen several decibels, and she bolted off the couch and strode across the room. "He was all right, he just needed looking after more than most. Your mom and dad agreed with me, and your mother helped me to take care of him. Skip was in the hospital for several weeks, but when he was released he and I stayed with your parents. There was someone with him all the time, and they taught me at the hospital how to give oxygen when it was needed. He got along just fine...."

Heath came up behind her and put his arms around her. "Sweetheart, I understand. Believe me, I do. The thought of the little guy going under the knife scares me as much as it does you, but it has to be done—"

"Not yet!" It was a cry of terror as she spun out of his embrace. "Later. When he's older, bigger, stronger..."

"Michaela, he's not going to get much older, bigger or stronger without the operation," Heath said brutally. He was going to have to give it to her straight. "His growth is already stunted to some extent, and it will get worse. He'll get progressively weaker and more breathless as his body tries to increase the amount of oxygen carried to the tissues. His fingers and toes will club—''

"No!" Michaela screamed, and clapped her palms over her ears. "Stop it! You just want to scare me into agreeing to the surgery because you can't stand the thought of having a son who's flawed. You want him to be a jock like you who'll play football and baseball and ice hockey. Who'll brawl, and drink and...and *make* every woman who crosses his path—''

Heath watched, shocked, as the veins stood out in her neck, her face got red and her eyes dilated. He'd never seen her lose control so completely, and he grabbed her by the shoulders and shook her. "Michaela, that's enough! You're not even making sense. What does my supposed behavior have to do with Skipper's heart condition?''

She was breathing heavily, and he could see the effort she was making to pull herself together and shake off the hysteria that had gripped her.

Dear God, what was he going to do? How could he put her through the agony of insisting on risky cardiac surgery for their little son? On the other hand, knowing what he did, how could he not?

Her whole body shook beneath his hands, and with a groan he gathered her to him and held her as he murmured soothing words of comfort. Everything but the five words he knew she most wanted to hear. *We'll forget about the surgery.*

Michaela's breath came in gasps as she leaned against Heath and fought to subdue her runaway emotions. He was right, she wasn't being rational. He'd unleashed the terror that had lived just below the surface of her being ever since she'd learned, only a few days after the birth of her baby, that he had a potentially fatal defect. She'd panicked as she always did when the beast within tore at her heart.

They'd told her then that there was a small chance he could die during the surgery to correct it. They'd also admitted that it could be postponed until he was older, and he'd been getting along so well. It's true he couldn't be as rowdy as other little boys, and sometimes he had trouble breathing and needed oxygen for a while, but he was alive and thriving.

Heath didn't know what he was talking about! If he did, he'd never insist that his son have an operation that might kill him!

Heath's caressing hands and voice began to get through to her, and she relaxed against the long length of him. He was putting on weight. His chest was broader and not as bony as it had been when he first came back.

She closed her eyes. He smelled good, too. She'd bought him some obscenely expensive cologne and shaving lotion in Bethesda one day when she and Irene Preston had gone shopping, and its musky fragrance blended with his natural scent to suit him perfectly. If only they could stay within the magic circle he was weaving around them and never again have to face the frightening fact of Skipper's malfunctioning heart.

Unfortunately that wasn't possible, and long before she was ready, Heath brought her back to reality with a question. "Are you all right now, sweetheart?"

She opened her eyes and raised her head to look at him. "Yes. I'm sorry I freaked out. I didn't mean all those things I said. I know you love Skip."

He rubbed his chin in her hair. "Next to you he's the most important person in my life. That's the only reason I'm putting you through this, believe me. If I felt there was any other way..."

"But he's getting along just fine." Michaela knew she sounded like a broken record, but it was true.

"No, honey, he's not. He's limited in his everyday activities, and extracurricular ones are out of the question. He'll be starting school in September, and he won't be able to play with the other kids, or take gym classes, or go with them on field trips...."

"He won't mind," she protested. "He'll just be in kindergarten."

"He'll mind, Michaela," Heath insisted. "Believe me, he will. He'll be different from the other kids, and they'll tease him about it. It will break his heart."

Michaela's own heart was breaking as she shook her head vigorously. "No. He's never been able to do all the things the other kids in the child care center do, but it doesn't bother him. You don't know—"

"Yes, I do know." Heath's tone was firm, unbending. "I know because I went through it when I was a child. I was raised as an invalid, and I hated it."

That brought her up short. She'd forgotten in the heat of her fear that Heath had also had a heart problem when he was growing up.

He led her back to the sofa and sat down with her as he told his story.

"I'm sure my parents have told you a lot of this, but if you don't mind, I'd like you to hear it from my side. I was seven years old when I contracted rheumatic fever. I ran a high temperature for a long time and was on bed rest and out of school for four months." He made a face. "The longest four months in my life. I was an active kid, always on the go, and when the temperature and the pain lessened it was torture to lie in bed and try to be quiet."

"I'm sure it was," Michaela murmured sympathetically.

"Then I began having other symptoms," he continued, "and the doctor said I had myocarditis, an inflamation of the heart muscle that often accompanies inflammatory diseases like rheumatic fever. My mom flipped." He chuckled. "She was sure I was going to die if I so much as turned over in bed."

Michaela frowned. "Shame on you. You mustn't make fun of her. She was worried about you."

He sobered. "Yes. I appreciate that, but she went way overboard. For years I wasn't allowed to do anything because of my 'bad heart.' I had to quit cub scouts, and forgo little league, camping, hiking. I wasn't even allowed to go outside for recess or take physical education classes. It was a real bummer."

"But you had to give your heart a chance to heal," Michaela pointed out.

"Hell, my heart had healed long before she'd admit it. She was convinced I was going to be an invalid all my life, and she damn near made me one."

Michaela gasped. "Heath, that's not fair! Your mother loved you."

"I never doubted that," he said, "but she was so afraid of losing me that she smothered me. The doctors told her that the type of myocarditis I had wasn't dangerous and I would recover fully, but she didn't believe them. All she knew was that her son had 'heart problems' and was therefore 'disabled.'"

He ran his hands over his face. "I hated those words!"

Michaela was appalled by the bitterness in his tone. "If it's true that she was overprotective, why didn't your father do something about it?"

This time Heath's chuckle was filled with irony. "Oh, yeah, sure. You know Dad. For one thing, he was seldom home but off on duty somewhere. But even when he was there he didn't interfere. He's a firm believer in men's and women's work. He fought the wars and made the living, and Mom kept house and took care of the kids. She didn't tell him how to plan battle strategy, and he didn't tell her how to raise Darren and me."

Michaela had never realized that his relationship with his parents was so tainted with resentment. She'd only met them briefly at the wedding when she and Heath were first married, and didn't come to know and love them until after he was lost and declared dead.

"When I was a sophomore in high school, I wanted to go out for football," he said, "but Mom wouldn't even allow me to take the physical. We'd moved several times in the intervening years, and my records got messed up so that each busy new army doctor just took her word that my heart was damaged.

"That time I rebelled." He grinned. "I was fifteen and a big strapping kid, certainly not the invalid type. I also had a girl friend whose father was a physician. He was a nice guy and seemed to like me, so I told him my problem and asked him to give me a complete physical."

"But wasn't that unethical?" Michaela asked.

Heath shrugged. "Not really. I had a right to a physician of my choice. He hesitated about it, but when he saw that it meant so much to me, he agreed. He found me strong and fit, but to be sure he asked a friend of his who was a cardiologist to examine me, too. That doctor did some tests and said that if my heart had been damaged, it was completely healed."

Michaela smiled. "I'll bet your mother was relieved when they told her."

He shook his head. "She didn't believe them. It took both of them plus the school doctor and the coach to convince her that I was fit enough to play football or do anything else I wanted to. Instead of rejoicing, she acted as though she was disappointed because I was finally out from under her thumb.''

Michaela winced. ''Heath! That's a dreadful thing to say!''

He shrugged. ''I agree, but that's the impression I got. She never once came to any of my games in high school. She said if I was going to fall over dead on the football field she didn't want to be there to see it happen.''

Michaela couldn't imagine Alice Tanner behaving in such a cold and hurting manner with either of the sons she adored, but Heath's pain, even after all these years, was too deep to be a misunderstanding.

Michaela put her hand on his thigh and rubbed lightly. ''I'm sorry you were so badly hurt, but try to understand that being told there's something wrong with your child's heart is a terrifying experience for a mother. She'd lived with the fear for so long that I can understand why it was difficult to let go. If a physician I didn't know came to me and told me Skipper no longer had a hole in his heart, I'd call him a charlatan.''

Heath put his hand over hers and held it against his leg. ''Of course you would,'' he said gently, ''because you've always known that his heart wouldn't heal itself, but it needed surgery to repair it. That's what we're talking about.''

Her nerves tightened, and with them the muscles in her stomach. Ah, yes, how could she have forgotten, even for a moment, that he was trying to talk her into agreeing to let a surgeon operate on her son's most vital organ. The one that pumped life into his veins.

She steeled herself as he spoke again. ''Honey, Dr. Oliver feels that we've postponed that surgery as long as we safely can. He'd like to set a date in two weeks to—''

"No!" She felt terror clawing at her as she withdrew her hand from under his. She knew what Heath was going to say and she couldn't bear it. "Absolutely not! He's too young!"

Chapter Twelve

Heath was torn between compassion and frustration. He'd been almost certain this was going to happen, but that didn't make it any easier.

God knows he was as scared as Michaela was. He hated the thought of subjecting his small son to such a life-threatening, traumatic experience, but they had no choice.

He still didn't truly understand why she was being so stubborn. She was an intelligent, well-educated woman. Intellectually she knew Skipper had to have the surgery, so why was she dragging her feet?

Heath took a deep breath and tried one last time. "Michaela, the longer we put this off the more dangerous it becomes. Delay is no longer an option, and he'll be starting school in September. If Dr. Oliver and his team operate within the next two weeks, Skip should be able to begin kindergarten with the rest of the class, but he'll have to take antibiotics for several days before the surgery."

He reached for her hand, which was now curled into a cold, tight little fist, and held it. "Sweetheart, I wish I could spare you this, but I can't. It's something you simply have to face. Our son needs corrective surgery on his heart, and it has to done as soon as possible."

Michaela seemed to have shrunk and drawn inward while he was talking. Her face was white with anguish, her features taut and her shoulders hunched. He ached to take her into his arms and reassure her, but he could feel the resistance that radiated from her and knew she'd tear herself away from him if he attempted it.

When she spoke her voice was icy. "Obviously you've managed to persuade Dr. Oliver that no son of yours will ever be happy with anything but an athlete's physique. Well, that's not good enough for me. I want another opinion."

Heath released her hand and stood. He'd known this was going to be difficult, but why was she making it impossible? "Dr. Oliver has already discussed Skipper's case with several of his colleagues and they agree with him. Skip is a good candidate for surgery, and it must be done soon in order to be totally successful."

"I want an independent physician of my own choice," she said. "Not a buddy of Oliver's who will probably get a cut of the astronomical fee."

Heath stiffened and clenched his jaw to keep from making an equally scathing reply. She was being unreasonable, but he didn't want her to have any doubts when Skip was finally wheeled into the operating room.

"Do you have someone in mind?" His tone was still sharper than he'd intended.

"There's a pediatric cardiologist at Stanford University hospital in California who's had a lot of success with this type of surgery," she said crisply. "I want him to examine Skipper and give us a second opinion."

Heath sighed and ran his fingers through his hair. More delay. He knew that was the reason she'd asked for a consultation, but he couldn't deny her request. "All right, Mickey," he said, his tone heavy with impatience. "I'll ask Dr. Oliver to set up an appointment with this other man, but it will have to be very soon."

The taxi pulled up in front of the Stanford Medical Center in Palo Alto, California, and the driver opened the door for Michaela as Heath got out from the other side. While he paid the fare, she walked on into the hospital with him.

Although he wasn't yet thirty, he felt old, and tired, and despondent. It had been five days since his talk with Michaela, and she'd hardly spoken to him since. He'd thought he'd had all the isolation he could stand during his imprisonment, but having her with him and not communicating was even more difficult.

Oh, she was very civilized about it. She gave curt answers to his questions, and when Skip was present she chatted with both of them so the child wouldn't notice the silence between his parents, but she was effectively freezing Heath out.

At least she was still sleeping with him, but that's all they were doing. Sleeping. Her frosty attitude warned him that she wouldn't respond to any advances in bed or anywhere else, and he wasn't going to put himself through the emotional wringer of trying and being rejected.

They'd flown to Palo Alto three days before, on Wednesday, and checked Skipper into the hospital. Now, on Saturday, they had an appointment to talk with the doctor, after which they would return to Seattle.

Then what? If this doctor agreed with the others, they'd schedule the surgery. But what if this doctor felt that it could safely be postponed?

Heath groaned and forced the subject out of his mind as he hurried to catch up with her. He wasn't going to borrow trouble. They would make a decision when they had all the facts.

Dr. Xavier was a young man, probably not much older than Heath, and his red hair and freckles gave him a mischievous, Tom Sawyer-type look, but he'd already earned a national reputation as a top-notch cardiovascular surgeon. He stood behind his desk as Heath and Michaela were ushered into his office and motioned them to the two chairs across from him.

When they were all seated, he looked from one to the other. "I know how anxious you must be, so I'll get right to the point," he said. "I've given your little boy a thorough examination and we've run all the pertinent tests."

His gaze swung to Michaela. "I understand your misgivings, Mrs. Tanner. Believe me, you're not the only mother who has them when heart surgery is advised for her child, but I have to agree with Dr. Oliver. If Skipper's heart isn't repaired very soon he's going to suffer irreparable damage to other parts of his body. I strongly advise that this be done while he's still in good health otherwise."

Heath had been watching Michaela closely as the doctor spoke, and he didn't miss the shock and fear that twisted her haggard face.

He waited for her to comment, but for a minute or two she was silent. He was beginning to hope that Dr. Xavier had managed to convince her of the urgency of the situation when she cleared her throat and said, "I want you to make arrangements for us to have our son examined at the Mayo Clinic before I make a decision."

The spark of hope died, and a blaze of anger replaced it. Obviously this time-consuming consultation had resolved nothing. She'd had no intention of accepting Dr. Xavier's diagnosis if it confirmed that of the other specialists. She wouldn't accept one from the Mayo clinic, either, and he wasn't going to put Skipper through an endless trek for a diagnosis that no reputable physician could make.

Apparently he was going to be forced to play the heavy father after all.

"No, Michaela." His tone was harsh and determined. "This is the end of the line. You wanted an opinion separate from that of Dr. Oliver and his consultants, and I didn't argue because I wanted you to know we'd done everything possible to be sure the operation was necessary. You told me Dr. Xavier was the best, and I accepted that since you'd had more experience with the current crop of cardiologists than I had—"

"But even the best can be wrong," she interrupted, her eyes wide with surprise at Heath's interference. "It can't hurt to have one more opinion. The Mayo Clinic is world-renown—"

"And what happens if they agree with all the others who have examined Skip?" Heath asked angrily as he got to his feet. "Where will you take him then? Johns Hopkins? How about England? France? I'm sorry, Michaela, but I won't allow it. All the travel and the stress would kill him. We're going back to Seattle and make an appointment to have the surgery as soon as it can be scheduled."

Heath had been too upset to recognize the fury building up in her until she jumped out of her chair and confronted him, fists clenched and brown eyes blazing. "*You* won't allow it? Who in hell are you to tell me what's best for my child?"

Her tone was strident. "I'm the one who gave birth to him alone and has taken care of him alone ever since. I'm the one who worried about him; who spent nights sitting beside his crib to make sure he didn't stop breathing; who spends all my free time with him because he can't play like the other kids his age do."

She raised one fist and shook it at him. "Where did you get the idea you could come back here and just take over? You were gone for six years. You didn't even know you had a son until a few weeks ago—"

"No, I didn't," he yelled back. "And whose fault was that? Suppose you explain why you didn't write and tell me you were pregnant even though you must have known it for quite some time before I was lost?"

It was the doctor who interrupted this time. "Now look, you two, I realize that you're both overwrought, but this is getting you nowhere and I have other appointments. Now please, be quiet and sit down. I can't allow you to take my patient out of the hospital unless you can both be calm and rational enough to understand that your quarreling will put a dangerous strain on his heart."

Ashamed of his loss of control, Heath lowered himself wearily into his chair and noticed that Michaela dropped into hers as though her knees and suddenly given way.

She put her hands over her face and murmured, "I'm sorry," but she was talking to the doctor, not to Heath.

"I'm sorry, too," he said, also to the doctor. "You shouldn't have to witness our childish fights."

Michaela dropped her hands from her face and looked at him. "Are you saying I'm being childish?" she snapped.

Heath closed his eyes and shook his head. "I'm saying we both are," he answered, "and Skip is the one who'll be hurt the most by it. It's time we grew up, sweetheart, and stopped playing one-upmanship with our son's life. We have three specialists who have examined Skipper, plus several others who have gone over his records, all urging us to have the corrective surgery. Now are you willing to give your consent?''

Michaela shook her head. "I can't help feeling that he's too young for such a serious operation. But I do realize it's necessary." Michaela dropped her head in her hands, and this time she cried quietly.

Heath felt as if his heart were being wrung dry. "In that case, I'll sign the consent form and arrange to have it performed as soon as possible."

Back in Seattle, Dr. Oliver scheduled Skipper's surgery for Tuesday of the following week and started him on a series of antibiotics. "Make sure he takes every one of these as directed," he said as he handed Michaela the prescription, then turned to Heath with an explanation. "It's a necessary precaution we take against bacteria entering the bloodstream and causing an inflammation of the inner lining of the heart called endocarditis. Skip's heart abnormality makes him more susceptible than the average child. Michaela is already familiar with it. It's not as grim as it sounds. We do it every time Skip has his teeth cleaned, and we gave him injections while he was in the hospital after his recent fall."

Heath began to feel the terror he'd recognized in Michaela. What was he subjecting his young son to? The further he got into this the more ominous it sounded. Had he made a mistake in convincing Michaela? Had she been right after all?

The chill between them had deepened, and now she seldom spoke to him even when Skipper was around. She moved about the apartment like a ghost and only came to life when taking care of the child.

If Skip didn't survive the surgery it would not only destroy their marriage, it would destroy them as well.

On the day Michaela started Skip on the antibiotic, she also told him about the impending operation. He already knew that someday he would have to have his heart "fixed." As a conscientious parent, she'd explained his condition to him as simplistically as possible when he was old enough to understand that there were a lot of things he couldn't do that other kids his age could.

He'd accepted it the way a small child accepts the knowledge that someday he'll grow up and go to work every day like Mommy and Daddy—a nonthreatening fact, because a preschooler hasn't the experience to envision time as other than "now" and a far-off "someday."

But "someday" had abruptly become "now," and Michaela was faced with the difficult task of telling him without scaring him. Subdued, Heath asked if he could be present and she nodded coolly. She couldn't forget that he'd pushed her on the most important decision of her son's life, and was unwilling to forgive him for it.

After a lunch that she and Heath merely picked at, as they did with all meals now, she took the bottle of medication from the cupboard and showed it to Skipper. She explained that he'd be taking it every few hours for a while, and he asked the obvious question.

"Why? Am I gonna have my teeth cleaned again?"

Michaela had rehearsed what she wanted to say over and over again, but still her heart pounded and her hand shook as she measured the liquid into a spoon. "Not this time, honey," she said, and put the spoon into his open mouth. He was familiar with the taste and didn't argue about taking it.

"Do you remember when I told you that someday the doctor would fix your heart so you could run and play like the other kids?" she asked, as brightly as she could manage.

"Yeah," he said, and wiped at his mouth with the back of his hand.

"Well, Dr. Oliver says you're old enough now, and he can patch the hole in your heart so that you can breathe easier and won't get tired so often."

The child's eyes widened with a mixture of joy and apprehension. "Yeah? How?"

She paused for a moment, thinking maybe Heath would say something, but he sat quietly across the table from her without indicating that he wanted to join the conversation. Even as she tasted the bile of bitterness, she noticed that he looked as frightened and ravaged as she did, and she felt a stab of guilt which she tried to banish but couldn't.

"How?" she said in answer to Skip's question. "Well, next Monday we'll take you to the hospital, but I'll stay right there with you. Then the next morning while you're still asleep, they'll wheel you into another room where Dr. Oliver and some other doctors and nurses will fix up your heart so it will never bother you again."

Skipper pondered that for a moment, then asked, "How can they do that when my heart's inside of me?"

Michaela was beginning to wish that Heath would help her out, but he remained silent. The doctor had gone over the whole procedure with both of them and she understood what would be going on, but she didn't know how to explain it to a five-year-old without frightening him.

She decided to settle for handling it the way Dr. Oliver recommended. "I asked the doctor that, too," she answered, "and he said that there's a lady at the hospital who will tell you and Daddy and me all about what they're going to do to make your heart well.''

Again he mulled it over in his bright little mind. ''Will it hurt?''

This time Michaela smiled. ''You'll be asleep, honey, so you won't feel anything then. Later it'll hurt a little, but it won't last long. Daddy and I will be right there with you, and pretty soon you'll be able to go home.''

She waited for his next question, but when he spoke, it was an emphatic statement of fact. ''I want Uncle Darren there. If he can't come now, we'll wait for him.''

It hit Michaela with all the force of a punch. She should have expected Skip to ask for Darren, he adored his uncle, but she'd been so upset by the rift between Heath and herself, as well as her constant misgivings about the surgery, that she hadn't been as quick as she should have been.

She glanced at Heath and saw the stricken look on his face. Again she felt the wave of guilt. She was so furious with him that she'd totally ignored the fact that Skip was his son, too, and he must be suffering almost as much as she was. If she sent for Darren it would be a slap in the face, and she couldn't do that to him. Still, how could she refuse her son's only request?

''Oh, Skipper, I don't see how—''

''Of course we'll send for your Uncle Darren, Skip,'' Heath interrupted, his tone reassuring. ''He loves you very much, and he'd never forgive us if we didn't.'' Heath stood and turned to bend over his son and cuff him playfully under the chin. ''I'll go make the arrangements right now.''

Skipper beamed. ''Hey, gee, thanks Heath.''

Michaela gasped at his impersonal use of his father's first name, but Heath continued to smile as he walked away.

He might be able to fool a five-year-old, but she'd seen the agony in his brown eyes.

Heath was gone all afternoon, and Michaela was left to face the persistent prodding of her conscience while Skip napped. She'd been pretty hard on Heath over this business with their son, but she had a right to be. She'd been his only parent up to a few weeks ago. She'd made all the decisions affecting him. It was unreasonable of Heath to think he could just walk back into her life and relegate her to the role of assistant, helpmate, the little woman, whatever. She was Skipper's mother, and she had a right to an equal say in matters concerning him.

The haunted expression on Heath's pale tight features burned in her mind. She was forced to admit that he hadn't attempted to step in and lay down his own rules or change her way of dealing with their son until he witnessed the frightening example of what could happen when Skip overexerted his fragile heart.

That would horrify any father, and she could certainly understand his concern, but he didn't know enough about the problem to make snap decisions of such magnitude. He hadn't lived with Skip all these years and seen his strengths as well as his weaknesses. So what if he was limited in some of the things he could do? He was alive, and that was more than the doctors could guarantee once they started operating on him!

Heath's unscheduled appearance at the executive offices of Darren's and Michaela's company caused quite a stir when he introduced himself. He'd never really gotten used to being a celebrity, but this time he was able to use it to his advantage.

After requesting that there be no news releases, he filled them in on some of the background details of Darren and Skip's relationship, then asked if they could arrange an overseas call to his brother.

They were more than cooperative, although it took a couple of hours to locate Darren. Finally the connection was made, and Heath was handed the phone while the office cleared to give him privacy.

There was a slight crackle on the line as he put the instrument to his ear and spoke. "Hello. Darren?"

The voice on the other end sounded harried. "Yes. Who's this? I understand you've been trying to locate me. What's the matter?"

Heath spoke quickly without giving himself a chance to react. "This is Heath."

For a moment there was silence, then Darren answered. This time his tone was anxious. "Heath? Is something wrong?"

It was the Darren Heath remembered. The big brother who'd been as disturbed as their parents about his baby brother's weakened heart, and just as protective.

Heath's mouth felt dry and he swallowed. "Well, yes and no."

He told Darren about Skipper's fall, the subsequent examinations and the doctors' recommendations for immediate surgery. "He's going into the hospital on Monday and the operation will be on Tuesday. He wants you with him. I've talked to the people here and they'll make arrangements to fly you home."

Again there was silence, which surprised Heath. He'd expected Darren to agree immediately.

"I'm not sure that's such a good idea, Heath," he said reluctantly. "After all, you're his father. He shouldn't continue to rely on me for that type of thing."

Heath was dumbfounded. "Are you saying you won't come?" he demanded.

"No! Of course that's not what I'm saying. If you and Michaela want me, I'll be there, but . . ."

"What Michaela and I want has nothing to do with it," Heath grated. "It's what Skipper wants. For God's sake, Darren, he may not survive the surgery. . . ."

"Hey, look, I'm sorry," Darren hurriedly assured him. "I was only trying to . . . Oh hell, I have some loose ends to tie up here, but I'll be home Sunday for sure. Now, let me talk to whoever's in charge there so I can get the ball rolling, but Heath . . ." Again he hesitated. "Don't sacrifice yourself. Make Skip understand that you're his father. He's special to me, but I can't and won't ever again be more than an indulgent uncle."

Michaela was poaching salmon and Skipper was setting the table for dinner when Heath came home. He glanced at her and nodded but spoke to the boy. "It's all taken care of, Skip," he said with forced cheerfulness. "I went to the office where Uncle Darren works and told them his family needed him. They arranged for me to talk to him, and he'll be back here sometime Sunday. He said to tell you to hang in there and do everything your mom and the doctor ask you to until he gets here."

A wide smile split the child's face, and he dropped the silverware on the table as he glowed with excitement. "Oh, boy, I knew he'd come. I knew Uncle Darren wouldn't forget me."

Michaela cringed. Is that what Skipper had thought? That Darren had forgotten him? How could she have been so blind and unfeeling as not to have guessed? Darren had never before left him so abruptly, and he'd always called at least every other day to talk to him, and to her.

In their eagerness to spare Heath's feelings, Darren hadn't called, and she hadn't even mentioned him to Skip or Heath. No wonder the little boy had felt abandoned. Obviously Heath, Darren and she were going to have to come to terms with their tangled relationship.

She could start by making peace with her husband. In her anguish over their disagreement about the best way to deal with Skipper's health problem, she'd lost track of the fact that Heath was still recuperating from an experience that would have shattered a weaker man. He'd been near the breaking point when he came home, and was still dangerously vulnerable.

She knew he loved Skip and only wanted what was best for his son. Who was to say he was wrong in insisting on the surgery? Certainly not the doctors. To a man, they'd agreed with Heath, so why was she so uncertain?

Was she the one who wasn't thinking clearly?

By the time Michaela pulled her mind free of the quagmire of her confusing thoughts, Heath had taken over setting the table, and Skip was chattering happily about his Uncle Darren, who was still the man he thought of as his father. She knew his monologue must be excruciatingly painful for his real father to endure, but Heath listened and joined in at the appropriate times.

Michaela belatedly realized that it was time to start taking charge of the situation. "Skipper," she said, interrupting his continuous stream of words. "Run along now and wash up. Dinner's almost ready."

The youngster took off toward the bathroom, and Heath started to leave the kitchen, too, when she stopped him. "Heath, I'd like to talk to you," she said gently.

He turned around to look at her, and she saw the wary expression on his face. Dear Lord, had her attitude really been so punishing that he was afraid anything she said would be painful for him?

She walked over to where he stood and put her hand on his arm. His muscles contracted under her palm, but he didn't move or speak.

"I...I just want to thank you for giving in to Skipper and asking Darren to come home to be with him when he goes to the hospital."

Even as she spoke she knew she was either saying the wrong thing or he misunderstood. He stiffened, and the wariness of his expression turned to ice. "There's no need to thank me, Michaela." His tone was equally icy. "In spite of what you think of me, I love my son, and I'll do anything I can to help him through this ordeal. Surely you must know that if anything happens to him because of my insistence that his heart be made whole again, I'll never forgive myself. Now, if you'll excuse me, I'll go wash up, too."

He turned again and walked away from her.

Darren arrived back in Seattle on Sunday as he'd promised, and Heath, Michaela and Skipper were at Sea-Tac airport to meet him.

It had been a difficult few days. Heath had continued to politely rebuff Michaela's timid peace overtures as he drew more and more into himself. She couldn't connect with him on any subject. Their roles had been reversed, and now he was the silent, withdrawn one. He was only animated when he talked or played with Skipper.

She could feel his pain but couldn't reach him to soothe it.

If they could make love it would probably help, but at night he stayed on his own side of the bed with his back to her, and she was too shy and intimidated to try to initiate anything.

She was being given a dose of her own medicine, and she was appalled at how much it hurt. No wonder he didn't want her anymore. She'd probably killed his desire as well as his love for her.

As the plane began to unload its passengers, Skipper danced with excitement. Michaela had dressed him in a color-coordinated outfit of burnt orange slacks, plaid shirt and cardigan, and with his sparkling dark eyes and the flush of excitement on his cheeks, he didn't look at all like a child in dire need of surgery.

Michaela and Heath were also dressed up. She in dusty rose, raw-silk slacks with a matching silk jacket, and he in dark blue slacks and a light blue blazer. They looked like an affluent young family just coming from church. If only their life were really that simple!

At last Darren appeared hurrying up the ramp, and Skipper took off at a run to meet him. With a whoop of welcome Darren swung him up in his arms and hugged him, then carried him back to where Heath and Michaela stood.

Michaela noticed that Darren looked tired and rumpled from his long flight. He seemed thinner, but it was difficult to tell with Skip hanging all over him. His eyes sought hers, then shifted to Heath before he spoke.

It was an awkward moment. Ordinarily Michaela would have hugged and kissed him. Not passionately, but with genuine pleasure at having him back. He'd been like a big brother to her before they became engaged. Now she stood tongue-tied and wondering what to do with her hands.

He seemed to be having the same problem. Fortunately the child in his arms would have made an embrace or a handshake unwieldy. Instead he leaned down and kissed her chastely on the cheek. "Hello, Mickey," he said softly. "You're looking beautiful, as always."

Then he turned to Heath, and the two brothers' gazes met and clashed, then softened. This time Heath was the first to speak. "Thanks for coming, Darren. I know it's really messed up your schedule."

Darren nodded. "Thank you for asking me to come. I can't tell you how much I appreciate it."

Heath shrugged. "Skipper needs you," he said simply.

Michaela saw the swift look of compassion in Darren's eyes before he blinked it away. "It's you he needs, Heath. He just hasn't realized it yet," he said firmly. "Give him a little more time."

Heath swallowed, and his mouth quavered as he turned away without trying to answer.

They took Darren back to their apartment, where Michaela had a roast beef in the oven for dinner. On the way, Darren sat in the back seat with Skipper and listened to the boy tell him about the trip to Victoria, the fall and the excitement of the two helicopter rides, blissfully unaware of the strained silence between the adults in the car.

Dinner was an uncomfortable ordeal. Everyone tried to hard to make it like a normal family gathering, and once more Skipper unwittingly acted as a buffer, with the adults directing most of the conversation to him.

Michaela's glance strayed occasionally to Darren. Furtively, because she was curious to know how well he'd adjusted to the traumatic events that had totally changed the course of their lives, but she couldn't ask and she couldn't chance the possibility that Heath would see her looking at his brother and think she was flirting with him.

At times she felt Darren's gaze on her, too, and knew he was equally curious, and equally cautious, about her.

When the meal was finally over, Michaela announced that it was time for Skipper to go to bed since they were scheduled to check him into the hospital early the next morning. Skip started to object, but Darren assured him that he was leaving right away to go to his own apartment and sleep, too.

"There's no place to lie down on an airplane," he told the child, "and I can't sleep sitting up, so I'm too tired to stay awake any longer."

"But you'll go to the hospital with us in the morning, won't you?" Skip asked.

Darren shook his head. "Not in the morning. Six o'clock is too early for me." He picked the boy up and hugged him. "Sleep well, little one, and I'll come see you at the hospital after lunch tomorrow."

Heath drove his brother home, and when the silence between them became oppressive, Darren broke it with small talk. "Did you have any trouble learning to drive again after you got back here?"

Heath shrugged. "Not much. It was mostly a matter of finding my way around." He slowed and looked at the street signs. "You'd better give me some directions for the next turn. I don't remember just where it is. I'd never been in Seattle before, and you can't go more than a few miles without running into the bay or a lake. And those floating bridges. I've never seen the likes of them before."

Darren chuckled. "And the hills. The damn city goes straight up from the waterfront. I can believe that they slid logs down the muddy streets and into the water in the early logging days." He suddenly changed the subject. "Oh, hang a right at the next turn."

Heath turned onto the next cross street, and after a few more minutes of silence Darren spoke once more. "It's good to see you again, Heath. I know our relationship is on shaky ground, but I missed you like hell all the time you were gone."

He paused and cleared his throat while Heath remained mute. "I just wanted you to know that I thank God every day that you're alive and well."

Again he paused and ran his fingers through his hair. "Damn, I don't know how to say this, but if I'd had a choice in this little drama you, Michaela and I are involved in, I wouldn't have changed the way it turned out. Michaela and I had a strong brother/sister-type relationship, but I've come to recognize that we both deserve more than that in a marriage. You were always her man, even when she thought you were lost to her forever, and I wish you two a long and happy life together."

Chapter Thirteen

At five-forty-five the following morning, Monday, Heath and Michaela arrived at the hospital with their grumpy, sleepy-eyed son.

Skipper had suddenly decided that he liked his heart just the way it was, and there was no need to fix it. He was having last-minute terrors, and so was Michaela. Her anger at Heath for putting them through such a frightening ordeal returned full force. She hoped he felt plenty guilty.

Heath didn't feel just guilty, he felt a monstrous remorse that threatened to overwhelm him. What had he been thinking of? Skipper was alive and doing reasonably well. That's all that really mattered. It tore Heath apart to see the fear that gripped both Michaela and Skip. Maybe he was too young after all for such major surgery! Maybe they all needed a few more years to get used to the idea. Maybe he should have stayed out of the situation and let Michaela handle it!

When they approached the registration desk to check Skipper in, the registrar informed them that there was a notation on his records that Mr. and Mrs. Tanner were to come to the office before proceeding further.

Michaela's already battered nerves threatened to snap. What now? Had they found something else wrong with Skip?

The woman directed them to the business office, and Heath took her arm as they walked along the corridor. His touch was warm and oddly comforting. In the large office complex Skip was given a seat and a picture book while Heath and Michaela were ushered into a small cubicle that held a desk and three straight-back chairs.

A few minutes later they were joined by a harried looking man carrying a file folder. "Good morning," he said, "I'm Harold Phillips, the business manager."

He took the seat behind the desk and opened the folder. He took out a sheet of legal-size paper, scanned it, then raised his head and looked at Heath. "I'm sorry to have to bother you at a time like this, but it's only just come to our attention that you're the political prisoner who was recently returned to the United States."

Heath nodded. "That's right, but what does that have to do with this?"

"It's mainly just red tape," the man answered, "but as we understand it, you were declared dead several years ago after a naval skirmish?" It was more question than statement.

"That's true," Heath said, "but as you can see I'm very much alive. The navy had every reason to believe I had drowned in a fall overboard during an attack at sea, so I was declared dead instead of missing. However, that's all been resolved, and I still don't understand—"

"I'm sorry. I know it seems like nit-picking, but with malpractice suits so prevalent these days, the hospital legal department feels that there's a legal gray area here. Even though you've been officially identified by the navy and are sitting here living, breathing and talking, we can't accept your signature on the consent form for you son's surgery."

Michaela felt as if the breath had been knocked out of her, and Heath's eyes widened with disbelief. "You what!"

The man held up his hand. "I know. I know. It sounds ridiculous, but the hospital has to be protected. You can go to court and petition to have your...uh...legal status reinstated, but we needn't postpone the operation." He slid the sheet of paper across the desk to Michaela. "There's no doubt about the child's mother's guardianship. If you'll just sign the consent form, too, Mrs. Tanner, everything will be perfectly legal and we can proceed as planned."

Michaela stared at the document, stunned. Then she raised her head and looked over the half-wall of the cubicle to her son sitting across the room leafing through the book he'd been offered. He looked pale and frightened. She could put an end to this nightmare that was haunting them all by refusing to sign the paper.

For a moment she felt as if a crushing weight had been lifted from her, but then, from somewhere deep in her subconscious, the picture flashed in her mind of Skip clutching his chest and gasping for breath just before he collapsed and fell at the Butchart Gardens. He'd only been running up the stairs as children do all the time, but he could have died from the exertion.

She closed her eyes and tried to dislodge the image, but another one took its place. This time she was seeing him a week later at the Stanford University hospital in California. The bruises from the fall were gone, but still his lips had a distinctly bluish cast. At the time she'd brushed it aside as just a result of the accident, but now as she looked at him even from across the room she could see that it was still there. She knew also that his fingernails were more mauve than healthy pink.

Had she deliberately shut these ominous symptoms out of her mind and refused to see them? Was she truly capable of taking dangerous chances with her precious child's life rather than face the fact that, while he may not survive the surgery, he would surely die without it?

A voice that seemed disembodied interrupted her broodings. "Mrs. Tanner? Will you sign the consent?"

Another voice, this time Heath's, harsh and disapproving. "Leave her alone. She mustn't be rushed. She can have all the time she needs."

He leaned toward her and caressed her shoulder as he murmured, "I'm sorry, sweetheart. I'd have taken this responsibility on myself if it had been possible. If you're not ready, just say so and we'll forget it for a while. Don't do anything you feel you might regret."

She tipped her head and rubbed her cheek against his gentle hand. She hadn't realized it before, but by being the sole parent to give the consent for Skip's surgery, he had taken the responsibility, and any guilt that may have followed, off her and onto himself. He'd been sparing her the terrible anguish of making a decision that had to be made but may result in the death of her child.

As he'd pointed out, the surgery had to be done, if not now then a year or two from now. Skipper was prepared for it now. If it were postponed, he'd have to go through the whole preoperative period all over again, and she wasn't going to put him through that just to spare her feelings.

It had finally occurred to her that it was never going to be easier for her whether he was five or twenty-five, and he probably wouldn't live to be twenty-five without it.

She turned her face and looked into Heath's tormented eyes. "It's all right," she said softly. "I know you and the doctors only want what's best for Skip, too. I'd prefer to wait, but it's gone too far to cancel now."

She reached for the paper and pen and signed her name.

Skip was checked into a room then put through a battery of tests that took all morning while his parents waited. Michaela didn't feel like trying to make pleasant conversation. Even though she'd signed the papers, she still felt a lingering resentment toward Heath for forcing the issue in the first place, and he'd once more retreated behind the barrier he'd erected between them.

They leafed through battered old copies of magazines they'd never have read otherwise and drank foul-tasting coffee from a machine.

After lunch, which was served to them in Skipper's room, Skip napped and Heath and Michaela found a small deserted waiting room down the hall, where she stretched out on the couch while Heath sprawled in an easy chair and watched an old Humphrey Bogart movie on television.

Michaela was asleep when a nurse came to get them. "Your son is awake now, and Mrs. VanGelder would like to talk to the three of you."

"Mrs. VanGelder?" Heath asked.

"She's the nurse-practitioner who works with the pediatric heart surgery patients and their parents. She'll explain to Skipper just what's going to happen tomorrow, and she'll answer any questions you may have," the nurse said.

Michaela sat up and rubbed her eyes. "Oh yes, she's the lady Dr. Oliver said would talk to Skip."

A few minutes later the three of them were in the sunny playroom when a short, plump woman with twinkling blue eyes and a wide smile walked in. "You must be the Tanner family," she said, putting out her hand. "I'm Johanne VanGelder. Just call me Josie."

Heath took the extended hand. "Hi, Josie. I'm Heath. This is my wife, Michaela, and our son, Skipper."

Within minutes Josie VanGelder had not only managed to relax them, but actually had them laughing as she told Skip a funny story about a puppy who got loose in the hospital after being smuggled in to see one of her small patients. As she talked, she casually picked up a Cabbage Patch-type doll that was lying on a doll-sized hospital bed near the rocker where she was sitting.

The doll had a boy's haircut and its own hospital gown that opened down the back. It also had an assortment of catheters and IV tubes fastened to its cloth body. Josie put it on her lap, then casually changed the subject when she finished her puppy story.

"This little guy is Butch," she said to an attentive Skip, "and he's here to help me show you and your mommy and daddy some of the things that will happen to you tomorrow."

As she spoke in words and phrases a five-year-old could understand, she illustrated on the doll how and where all the tubes and patches would be placed on Skipper the following day. When she'd finished he looked at her and said, "After they sew up my heart, they won't leave the needle in it, will they?"

Josie's eyes sparkled, but her tone was serious. "No. You don't have to worry about that. The doctors and nurses are very careful."

She handed him the doll. "Here. Would you like to play with Butch for a while? I'll bet he'd like you to take his temperature."

Skipper eagerly took it from her and wandered across the room to sit on the window seat with his new toy. She turned to Heath and Michaela and spoke in a low but optimistic tone. "No matter how well prepared you think you are, it's going to be a shock when you see your son after the surgery. He'll be unconscious and have all this stuff that I've shown you attached to him. We try to prepare you, but I have to warn you that when you're actually looking at your own child in that state…well, it's rough."

Michaela was trembling, and it was all she could do not to rescind her consent. Dear God, why did he have to go through this horror? Why couldn't he have been born whole like all the other babies born in the hospital that day? Why couldn't she have the surgery for him?

"It's a long operation," Josie continued, "but we're going to help you get through it. We'll keep you posted every hour, and when it's over we'll get you into the recovery room and intensive care unit as soon as we can."

Michaela's brave front crumbled, and her shoulders shook as she broke down and sobbed.

Heath reached her in seconds and cradled her in his arms. He was trembling, too, but although his chest heaved he managed to hold on to his self-control.

When the storm was finally over and she requested a tissue he handed her his handkerchief. For the first time they both noticed that Josie VanGelder had left the room and taken Skipper with her.

Michaela apologized for her loss of control, and Heath said it was nothing to be ashamed of, but when he released her he stepped away. The feeling of oneness that had existed between them in their mutual anguish just moments before was broken. They didn't touch as they walked out of the playroom and entered the separate restrooms to try to repair their ravaged faces.

Later that afternoon, Darren came to visit, as he'd promised Skip he would. He played board games with the child and told him about how the children in Japan lived. Michaela joined in the conversation while Heath sat back and watched.

Seeing Darren again made Heath uneasy. He felt more than a little ashamed that he hadn't made a reply to his brother's impassioned plea for understanding the night before. It wasn't that he didn't want everything to be right between them again. He did, but the thought of Michaela in Darren's arms made Heath burn with a jealous rage.

Had they ever gone further? That was the question that still drove him crazy. They both denied that they had, but Darren was a man with strong appetites, and Michaela was a passionate woman. Both had thought Heath was dead, so why would they have restrained their natural desire?

He couldn't tear his gaze away from them sitting on either side of the hospital bed laughing with Skipper. If Heath were still an anonymous prisoner thousands of miles away, the three of them would be a family now, and Skip wouldn't be facing life-threatening surgery in a few hours. That fact made him cringe as Michaela's laughter filled the room. He knew that Darren would never have gone against her wishes where her son's health was concerned.

Darren could make Michaela laugh at this tense time, but all Heath had done was make her cry. And now, since she'd been more or less forced to sign the consent form, she'd feel responsible if anything went wrong tomorrow.

No wonder she still preferred his brother to him.

Darren stood up to leave when they brought the dinner trays. "Aw, Uncle Darren, don't go," Skip whined. "The nurse will bring you some food, too, if you ask her."

Darren patted his dark head. "Sorry, Tiger, but I have to go back to the office. A lot of work piled up while I was gone, but I'll come back early in the morning. Okay?"

Heath saw his son's disappointment and sighed. It was going to be a long, lonely night.

Skipper's surgery was scheduled for seven o'clock, and Heath and Michaela arrived at the hospital at six.

Michaela had wanted to spend the night there, but Dr. Oliver refused to authorize it. "The boy has to rest," she'd been told. "We'll give him a light sedative and he'll sleep through the night. You two go home and try to sleep, too. Do you want me to give you something to help?"

She'd refused and so had Heath, but it was a hellish night. They tried watching television, reading, Michaela made cookies and Heath fixed a dripping faucet in the bathroom, but by one o'clock they were still wide awake and nervous wrecks.

At two o'clock, Heath insisted that they both go to bed. "I know we won't be able to sleep," he said, "but tomorrow is going to be a grueling day. We'll never survive it if we don't at least get some rest."

Michaela agreed because she hoped that if they lay down, he, at least, might sleep, but she'd hardly settled between the sheets before the alarm rang.

They'd both slept deeply for three hours.

Skip was awake when they got there, and Darren appeared a few minutes later. Whereas the night before had been interminable, now the time flew, and much too soon a gurney was rolled into the room with Josie VanGelder right behind.

"Good morning, Skipper," she greeted the groggy child. "Time to get your heart fixed."

The sedative he'd been given a few minutes earlier worked fast, and he could hardly hold his eyes open as she continued cheerfully, "Remember yesterday we showed you this table with wheels called a gurney and told you we'd give you a ride on it today? Well, this husky fellow here—" she nodded toward the orderly "—is going to lift you onto it and then we'll go. Mommy and Daddy will walk right along beside you and hold your hands until you fall asleep. When you wake up again your heart will be all well."

If he wakes up, Michaela thought, and fought back the overwhelming desire to pick up her child and flee.

Chapter Fourteen

Heath, Michaela and Darren were shown to the nearest waiting room and told that it would probably be a couple of hours before there was anything to report, but from then on they would be notified every hour about the progress the surgical team was making. The nurse also suggested that they go down to the cafeteria and have breakfast, since it would be a long, difficult day and they'd feel better if they took nourishment at regular times.

"I couldn't possibly eat," Michaela said.

It was Darren who finally convinced her. "Sitting up here in this room tearing your heart out with worry isn't going to help Skip a bit, and you'll be a basket case later when he does need you. Now come on. Meals are on me today, so take advantage of it."

She agreed mainly because Heath wouldn't go without her, but once she got a whiff of the aroma of bacon, eggs and fresh coffee, she not only ate a full breakfast but enjoyed it.

By noon, however, when the volunteer who manned the coffee cart and relayed the telephoned reports from the operating room suggested they should have lunch, none of them were willing to either leave or eat even if it were brought to them.

Michaela felt as if her nerves were wound more tightly with every hour that passed. So far the news had been encouraging. Everything was going as expected, but why was it taking so long? How much time could it take to sew up a small hole in the heart?

Even as the question formed in her mind she knew it was ridiculous. Heart surgery, especially on a child, was complicated beyond anything she could imagine. A generation ago it hadn't even been possible.

She shifted to a more comfortable position and looked around the room. During the morning other people had come in, but even so it was quiet and tension crackled in the air.

Michaela was finding out that a surgery waiting room was a little corner of hell right here on earth. No matter how many people arrived together, including the three Tanners, after a while each was alone with his or her fears, and guilts, and frantic prayers.

She stole a sideways glance at Heath sitting hunched on the sofa beside her. His hands were clenched, and his face had a strained, pinched expression that accentuated the premature lines his prison experience had put there. His shoulders slumped forward, but there was a line of tension in him that held him immobile.

She wanted to reach over and touch him, but he'd closed himself off from her. She was almost certain she'd be intruding if she tried to comfort him.

Her gaze moved to Darren sitting in a chair on the other side of her. He held an open magazine in his lap and seemed to be reading, but his eyes had a shuttered look, and he'd stopped turning pages long ago.

She wished she could touch him, too. There'd always been a special bond between him and his young nephew, and she knew that his anxiety was almost as great as hers and Heath's, but he, too, was drawn inward and suffered alone.

Why couldn't they all forget the past and support and comfort one another the way families were supposed to do?

By now her gaze was drawn every few minutes to the hands of the clock on the wall of the room, and it seemed to take them forever to move from hour to hour. When the phone rang at one o'clock, she waited eagerly for the report, but the call was for the middle-aged man whose wife was having a hysterectomy.

Michaela waited anxiously, willing the phone to ring again, but when it did it was for the elderly couple whose son had been injured in a car accident.

A wave of panic swept over her, and it was all she could do not to scream. Why didn't they get a report on Skip? Had something gone wrong?

By fifteen past the hour she couldn't stand it any longer. Just as she was about to get up Heath stood and approached the pink-clad volunteer. "It's been well over an hour since our last report," he said tersely. "Could you please call the operating room and find out what's going on?"

The woman nodded and picked up the phone. "I'll try, Mr. Tanner," she said and dialed.

Michaela walked over to stand beside him while the volunteer held the instrument to her ear. After several tension-filled seconds she put it back in the cradle. "I'm sorry," she said softly, "they don't answer."

Michaela gasped and Heath caught her in his arms as she swayed.

The woman hurried to assure them. "You mustn't panic. This isn't all that unusual," she said soothingly. "There's a lot going on during this type of surgery, and sometimes there just isn't anyone available to make or receive phone calls. I know it's frightening, but I'll try again in fifteen minutes. Meanwhile hold on to the thought that this happens sometimes, but it seldom means there's a problem."

Heath led Michaela back to the couch and held her as the minutes ticked by with agonizing slowness.

It wasn't a very comforting embrace, however. He was as tense as she was. Leaning against him was like cuddling up to a statue, except that she could hear the heavy pounding of his heart under her ear.

My God, how much longer could they endure this waiting!

At one-thirty, the volunteer called the OR again, and there was still no answer. Michaela broke down and cried.

"Would you like me to page Mrs. VanGelder?" the woman asked. "Maybe she can find out something."

"Yes, please," Darren said before either Michaela or Heath could answer.

It took only a few minutes for Josie VanGelder to arrive, and when she did she went right to the Tanners. "What's the matter?" she asked quietly.

Michaela was grateful when Darren explained since neither she nor Heath could trust their voices.

"I'll see what I can find out," Josie said in a crisp, confident tone as she turned and hurried out of the room.

Michaela made a massive effort to pull herself together. She just made it harder on Heath and Darren when she cried, and it didn't do anyone, herself included, any good.

Besides, she could see that Heath was on the ragged edge of his own despair and needed support even more than she did. She sat up and forced herself to stop sobbing as she dried her eyes.

It was another twenty long minutes before Josie reappeared, but when she did she was smiling. "They're closing now and everything's going well," she told them. "It will be a while yet, but they'll take your little boy to the recovery room when they're finished in surgery and then you can see him."

"Oh, thank God," Michaela murmured. She felt the room begin to tilt and grabbed the arm of the sofa to steady herself. "But what happened? Why didn't they report on time? Why didn't they answer their phone?"

Josie paused for just a few seconds, but it was long enough to alert Michaela that there was something she wasn't going to discuss with them. "Dr. Oliver will be in the recovery room with Skipper when you get there, and he'll tell you all about the surgery. Now, please, relax and have a cup of coffee. I'll be up in half an hour or so to take you to see your little son."

Josie left, and Michaela looked at Heath. He was white as death and made no attempt to speak.

She took his hand, and it was cold as she pressed it against her chest. "Darling," she said, "everything's all right. The operation's almost over, and Josie says we can see Skipper soon.''

He still didn't look at her, just stared off into space as he nodded. "Yes, I heard," he said in a monotone.

A feeling of foreboding gnawed at her as she watched him. She could understand why he didn't relax and rejoice. None of them were doing that. They all knew that performing surgery on the heart of a child was still a high-risk procedure that could go sour even at the last minute. They couldn't truly assume that Skipper was out of immediate danger until he was doing well enough to be moved from recovery to the pediatric intensive care unit. That time might be hours away.

Still, Heath wasn't just tense, he seemed to be in shock. His eyes were wide open and staring, and his skin was dry and cold. She looked over at Darren and saw by his expression that he'd also noticed.

He came over to hunker down in front of his brother and put his hands on Heath's shoulders. "Heath? Are you okay, fella?"

To Michaela's great relief Heath blinked and looked straight at Darren. "Yeah," he said, and cleared his throat. "I'm all right, just cold." He shivered.

The room temperature was almost uncomfortably warm, but his hand under Michaela's was still icy.

Darren frowned. "I'll get you some coffee," he said as he stood and headed for the coffee cart.

Heath drank two cups of the hot liquid before he stopped shivering, and a short time later Mrs. VanGelder returned. "Skipper's in the recovery room now, and he no longer has a hole in his heart," she said happily. "If you'll come with me I'll take you to him. Now remember, I told you he'd look pretty frightening with all the tubes and stuff, but he's doing just fine. Dr. Oliver's with him, and he'll tell you all about it."

Without being obvious, Darren helped Heath stand up, and Michaela took his arm as Josie led them down the long corridors. Although their strain had eased a little, it hadn't gone away. Michaela knew it wouldn't until they'd seen Skipper and assured themselves that he was all right.

Josie finally stopped in front of an open doorway and spoke softly. "Skip is awake, but his reaction time is still pretty slow. Don't hesitate to talk to him; we want him fully conscious as soon as possible. He'll know you, but don't be surprised if later on he doesn't remember that you were here. Don't stay longer than five minutes this time. We want to be sure he's stabilized before we move him into pediatric ICU."

She stepped aside and motioned Heath and Michaela in. Darren followed, and the three of them approached the bed.

The child lying on the bed had his eyes closed and was connected to numerous tubes and catheters just as they'd been told he'd be, but Michaela wasn't prepared even so. Josie had been right. Seeing a doll in that condition was a whole lot different from watching her son hooked up to the machines.

A moan escaped her before she could stifle it, but she walked to the side of the bed and stood looking down. "Skipper," she said softly, "it's Mommy. Are you awake?"

Skip's eyelids fluttered, then opened, but his glazed eyes focused straight ahead.

She touched his face, which seemed to be about the only place she could see that wasn't bandaged. "Over here, honey. Can you wake up for a minute and talk to me?"

He turned his head and looked at her. A tiny smile lifted the corners of his mouth. "Hi, Mom," he said in a little more than a whisper. "I'm thirsty."

Her eyes misted with tears of happiness. He really was all right!

She brushed a lock of hair off his forehead. "The nurse will give you something to drink pretty soon," she assured him. "Daddy and Uncle Darren want to say hello to you before you go back to sleep."

She moved aside and Heath took her place. For a moment he just stood there as though uncertain of what to do. When he spoke, his voice was hoarse. "Hi, Skip," was all he said, and although his hand hovered over his son's head he didn't touch him.

"Hi," Skip answered. "Can I have a Coke?"

Michaela recognized the ploy and smiled. He knew she seldom let him have soft drinks, so he was appealing to Heath.

She was standing close enough to feel the tremor that shook her husband before he answered tremulously. "Sure. Just as soon as the doctor says it's okay."

He turned abruptly and walked away, making room for Darren. The boy looked at his uncle and asked a question. "Are you gonna marry my Mom?"

Darren patted him on the shoulder. "No, Skipper. Your Mom is already married to your Dad, but I'll always be your uncle."

Skip's tired eyes dropped. "Okay," he said, and drifted off to sleep again.

Michaela looked up just in time to see Heath stride out the door. There was a jerkiness in his movements that alarmed her, but she was wedged into a small space at the head of the bed and it took time for her to maneuver around furniture and equipment to get out.

She made it to the hall just in time to see him disappear into another room. She called to him, but he didn't answer. She hurried after him, but when she came to the open doorway it looked as though the room was empty. It was a duplicate of the one she'd just left, except the bed was made up and there was no one in it.

Then she heard a sound and looked to her left. Heath stood against the wall with his hands covering his face and massive sobs convulsing him!

"Oh Heath," she cried as he slid slowly down the wall to sit on the floor with his knees drawn up against his chest.

She knelt on the floor facing him and put her arms around him. "Darling, it's all right," she said anxiously. "The operation's over and Skipper's going to be well and strong just like you said he would."

She wasn't sure she was getting through to him. He didn't acknowledge her presence in any way but sat all huddled up and closed off from her as his sobs continued to rock them both.

Michaela had never seen anyone weep like this before. The anguish he'd been holding in for so long was finally spewing out of him, but it was tearing him apart in the process.

She stroked her fingers through his hair. "Sweetheart, I want to help you. Don't shut me out. Put your arms around me. Let me hold you close and comfort you."

For a moment he didn't respond, then slowly he removed his hands from his face and raised his head. His eyes were red and tears gushed down his cheeks as he lowered his bent legs to the floor and took her in his arms. He clasped her hard against him, then buried his ravaged face in her shoulder and gave himself up to the wracking sobs.

It was a long time before he was able to bring his torment under control, and during it she murmured endearments, planted little kisses on any area she could reach and gently massaged his shoulders and the back of his neck.

Early on she was aware that a nurse and Darren had come to the door and looked in, but they'd backed out immediately and given Michaela and Heath the privacy they craved.

Finally Heath's sobs diminished, but they still sat on the floor, wrapped in each other's arms, until they were both relaxed and in danger of going to sleep. It was then that Heath straightened up and released her to reach in his pocket for a handkerchief.

He blew his nose and mopped at his face before he spoke. "Michaela, I'm sorry. I've never lost control like that before...."

She took the hem of her full cotton skirt and dabbed at his eyes with it. "You've nothing to be sorry for, love," she said as she brushed away more tears on either side of his nose. "I've been crying for days, but you held it all in. I'm glad it finally broke loose. You'll feel better now."

He reached out and gathered her to him again. "If anything had happened to Skipper because I insisted on that surgery I—"

She put her fingers to his lips. "Shhhh," she murmured. "Nothing did happen, and now he'll grow big and strong and have a normal life span. You were brave enough to give him the one gift that I couldn't bring myself to chance...."

He bent his head and covered her mouth, cutting off the rest of her sentence. "I love you," he whispered against the corner of her lips.

Her arms around his neck tightened. "I love you, too," she whispered back.

He brushed her lips with his. "You're sweet to say that," he said, "but I'm all right now. I can take the truth."

Michaela's eyes opened. "The truth? But I—"

Darren's voice coming from the doorway interrupted her. "I hate to intrude, you two, but the doctor has to leave in a few minutes and he'd like to talk to you."

Heath and Michaela sprang apart and got up off the floor looking a little sheepish.

Back in the recovery room, Skip slept while Dr. Oliver spoke quietly with his parents. "We won't be moving Skipper into ICU for at least a couple of more hours, so why don't you folks go on home, get a good night's sleep and come back in the morning? He won't be with it enough until then to know what's going on, anyway, and, to put it bluntly, all three of you look worse than he does. We'll call you immediately if there's any change, you have my word on it."

Michaela was reluctant, but Heath and Darren managed to persuade her that the doctor was right.

Heath spoke little on the way out of the hospital, and as they approached the parking lot he stopped and turned to Darren. "I . . . I need to be alone for a while," he said hesitantly. "Do you mind driving Michaela home?"

She gasped. "Heath, what's the matter? Where are you going?"

He turned to look at her. "Do you remember my telling you that there are times when I simply have to get away by myself?"

She nodded. "Yes, but—"

"Well, this is one of those times. There's nothing the matter, and I don't know where I'm going. Somewhere peaceful and quiet where I can think."

He shouldn't be alone, he was too upset. "Let me go with you," she pleaded. "I won't make any noise...."

"No, honey," he said reluctantly. "Please understand. I'll only be gone a few hours. When I get home we'll talk."

Talk about what? She thought they had everything straightened out! Was something still bothering him? "Heath, I—"

He lifted her chin with his hand and kissed her. "Later, sweetheart," he said and walked away.

On the drive to her apartment Michaela and Darren were alone together for the first time since Heath's return from his imprisonment, and she knew there were a lot of things she'd wanted to discuss with him, but her mind had been wiped clean of everything but Heath. Why did he want to get away from her? Where was he going? Why was he acting so strangely?

When they got to the apartment, Darren offered to come in and stay with her until Heath returned, but she sent him away, telling him she was going to rest.

She telephoned both sets of grandparents first to tell them the good news, then took a leisurely warm bath and put on a long royal-blue caftan. She lay down, but sleep wouldn't come. Every time she closed her eyes she saw Heath's drawn, white face and heard the gut-wrenching sobs that seemed to be torn from his very soul.

She could understand why he'd been so upset. He'd stored up so much agony in the past six years, and now he felt responsible for anything that might have gone wrong during the surgery since he'd insisted on it.

But nothing had gone wrong! Even the tense hour between one and two o'clock when there'd been no report from the operating room had been explained by Dr. Oliver as simply a point in the surgery where they couldn't spare any of their highly trained personnel to make or answer a phone call.

There was every reason to believe that Skipper had come through the experience with no complications, and the little boy had the prospects of a long and healthy life, so what was bothering Heath?

By six o'clock, he'd been gone for three hours, and Michaela's nerves were raw from listening for the car to turn into the driveway. In desperation she'd finally turned on the television to banish the silence.

That's why she didn't hear anything until the front door opened. She jumped to her feet just as Heath strolled into the living room. He was carrying two large white paper sacks from the carryout chicken place a few blocks away, and he grinned as he held them out to her.

"I know you don't usually eat fast food, but since we don't have to worry about Skip's diet tonight, I thought we could pig out on fats and cholesterol."

She was so relieved to see him that she forgotten she'd been working up a good head of anger at his seeming indifference to her anxiety. "I guess we can both afford to put back on some of the weight we've lost the past week or so," she said with a smile that vanished as she turned serious. "Heath, are you—"

He shook his head and interrupted. "Not now. Wait until after we've eaten, and then I'll tell you what I've been thinking about."

She decided not to argue. Whatever the problem was, he wanted to discuss it in his own way and his own time. She could wait.

They sat on the couch in front of the television and ate their fried chicken, mashed potatoes and gravy, cole slaw and biscuits off the coffee table while watching the evening news. Michaela found parts of the program unappetizing, but Heath was still fascinated by what was going on in the world around him.

When they were finished he disposed of the paper and plastic dishes. He was gone longer than she'd expected, and she was about to call to him when she heard him come in the back door. He was marking time again, but why?

His tension communicated itself to her as soon as he came into the room, and her own muscles tightened as he turned off the TV and this time sat down in a chair on the other side of the room.

He seemed to be trying for a casual tone when he spoke, but it came out tight and jerky. "Michaela, I've done a lot of thinking since we started living together again. I realize now that my original expectations were unreasonable. We're neither of us the same people we were six years ago."

She didn't like the way this was going and started to protest, but he stopped her. "No, please, let me finish. Lately I've begun to remember more of the way it was when we were first married, and you're right. I was an arrogant bastard."

"Heath, dammit—"

"Just hear me out. I was self-centered and totally wrapped up in sports and partying. It probably started when I finally broke out of that velvet prison my mother encased me in because of my heart condition. Once I was free of that I went a little crazy. I didn't know how to handle just being a normal carefree teenager, and I went overboard. I didn't even know how my behavior was affecting other people."

He shrugged and looked at his hands. "Because I was a good athlete, the other kids put up with me. They even went along with it, and I guess I just expected you would, too."

Michaela squirmed with impatience. "I'm trying to tell you—"

He continued as though she hadn't even spoken. "I remember now when you left me. Two of the other graduating athletes and I had been raising hell for three days, and I knew you'd be mad, but I didn't expect you to pack up and leave. That sobered me up in a hurry, but by then you were gone and you wouldn't see or speak to me."

Even now Michaela cringed in remembered pain at what she'd considered her new young husband's desertion. She'd been so sure she hated him until he'd come to her shortly before he was due to ship out for six months of sea duty.

"That was a long time ago," she said, determined to have a say in this conversation, "and we did spend the week together before you went to sea."

"But apparently we didn't resolve anything," he answered firmly. "Why didn't you write and tell me you were pregnant?"

She hung her head in shame. "Because I was only nineteen and still a little vindictive. I thought we were both immortal and would live forever, so I was going to take my time about sharing the news with you. You'd hurt me badly, but that's no excuse...."

"We were both young and impulsive," he said regretfully, "and now that we've grown up and matured, we're different people. It was stupid of me to think that everything would remain the same for all those years I was gone. That's what I want to talk to you about."

He shifted restlessly in his chair, then stood and turned away from her. "Michaela, I've decided to reenlist in the navy."

She blinked with surprise. "Oh. I thought you were going to wait awhile before making a decision on that."

"I was, but it's time I got back to work. I'll request an immediate assignment somewhere on the East Coast, and then I'll . . . I'll file for divorce."

Michaela heard him, but she was sure she'd misunderstood. Divorce? What on earth was he talking about?

Before she could catch her breath, he continued, "I'm sorry I came home and interrupted your and Darren's wedding. I'm even sorrier that I more or less forced you to stay with me. Maybe it won't even be necessary to get a divorce. Apparently I'm legally dead. . . ."

"Dammit Heath, shut up," Michaela yelled as she jumped to her feet. "Just be quiet for a minute and let me catch up with what you're saying."

He whirled around just as an attack of dizziness struck her and made the room spin. She reached out for something to hold on to, and he caught her around the waist.

"Take it easy, honey," he said and sat her back down on the couch. "I know I'm doing this badly, but I . . . Look, if it's custody of Skipper you're worried about, don't be. He . . . he doesn't even like me. He thinks of Darren as his dad, and that's good. When I'm gone he'll forget all about me. After you and Darren are married I . . . I may even let him adop . . . adopt him. . . ."

Heath's voice broke and he quickly turned away again and walked across the room.

Michaela's heart was pounding and her breath came in gasps, but she finally found her voice again. "Don't you want to be married to me any longer, Heath?" she asked shakily.

It took him a moment to answer, and when he did his tone was scratchy. "It doesn't matter what I want. It's too late for us. You've made a new life for yourself and our son. You both love Darren. Neither of you would be happy with me. I should have been prepared for all the changes that come with six years of living."

"Does it matter to you what I want?" she asked.

He turned back to look at her with a puzzled expression. "Of course it does. That's why I'm giving you your freedom."

She sighed. "Don't you think you should ask me if I want my freedom before you throw away our marriage?"

He frowned. "Mickey, I know you think you owe me—"

"I don't owe you a damn thing," she said tautly and got to her feet. "Just a few hours ago you told me you loved me. Were you lying?"

He ran his fingers through his hair. "No, I wasn't lying. I do love you, but—"

"And I told you that I loved you, too," she interrupted. "Are you accusing *me* of lying?"

He stared at her in bewilderment. "Michaela—"

"Are you?"

He shook his head. "Not exactly. I think you were telling me what you knew I wanted to hear because you felt sorry for me."

"Why should I feel sorry for you?" Her tone was brisk. "You've regained your freedom, you have a wife who adores you, and a son who'll now be able to lead a normal life."

"Dammit, Michaela, don't give me that," he exploded. "You know it will destroy me if I have to give you up—" He stopped abruptly. "What did you say?"

She could hardly keep from grinning. "I said you have your freedom, a wife who adores you, and—"

She didn't get a chance to finish. He was across the room and grabbed her by both arms. "Are you saying that you don't want a divorce?" he demanded.

He looked so dumbfounded that she could no longer hold back a smile. "Of course that's what I'm saying, love." Her tone was low and husky. "For someone so bright you're awfully dense," she teased. "Whatever made you think I did?"

He still looked skeptical. "But you were so happy when... I mean, you were so mad at me when I insisted that Skip have the surgery, and it wasn't until I asked Darren to come back home that you were willing to forgive me. I thought—"

She put her arms around his neck and raised her face to look at him. "You think too much, Lieutenant. If we had a little more action around here I might be able to convince you that it's you I want to be married to, not your brother."

With a groan he put his arms around her and hugged her to him. "You'd better be sure, sweetheart," he murmured against her temple, "because if I take you to bed now, it's going to be a lifetime covenant."

"Then what are we waiting for?" she whispered, as his mouth descended to silence hers in a kiss that removed for all time any doubt about the depth of their love for each other.

Parting is all we know of heaven
And all we need of hell.

Emily Dickson

* * * * *

Double your reading pleasure this fall with two Award of Excellence titles written by two of your favorite authors.

Available in September

DUNCAN'S BRIDE
by Linda Howard
Silhouette Intimate Moments #349

Mail-order bride Madelyn Patterson was nothing like what Reese Duncan expected—and everything he needed.

Available in October

THE COWBOY'S LADY
by Debbie Macomber
Silhouette Special Edition #626

The Montana cowboy wanted a little lady at his beck and call—the ''lady'' in question saw things differently....

These titles have been selected to receive a special laurel—the Award of Excellence. Look for the distinctive emblem on the cover. It lets you know there's something truly wonderful inside!

From *New York Times* Bestselling author
Penny Jordan, a compelling novel of ruthless passion
that will mesmerize readers everywhere!

Penny Jordan

Silver

Real power, true power came from
Rothwell. And Charles vowed to have it,
the earldom and all that went with it.

Silver vowed to destroy Charles, just as surely and
uncaringly as he had destroyed her father; just as he had
intended to destroy her. She needed him to want her . . .
to desire her . . . until he'd do anything to have her.

But first she needed a tutor: a man who wanted no one.
He would help her bait the trap.

**Played out on a glittering international stage,
Silver's story leads her from the luxurious comfort of
British aristocracy into the depths of adventure,
passion and danger.**

AVAILABLE IN OCTOBER!

 HARLEQUIN

PASSPORT TO ROMANCE VACATION SWEEPSTAKES

OFFICIAL RULES

SWEEPSTAKES RULES AND REGULATIONS. NO PURCHASE NECESSARY.

HOW TO ENTER:

1. To enter, complete this official entry form and return with your invoice in the envelope provided, or print your name, address, telephone number and age on a plain piece of paper and mail to: Passport to Romance, P.O. Box #1397, Buffalo, N.Y. 14269-1397. No mechanically reproduced entries accepted.

2. All entries must be received by the Contest Closing Date, midnight, December 31, 1990 to be eligible.

3. Prizes: There will be ten (10) Grand Prizes awarded, each consisting of a choice of a trip for two people to: i) London, England (approximate retail value $5,050 U.S.); ii) England, Wales and Scotland (approximate retail value $6,400 U.S.); iii) Caribbean Cruise (approximate retail value $7,300 U.S.); iv) Hawaii (approximate retail value $ 9,550 U.S.); v) Greek Island Cruise in the Mediterranean (approximate retail value $12,250 U.S.); vi) France (approximate retail value $7,300 U.S.).

4. Any winner may choose to receive any trip or a cash alternative prize of $5,000.00 U.S. in lieu of the trip.

5. Odds of winning depend on number of entries received.

6. A random draw will be made by Nielsen Promotion Services, an independent judging organization on January 29, 1991, in Buffalo, N.Y., at 11:30 a.m. from all eligible entries received on or before the Contest Closing Date. Any Canadian entrants who are selected must correctly answer a time-limited, mathematical skill-testing question in order to win. Quebec residents may submit any litigation respecting the conduct and awarding of a prize in this contest to the Régie des loteries et courses du Quebec.

7. Full contest rules may be obtained by sending a stamped, self-addressed envelope to: "Passport to Romance Rules Request", P.O. Box 9998, Saint John, New Brunswick, E2L 4N4.

8. Payment of taxes other than air and hotel taxes is the sole responsibility of the winner.

9. Void where prohibited by law.

PASSPORT TO ROMANCE VACATION SWEEPSTAKES

OFFICIAL RULES

SWEEPSTAKES RULES AND REGULATIONS. NO PURCHASE NECESSARY.

HOW TO ENTER:

1. To enter, complete this official entry form and return with your invoice in the envelope provided, or print your name, address, telephone number and age on a plain piece of paper and mail to: Passport to Romance, P.O. Box #1397, Buffalo, N.Y. 14269-1397. No mechanically reproduced entries accepted.

2. All entries must be received by the Contest Closing Date, midnight, December 31, 1990 to be eligible.

3. Prizes: There will be ten (10) Grand Prizes awarded, each consisting of a choice of a trip for two people to: i) London, England (approximate retail value $5,050 U.S.); ii) England, Wales and Scotland (approximate retail value $6,400 U.S.); iii) Caribbean Cruise (approximate retail value $7,300 U.S.); iv) Hawaii (approximate retail value $ 9,550 U.S.); v) Greek Island Cruise in the Mediterranean (approximate retail value $12,250 U.S.); vi) France (approximate retail value $7,300 U.S.).

4. Any winner may choose to receive any trip or a cash alternative prize of $5,000.00 U.S. in lieu of the trip.

5. Odds of winning depend on number of entries received.

6. A random draw will be made by Nielsen Promotion Services, an independent judging organization on January 29, 1991, in Buffalo, N.Y., at 11:30 a.m. from all eligible entries received on or before the Contest Closing Date. Any Canadian entrants who are selected must correctly answer a time-limited, mathematical skill-testing question in order to win. Quebec residents may submit any litigation respecting the conduct and awarding of a prize in this contest to the Régie des loteries et courses du Quebec.

7. Full contest rules may be obtained by sending a stamped, self-addressed envelope to: "Passport to Romance Rules Request", P.O. Box 9998, Saint John, New Brunswick, E2L 4N4.

8. Payment of taxes other than air and hotel taxes is the sole responsibility of the winner.

9. Void where prohibited by law.